The Language

of Threads

ALSO BY GAIL TSUKIYAMA

Night of Many Dreams

The Samurai's Garden

Women of the Silk

Gail Tsukiyama

The Language

of Threads

St. Martin's Press   New York

Book design by Ellen R. Sasahara

Library of Congress Cataloging-in-Publication Data

Tsukiyama, Gail.
    The language of threads / Gail Tsukiyama.—1st ed.
      p.   cm.
    ISBN 0-312-20376-4
    1. World War, 1939–1945—China—Hong Kong Fiction. I. Title.
PS3570.S84L3   1999
813'.54—dc21   99-22212
                                                 CIP

First Edition: October 1999

10 9 8 7 6 5 4 3 2 1

For Grace

Acknowledgments

I am deeply grateful to my agent, Linda Allen, my editor, Reagan Arthur, and to Sally Richardson and Joan Higgins at St. Martin's Press for their ongoing trust and guidance.

Again, my thanks to Catherine de Cuir, Cynthia Dorfman, Blair Moser, and Abby Pollak for the many years of wit and wisdom. And to my family, immeasurable gratitude.

*As I look at the moon
my mind goes roaming,
till I live again
the autumns that I
knew long ago.*

—SAIGYO

Pei

Pei glanced down into the dark, glassy water of Hong Kong harbor and suddenly felt shy and wordless. She saw herself as a child again, whom, at the age of eight, her father had taken to the girls' house in the village of Yung Kee. Compared to their small farm, everything had been big and frightening. For nineteen years, Pei had lived and worked with Lin doing the silk work, only this time, Lin's patience and kindness wouldn't be waiting for her when she arrived.

Now, she alone would have to care for Ji Shen in the big, vibrant city; the thought terrified her. At fourteen, Ji Shen was almost half Pei's age, and had already been orphaned once, fleeing from the Japanese devils in Nanking. She had miraculously found her way to the girls' house, where Pei and Lin had nursed her back to health. As the Imperial Japanese Army closed in on Canton, they'd made a desperate run to Hong Kong without Lin to guide them. That the past weeks had been spent in constant movement was a saving grace. Pei's days had been filled with the needs of Ji Shen and with their impending voyage.

When the ferry groaned and finally docked, it swayed from side to side, knocking and creaking against the wooden pier. As the crowd pushed to disembark, Pei stopped abruptly at the railing and stared down at the clapboard ramp that led to the crowded pier.

"We have to keep moving," Ji Shen whispered, gently urging her forward.

Pei held onto her cloth sacks and inched toward the ramp. High shrieking voices pierced the air, attacking them from every direction. Pei felt a sharp jab from someone behind, then stepped down the ramp into the dizzying, hypnotic life that would now be hers and Ji Shen's.

"Hong Kong's so crowded," Ji Shen said, clutching the sleeve of Pei's white tunic.

"Yes." Pei smiled wearily. She hoped Ji Shen couldn't see how afraid she was. Everything around them hummed and buzzed with movement. Ships from all over the world were docked in Hong Kong harbor, ships with long, complicated names written on their sides. Sampans huddled together, filled with families who lived their lives on the boats crowded, swaying decks. Faces glared at them, then quickly turned away. There were more Westerners than Pei had ever seen. Even many of the Chinese women were dressed in Western clothing.

From the pier they turned left and walked down the crowded street, sidestepping swarms of people as if in a dance, sweating in the humidity. The salty pungent smells and high whining voices were overwhelming. They passed endless stalls of merchants, selling silk stockings, flowers, fresh fruit, and hot noodles in soup. Filthy, toothless beggars thrust their wooden bowls out, hoping for a coin or two. Ji Shen squeezed Pei's arm tighter as they fought their way through the crowd. A long, jagged line of rickshaws and their drivers snaked from one end of the street to the next. Pei felt her pocket for their envelope of money and the letter Chen Ling had given her with the names and addresses of other silk sisters who had made their way to Hong Kong. "Go to the address at the top of the list," Chen Ling had directed. In her other hand, Pei grasped her belongings, including the cloth bag Moi had insisted she take. Pei carefully swung it over her shoulder, the jars of herbs and dried fruits clinking against one another.

"Ride, missees? Cheap deal!" A barefoot boy wearing once-white cotton pants and shirt—he was no older, Pei guessed, than thirteen or fourteen—stopped in front of them. A pointed straw hat hung from a string around his neck, thumping against his back. He pointed to a red-and-green rickshaw, which sat next to a nearby stone wall. On the ground beside it, an older woman in mismatched, soiled clothing cradled two smaller children on a straw mat.

"I'll give you a much better price!" another voice, belonging to an older, bigger man interjected.

"No, no, thank you." Pei took a step forward, but neither rickshaw driver moved.

"Cheapest deal in Hong Kong!" the boy repeated.

Pei pulled Chen Ling's letter from her pocket and looked past Ji Shen and the rickshaw drivers toward the crowded street ahead. In the weeks before Lin died, she had told Pei of going to Hong Kong with her father as a little girl. Across the street was a large open space—the one Lin had said was Statue Square. Statue Square was where the Government House and city hall stood, flanked by the precipitous green hills that loomed over everything. Pei caught her breath at the sight.

"Where are we going?" Ji Shen asked.

Pei cleared her throat. "Over there." She straightened her shoulders and began walking toward the square.

"Please, missees, cheapest deal in all of Hong Kong!" The boy was still following them.

"Don't listen to him." The older man laughed. "He's too scrawny to pull you more than a few feet!"

Pei stopped. She put down her belongings and looked up at the darkening sky. It was getting late. Statue Square would have to wait until another day. From the corner of her eye, Pei could see another rickshaw driver approaching them. She turned toward the boy. His smile grew wide now that he'd gained Pei's attention. She pointed to the address at the top of Chen Ling's letter. "Do you know where this is?"

The older rickshaw driver coughed and then spat on the ground in front of them. "Only a fool would choose a boy to do a man's job!" he said, stomping away.

The boy studied the letter for a few moments. Finally, he nodded his head in recognition. "In Wan Chai, not so far from here. No problem. I'll have you there in no time," the boy boasted. He glanced quickly at Ji Shen.

Pei hesitated. "Are you sure you know how to get there? Maybe we should try—"

"Yes, yes, right away." The boy nodded again. He ran back to the woman sitting on the ground, whispered some words to her, then grabbed the rickshaw and quickly pulled it toward Pei and Ji Shen. "Right away, right away! I know just the place. No need to worry." He stepped aside, offering Pei and Ji Shen help up into his rickshaw.

Pei suddenly remembered the stories she'd heard of rickshaw pullers doubling and even tripling prices once they arrived at their passengers' destination. Lin had told her to settle on a price immediately, before climbing up into the seat.

"How much?" Pei asked, fingering the Hong Kong coins she'd gotten at the exchange in Canton. She kept her voice low and confident.

"Don't worry, missee." The boy smiled. "I'll bring you there for a fair price."

When they'd settled on a fare, Ji Shen stepped up into the rickshaw. Then Pei squeezed into the torn leather seat next to her, proud of her first Hong Kong transaction.

The boy jumped between the wooden poles, squatting low to grip a pole in each hand. "Don't worry, Quan will get you there."

Pei felt sorry for him and wondered how such a skinny boy would be able to pull them more than a few feet, but Quan straightened his back, tightened his leg muscles, lifted up the poles, and moments later had them gliding smoothly down the crowded street. He called out, "Coming through! Coming through!" to urge the crowds and waiting rickshaw drivers out of his way. Ji Shen let out a scream and covered her eyes when they barely missed knocking down another driver. "I'll kill you next time!" the man shouted after them, raising his fists at them, but Quan simply turned around and yelled back, "You have to catch me first!"

All the colorful, crowded shops that lined the busy street Quan had turned on to mesmerized Pei. In the fading light of early evening, the street seemed to open up and come alive right before their eyes. Bars, curio shops, food stalls, fish stands, a shoe repair shop, a dress shop all blended together. Bright, harsh lights hissed and flashed—garish red, green, and yellow against the oncoming darkness. Pei had never seen anything like it, not even when she'd visited Canton with Lin. A quick spirit seemed to live here in Hong Kong, making everyone and everything move faster and louder than they did anywhere else she'd been.

After weaving in and out of dozens of streets, Quan rounded a corner down a narrow lane, which, though quieter, was just as dense with people and brightly lit shops. He drew the rickshaw to a stop, then turned around to face them.

Pei looked up at the narrow, grayish building, which rose four or five stories above an herbalist's shop. Signs plastered across the front window advertised ginseng and snake gallbladders and deer horn. To the side of the shop, an entrance led upstairs. The small window in the door was covered with a flimsy lace curtain. At one time the door must have been painted an auspicious bright red; now most of the paint had flaked down to the pale brown wood. In the fading light, the building looked tired and forlorn.

"Here, missees, this is the place." The boy carefully lowered the wooden poles and offered his dirty, callused hand to help them down from the rickshaw.

Pei accepted his help. "Is it safe here?" The words slipped from her lips.

"As safe as anywhere in Wan Chai. Just don't go wandering

around alone at night. There are many foreign-devil sailors looking for a good time, and bad men roaming the streets at night." Quan shook his head from side to side as if to make his point, his hands brushing against Ji Shen's long braid as he helped her down and signaled for them to follow him. "I think it's this way," he said.

Pei and Ji Shen followed Quan as if he were an adult, not a young boy barely older than Ji Shen. Strangely, Pei had felt comfortable with him from the moment she touched his callused hands. He swaggered up to the door and rapped hard three times. When no one answered, he knocked again, harder and louder. Pei held the letter up against the dim light to see the name and address again. "Song Lee" was written in neat black characters. Chen Ling told her Song Lee had been in Hong Kong for over eight years now, and would help Pei just as she had helped other sisters who had left Yung Kee. "She was a good worker," Chen Ling had said. "Tell her that I gave you her name. The last thing I heard was that she had found work in a good household."

At last, they heard the slow scrape of footsteps. Ji Shen held tightly onto Pei's arm. Then an irritated voice called out, "I'm coming, I'm coming!" The lace curtains parted and dark, suspicious eyes glared out at them.

"I beg your pardon." Pei stepped forward. "We are looking for a Song Lee. I was given this address as a place I might find her."

The lace curtains fluttered closed, and in a few moments, they heard the door unlatch and open just a crack. "What village are you from?" the woman asked.

"The village of Yung Kee."

"Are you from the sisterhood?"

Pei nodded. "Yes. I was told by Chen Ling that Song Lee might be able to help us."

The door swung open wider, and they stood in front of a thin, wiry woman in her forties who glanced at Pei's clothing and lacquered-black hair and chignon, then at Ji Shen's long single braid. "Come in, come in. I'm sorry for all the questions, but you must be careful in this area. Beggars will rob you blind if you let them!"

Pei stepped in, then turned around, remembering Quan. "No, no, I'll carry this up for you," he said, stepping in behind them. "All part of the service."

Single file, they followed the woman up a dark, narrow stairway, their steps resonating. Once upstairs, the building was slightly more inviting. The first floor had a high ceiling, which at least kept the building cool and comfortable. Doors to other rooms opened in three directions.

The woman didn't say another word until they reached the landing. "This way," she said. She led them through the middle door into a small, yet comfortable sitting room. There was an old sofa, a few chairs, and a small cabinet, which held a few small jade pieces. "You must be thirsty. Let me bring you some tea."

Quan smiled, then spoke to the woman in a cheerful, bargaining voice, a street voice. "These missees need a cheap and clean room."

The woman bowed her head slightly toward Pei and Ji Shen. "We will talk about that when I return with tea." She smiled. "Please, make yourselves comfortable."

Pei looked around at the worn furniture. Her tongue flicked across her parched lips. She reached deep into her pocket and brought out a small silk pouch, from which she extracted several coins. "Here, this is for you," she said to Quan. "You've been very kind to help us."

Quan glanced at the money. "Too much," he said. "Just what we agreed on."

"Please, take it," Pei insisted.

Quan hesitated, then quickly pocketed the coins. "I'll stay a little longer. Just in case you need me to bring you somewhere else tonight," he said shyly, watching Ji Shen.

When the woman returned, she sat down, poured each of them a cup of tea, and spoke words Pei suspected she had repeated many times before. "I am Ma-ling Lee. I was also a member of the sisterhood, though I left it many years ago to come to Hong Kong. When other sisters began migrating to Hong Kong, I decided that they might need a place to stay while they decided what to do. Hong Kong is a large, sometimes frightening place." Ma-ling sipped her tea. "You can stay here as long as you like, but there is a small fee. Many sisters have passed through this way. Most of them find work in a household within a few months. The less fortunate ones find whatever work they can."

"What kind of work?" Ji Shen asked.

Ma-ling smiled. "We'll talk about that another time. You two must be tired. Let me show you where you can sleep."

"And Song Lee?" Pei asked.

Ma-ling stood. "You can see her tomorrow. Right now she's working as a domestic for a household up on the Peak. I'll try to get in touch with her first thing in the morning," she offered.

Pei smiled. "We're very grateful."

Quan parted with them at the foot of the stairs. "I'm sure you'll be all right here," he said. "It looks as if she can get in touch with your friend."

"Thank you," Ji Shen said.

Quan blushed. "If you ever need anything, just ask for Quan. I'm around Wan Chai a lot. People here know me." He backed slowly down the stairs. A moment later, they heard the front door open and quietly click behind him.

The room Ma-ling brought them up to was not what Pei had expected. Once a large, open space, it was now divided into numerous smaller rooms by thin wooden partitions that didn't reach the ceiling. If Pei stood on her toes she could look over the partitions from one space to the next. They walked down the narrow aisle that separated the cubicles. At the entrance to each space hung a white cotton curtain most of the curtains were askew. Bare and clean, each small cubicle held two single cots and a wooden chair. Ma-ling told them there were some larger cubicles in the back with two sets of bunk beds.

"You can have this room." Ma-ling stopped and pointed to a cubicle with a curtained window that looked out on a small, colorless concrete courtyard. For a moment, Pei stood looking out at the graying darkness.

"Thank you." She tried to smile, grateful at least for the window.

"Everything will look better in the morning," Ma-ling assured her. "The bathroom is down the hall. There are only a few other sisters staying with us now, so it should be quiet. The kitchen is downstairs. I'll bring you up some tea and sweet buns in case you're hungry."

"Thank you for everything," Pei said, too exhausted to say anything else.

Ma-ling closed the door behind them, leaving Pei and Ji Shen by themselves. Pei couldn't believe they had come so far from their life in Yung Kee and the silk factory. With the Japanese now occupying most of China, she wondered whether Chen Ling and Ming were safely hidden away at the temple in the countryside where they'd taken refuge, and whether Moi would be all right by herself at the girls' house. Pei tried to push these thoughts out of her mind. Yet she couldn't stop wondering if she had made the right choice leaving Yung Kee. Her doubt was like the constant prickling of bristles.

"It's as if everything's alive here." Ji Shen's voice rose and filled the small space.

Pei inhaled, the warm air tasting slightly stale. "I suppose it's time we join in," she heard herself respond. She looked around at the bare, colorless cubicle that was now their home, then hurried to open the window, letting in the demanding, boisterous voices from outside.

* * *

That night, in a restless sleep, Pei dreamed of Lin. Once again she heard her friend's sweet, calm voice telling her that everything would be all right. At twenty-seven, Pei had spent almost twenty years of her life with Lin, first at the girls' house with Auntie Yee and Moi, and then at the sisters' house, where their life took on the comfortable rhythm of work at the silk factory. Pei was amazed at how easy it was to forget. Suddenly gone were the raw, sore fingers from soaking the cocoons in boiling water, the long, grueling hours of standing on damp concrete floors, the lives that were lost in their union's struggle against the rich factory owners. And Lin's death. It wasn't just Lin's death that tormented her, but how she had died, and what had gone through her mind as she gasped for breath, slowly suffocating in the devastating fire that destroyed the silk factory. In the past month, Pei had learned what to hold on to, and what to discard.

Instead, Pei dreamed moments of pleasure. How Lin always found answers to her smallest questions, even before Pei could ask them. When she first came to work at the silk factory, the steamy, sweet-sweaty smell of the soaking cocoons seeped into every pore of her skin, clung to her clothes, hung on every strand of her hair. It was so persistent, yet so subtle a scent, Pei thought it wouldn't ever wash out.

"Wash your hair with this," Lin had told her one evening when they'd returned to the girls' house. She held up a bottle filled with an amber liquid. When Lin shook it, white jasmine petals drifted through the liquid, floating slowly back down to the bottom of the bottle.

"Does it work?"

Lin stepped closer. "Here, smell," she directed.

From that day on, the scent of jasmine became a part of Pei's everyday life. Just after the girls had washed their hair, the strong, sweet smell rose up and filled their room at the girls' house; she couldn't help but think of Lin. Even the clean smell of Auntie Yee's ammonia was no match for the jasmine.

Again, Pei smelled jasmine in her dreams. Ammonia. Cocoons

boiling in hot water. The fragrance of Moi's cooking wafting from under the kitchen door they were forbidden to open without knocking first. Again, Pei stood at the bottom of the wide wooden stairway that led up to their rooms. She heard a sound, a small intake of breath, and looked up to see Lin, radiant in her white burial gown, walking down the steps toward her.

"I've been waiting for you," Lin said, smiling.

Pei opened her mouth, but at first no words emerged. She felt so dizzy she thought she might faint.

Lin answered her question even before she had asked it. "Yes, it's me."

"I've missed you." Pei finally found her voice. "More than you can know."

"I do know." Lin took her hand. "Now come along. Everyone is waiting."

Pei held onto Lin's hand, never wanting to let go. It seemed so real in hers she squeezed it tighter, feeling Lin's warm softness in her own large, rough hand. "But who's waiting?" she asked.

"Still so curious." Lin smiled. "You'll soon see." She swept a strand of Pei's hair away from her face, then swung open the double doors to the reading room.

Pei's heart raced. She glanced around the crowded room. The smell of burning incense was overpowering. Shadows flickered across the walls. The chairs were filled with women dressed in the white cotton trousers and tunic of the sisterhood. Pei closed her eyes and opened them against the thick, stinging air. She touched Lin's sleeve to make sure she was really there beside her. Faces from the past appeared fresh and young.

"Come, come in," called a high, shrill voice. Pei knew it immediately: It belonged to Auntie Yee.

Pei rushed toward the older woman, fell to her knees before her chair, and threw her arms around her. She breathed deeply. The faint clean smell of ammonia rose above the incense. "It's been so long," Pei whispered into Auntie Yee's neck.

Auntie Yee squeezed her tightly before letting go. "You've grown into a fine young woman, just as I knew you would."

"Yes, you have," another voice added.

Pei faintly remembered it. She stood up and looked closely at all the faces that surrounded her. "Who?" she asked.

"It's me," the voice said. Moving out and away from the other sisters was Mei-li, who appeared just as she had so many years ago, before she had drowned herself.

"Mei-li?" Pei asked.

"And don't forget me," another voice rang out.

Sui-Ying stood by the side of Mei-li—kind, sweet Sui-Ying, who had been killed during their strike for better hours.

All through the years Pei had prayed to the gods that these two friends would find the peace they so richly deserved. Like Lin's their lives had ended much too soon.

Then, from the corner of her eye, Pei saw movement from behind the others. The flash of gray hair stood out among the rest. Pei strained to see beyond the sisters in front of her, hoping to catch another glimpse. She wondered if this could really be. The last time Pei had seen her mother, Yu-sung, she had been so thin and fragile. "Ma Ma," Pei said softly, then again, louder. The hum of voices died down around her.

Yu-sung stepped forward. Her gray hair was neatly combed back. She smiled widely and said, "Yes, my tall daughter. I'm here."

Growing up, Pei had rarely seen a smile cross her mother's lips, Now it glowed before her as bright as any light. Pei took a step forward and began to say something, but the words became confused and caught in her throat. Tears blurred and burned behind her eyes.

"It's all right," Ma Ma said. "You have done well in life, just as I always knew you would. After you and Lin visited, I knew I could leave your world in peace."

Pei hung on to her mother for as long as she could, but soon she felt Lin lean near and heard her whisper, "You have to leave now."

Pei shook her head. "I don't want to leave. I want to stay here with all of you."

Yu-sung pulled away. "That can't be. It isn't your time yet. There are too many things you must still do. Don't forget your baba, and your elder sister, Li."

Pei began to cry, at first softly and then without restraint. She felt Lin take hold of her arm, pull her gently away from the others. Ma Ma stood before her, whispering words she could no longer hear.

Once outside the closed door, Pei held tight to Lin. "Not you, too," she said, through tears. "Not again."

"You have to go on with your life in Hong Kong, just as we planned. We will be together again one day," Lin whispered. "I promise."

Voices. Footsteps. A dull thump against the fragile partition. Pei awoke. In the darkness she felt lost. A thin, pale light filtered into the room. Ji Shen slept soundly in the bed across from her. Pei closed her eyes again, struggling hard to hold on to the memory of Lin's sweet, lingering fragrance of jasmine.

Song Lee

Song Lee quickened her steps, already late to meet the two new sisters waiting for her at Ma-ling's. Wan Chai was crowded and noisy. In the past year, since the Japanese devils had seized Beijing and continued their march southward, more and more people had flowed into Hong Kong from Canton. Along with the crowds, the heat and humidity already felt unbearable. The pounds she had gradually put on in the eight years since she had arrived in Hong Kong left Song Lee gasping for air.

That morning, when the young boy with Ma-ling's message arrived at the gate of the house she worked at, Song Lee had already made plans for her Sunday afternoon. She'd intended to meet some of her other sisters at the Go Sing Teahouse in the Central District. There, the latest news and gossip were eagerly delivered. The sisterhood from Yung Kee and other villages had remained strong in Hong Kong. Most of the sisters were known to be clean and hardworking. Nearly all were enthusiastically accepted as amahs and servants in wealthy households, both Chinese and British. The majority of the sisters now working in Hong Kong had been in the sisterhood back in the delta region of Guangdong province for many years, and had gone through the hairdressing ceremony, pledging their lives to the silk sisterhood. Song Lee knew the Hong Kong Tai tais had their own term, *sohei,* to describe their vow never to marry. Their vow meant the sisters were less at risk of attracting philandering husbands, and their services quickly grew in value.

Some sisters couldn't adapt to domestic work and were soon replaced. But for the most part, the sisterhood continued to thrive in Hong Kong. Organizing themselves much as they had in the silk work, they remained strong in numbers. Loan associations and retirement committees were quickly formed to help sisters who found their way to Hong Kong. In no time, Song Lee became an active participant in helping the new arrivals adjust to living and working in Hong Kong.

Like most of her sisters, Song Lee had had a lifetime of adjusting. She was the only daughter of a poor farmer and his wife. Her two older brothers were granted what little her parents had to offer them, both materially and emotionally, while Song Lee was given to the silk work when she was six, earlier than most. For months she refused to speak to anyone and cried herself to sleep every night. She lay small and voiceless in one of ten beds that lined the long, narrow room. Then one night Song Lee heard another girl crying, the soft hiccuping breaths drawing her attention away from her own misery. She listened in the darkness, mesmerized by the strangely comforting lullaby. For the first time, she realized that she wasn't alone. Every girl in the room had been abandoned by a family she loved. A dozen years later, Song Lee had pledged her life to helping her sisters in whatever way she could.

By the time Song Lee reached the boardinghouse, she was hot and thirsty. The two new sisters were waiting for her as Ma-ling ushered her into the sitting room.

"Please, please, don't get up," Song Lee said. She let her thick body fall onto the sofa next to the young girl, across from the older, strikingly tall sister, who watched Song Lee's every move with sharp, inquisitive eyes.

"Thank you for coming all this way," the tall Pei said, relaxing into a slight smile. "I wouldn't know where to begin looking for work. Hong Kong is so big, so crowded."

"I hope I can make your transition easier." Song Lee smiled. She rummaged through her bag for the red, gold-trimmed paper fan at the bottom, and snapped it open. The slight movement of sticky air brought her little relief.

Song Lee watched Pei closely for a moment. She must have helped more than a hundred sisters relocate and find domestic positions since she herself had come to Hong Kong. Now she prided herself on reading each woman's face as if it were a map of her life, with hints in every line and crevice. Even if Song Lee didn't know a woman's final destination in life, she could guess in which direction she was headed. Sometimes the clue was as subtle as a young woman's slightly protruding forehead, or the delicate downward curve of her lips. Each small feature foreshadowed a person's destiny.

So many times Song Lee's heart ached when she detected future problems. One eighteen-year-old sister, whose eyebrows were like two sharp knives pointing upward, had foolishly played up to the master of the house, become pregnant, and been kicked out by his wife. Afterward, the sisterhood had a hard time placing her. Word had spread, and no Chinese Tai tai would take her. She eventually found work washing clothes for an English family. Another young girl, whose eyes were always moist and watery, cried suddenly at the slightest word or glance. Her employers were at a loss for what to do with her, and when she returned to the sisterhood in tears, Song Lee was exasperated, too. In cases like these, Song Lee simply had to look the other way. There was little she could do against a fate that had already been set. She could only hope that what she detected as a flaw would be balanced by some other favorable feature she hadn't seen. Song Lee's own life had been no less difficult, and though that didn't show on her round, prosperous face, it was evident in the large, dark mole she carried on the back of her neck. If the same mole had been on the front of her neck, and carrying her, Song Lee's life might have followed an easier path.

The face of this woman, Pei, told a different story. Song Lee saw a quiet strength in the bridge of Pei's nose, along with intelligence in the deep-set eyes. If Ji Shen—whose face lacked a certain definition, with its flatter nose bridge and sloping forehead—minded Pei, then she too, would be all right. Pei was also old enough not to make some of the foolish mistakes that other younger sisters had. Song Lee saw a complex journey ahead, but one Pei could most likely manage.

Over the past years, Song Lee had learned to move slowly, leading each woman carefully into the specifics of her new life. She drank down her tea, cleared her throat, and spoke in her high, melodious voice. "The sisterhood has been good to me, and the least I can do in return is to help other sisters. Besides"— Song Lee smiled—"I have always believed good fortune will someday return to me. But tell me, how are Chen Ling and Ming?"

"Well, we hope," Pei said, her smile disappearing. "They have given themselves to the Buddhist faith and joined a vegetarian hall in the countryside. They were to leave the day after we left Yung Kee. I can't help wondering whether they're all right."

Song Lee leaned forward. "If anyone will be all right, it's Chen Ling. She has the strength of a dozen men!"

Pei and Ji Shen relaxed. They spoke of Yung Kee and the silk work, until Song Lee sat back and raised her hand as if to wave away the recollection.

"Most of the sisters who have come to Hong Kong do domestic work now," Song Lee said. She poured herself another cup of tea. "It is a small island, after all, and word spreads quickly from one household to another that a sister is looking for a position. Most families prefer us above all others as their children's amahs."

"Why?" Ji Shen asked.

"Because we have come from a working background, and we've proved to be stable and reliable," Song Lee answered.

"Will I be able to work, too?" Ji Shen asked. It was the first time she had uttered a full sentence since Song Lee had arrived.

Song Lee smiled at the girl. "I'll have to talk to some of the other sisters, but I'm sure we can find you a place—"

"No," Pei quickly said. "I'm sorry to interrupt, but I would like Ji Shen to finish her education."

"But—" Ji Shen began.

"You're still young enough to choose another path. It's important to me," Pei continued, lowering her voice seriously. "In a few years, you can do whatever you want." Then, turning back to Song Lee, she said softly, "For now, I'm the only one who will need to find a position."

Song Lee nodded. She sipped the slightly bitter tea, then adjusted the collar of her tunic, which was getting too tight. Perhaps she had been wrong; this tall sister's strength was not so quiet after all.

Fragrant Harbor

Three days later, Pei followed the directions Song Lee had given her to the Bing Tao Fa Yuen, the botanical gardens across from the governor's palace. She had thought about hiring Quan to take her up, but decided she should learn the streets of Hong Kong as fast as she could. Walking would assure her of a quick challenge. After making sure Ji Shen would be comfortable staying with Ma-ling, Pei set off to meet Song Lee and the other sisters who would help her seek work.

"Come meet some of the other sisters on the committee," Song Lee had said. "It is important to make as many connections as you can here in Hong Kong. You can never know when you'll need them."

Pei nervously agreed, wondering if she'd even be competent to do domestic work. With the help of Song Lee, she had no choice but to enter this new world, of which she knew so little.

A crush of people enveloped her as soon as Pei rounded the corner from the boardinghouse. She suddenly became acutely conscious of her surroundings. The sour smells of sweat and urine, the oily odor of Chinese doughnuts frying, the heady fumes from the many motorcars, the high-pitched voices of vendors. In the quivering afternoon heat, even the bright daytime blend of garish color was jarring. Pei had never seen so many big, dark motorcars, which roared and raced at her from every direction. "Metal monsters," she muttered under her breath as she dodged across a crowded street.

The crowds thinned and Pei's panic calmed as she left the noisy streets of Wan Chai and began the upward climb along paved streets toward the gardens. Beautiful brick and stucco houses stood large and imposing on each side of the street. Pei felt the muscles of her legs pull as she walked briskly up the incline. The flat, open space of Yung Kee had had almost no hills; climbing the streets of Hong Kong left her hot and breathless. As the streets grew gradually steeper, she tried to imagine making her way back down again. One slip, and she might roll all the way back to Wan Chai!

When she was high enough to see the shimmering blue-gray water below, Pei paused and turned around. Ships dotted the harbor. Across from it rose the dark landmass that was Kowloon, and beyond Kowloon lay China. Pei was amazed by all she could see. She swallowed the dull pain of wishing Lin were there with her.

At a soft shuffling of footsteps behind her, she turned around. An old woman dressed in a servant's dark tunic and trousers, carrying a bulging bag in each hand, walked slowly downhill toward Pei. She seemed to stare at her with disdain, mumbling under her breath. Pei made out the words "young and strong" and "take our positions," as the old woman quickened her steps down the hill.

The botanical gardens were on Upper Albert Road. Ahead, Pei could already see a cluster of green among the concrete roads and houses. She began to walk more quickly, promising herself the cool shade of the trees once she had arrived. Song Lee had told her that the sisters would wait on the grass just to the right of the entrance.

Near the gardens, Pei stopped and caught her breath. She liked sweet-voiced Song Lee and hoped for the best in dealing with the other sisters, but Pei remembered all too well the different personalities that had affected her life, first at the girls' house, then at the silk factory and sisters' house. Dealing with so many people was often like playing a game of chess. There were so many pieces, all moving in different directions. It was always wise to guard all sides against capture.

The sisters were waiting right where Song Lee had said. From the distance they resembled a flutter of black-and-white birds in their black trousers and white tunic tops, not unlike the clothing of the silk sisterhood. For a moment, Pei felt she could be back in Yung Kee. She took a deep breath and dusted off her own white trousers.

"Ah, Pei, you've found your way." Song Lee ran over to meet her. "I hope you didn't have any trouble."

Pei smiled, a bead of sweat running down her forehead. "No, your directions made it easy. I just didn't realize how steep the hills are."

Song Lee laughed. "You'll get used to them. You'll have no choice, going up and down to the market and picking up the little ones from school." She took Pei's arm and led her back to a small group of women waiting by a shady boulevard, surrounded by flower beds. "Don't worry," Song Lee whispered, "they won't bite."

Of the six or seven women gathered there, Pei could only remember the names of two: Luling, who was roughly the same age as herself, and a younger-looking sister who preferred to be addressed by her newly adopted English name, Mary. The others greeted her, poured her tea from a thermos, and handed her rich-tasting almond cookies, whose flaky crumbs tickled her throat as she tried to answer all the sisters' questions.

That night, as Pei lay in her cot next to Ji Shen's, she thought of what a different impression Lin would have made that afternoon. Although she was shy, Lin would have spoken eloquently, made them listen to her and recognize her gifts. But Pei felt as if all her words had been short and dry, falling to the ground like stones. Hong Kong is *hot, big, crowded*. Yes, I can *cook, wash, dust*.

Pei shifted on the uncomfortable cot. She felt the slight ache of her strained leg muscles, and winced again at recalling Ji Shen's excited, happy voice when she returned.

"What did they say?"

"They wanted to know how we like it here in Hong Kong," she answered wearily.

"Have they found you a position yet?"

"I've only just met them."

"When they do, will we live there?"

Pei forced herself up the stairs. "I don't know," she said, her voice barely audible.

Two days later, Pei went downstairs to find a note from Song Lee waiting for her. She turned it over in her hands, as Ji Shen urged her to hurry and open it. When Pei finally did, she read:

> *We have found you a good position in the Chen household. Be at the address below at two o'clock tomorrow afternoon. Use the back entrance.*
>
> *Song Lee*

Pei studied the address on Po Shan Road. She wondered if it was like one of the big brick and stucco houses she'd passed on the way to the botanical gardens, whether it had many rooms with the same thick, soft carpets she'd seen in Lin's house, and a view of the harbor. She kept the note tucked safely in her pocket all day.

For dinner, Pei and Ji Shen went to the nearby Star Village Restaurant to celebrate their good fortune. That night, Pei was too excited to sleep. Her heart raced. Their new life in Hong Kong would begin tomorrow. Pei inhaled the musty air, tried to find a comfortable position on the sagging cot, and then closed her eyes against all her fears.

1938

Pei

The house on Po Shan Road was larger than Pei had expected. It stood grand and imposing behind a black iron fence that isolated its wide green lawn from the rest of Hong Kong. Beyond the gate was a long gravel driveway that led to its front door. Even from a distance, the house appeared enormous—three floors of white stucco with massive white columns gracing a large veranda, which wrapped around the house like protective arms. Pei stopped at the gate to catch her breath. All the blinding whiteness made her want to turn and run away, even as her hand pushed against the sun-warmed metal and the gate whined open.

Pei's quick steps crunched through the gravel up to the house. The grounds were well-manicured, with bauhinia, chrysanthemums, and pink and purple azaleas blooming neatly in place. Only when Pei had climbed the steps and reached the intricately carved front door did she remember she was supposed to go around and enter through the back.

"Can I help you?"

The voice startled Pei. She turned around to see a man in his fifties dressed in a baggy shirt and pants, wearing a straw hat and holding a shovel in his hands.

"I'm looking for the back entrance," Pei answered.

The man squinted and smiled. "Then you've found just the opposite!" He pointed to a flagstone pathway that twisted around the house. "Just follow that walk," he directed with a wave of his hand.

Pei shifted from one foot to the other, trying to smile despite the heat. "Thank you."

The man nodded. Pei turned, nervous, and hurried down the steps to the stone path that led toward the back of the house.

"Oh, missee," he suddenly called after her. "Be sure you ask for Ah Woo. Ah Woo will take care of you."

"Thank you." Pei relaxed and smiled. "I will."

With its faded brown color and unornamented wood, the back door might as well have been attached to another house. Pei looked around as if she were in yet another world. Not far from the door near a stone well, a large wooden washtub lay on its side. A cluster of chairs and baskets sat beneath a large willow in the near distance. Unlike the front yard, the back was spare and devoid of flowers.

Pei knocked lightly on the door, then harder still when no one answered. Her heart was beating so fast she couldn't catch her breath, and after a moment, she hurried over to the well for a sip of water.

Just then the door swung open and a voice, sharp and stern, filled the yard. "Yes, what is it you want?"

Pei looked up, still clutching the wooden ladle in her hand, water dripping from her chin onto her tunic. The woman who glared at Pei was no older than she, dressed in a white tunic and dark trousers, her hair pulled back in a chignon. "I'm here to see Ah Woo about a position in the household." Pei quickly replaced the ladle in the wooden bucket. "I was sent here by Song Lee."

The woman studied Pei closely, her three-cornered eyes narrowing as they searched Pei's face. "Wait here," she finally said, and disappeared back into the house.

Pei stood by the door, feeling hot and uncomfortable at the cool reception. She wondered if all the servants in the Chen household were as hostile as this woman with the dark, piercing eyes.

The door swung open again and another voice sang out. "Ah, you've arrived! I'm Ah Woo. Song Lee told me you would be coming. It's hot outside. Why in the world didn't Fong have you wait inside? Come in, come in!" Her round, open face appeared ageless around her warm smile.

Pei followed Ah Woo into the cool, cavernous kitchen, which smelled of garlic and green onion and something slightly foreign. Just being out of the sun brought her relief. When her eyes had adjusted to the dim light, Pei saw a large, open room with unlit charcoal fires for several woks set in a wide, concrete counter. On top of the counter a swath of long-leafed mustard greens and turnips lay beside a freshly killed chicken. To one side of the room was a round wooden table with the remains of lunch—the thin translucent bones of a steamed fish, some bits of ground pork with pickled vegetables, a few hardened grains of rice clinging to the sides of bowls. Pei's mouth watered. She wondered if the Chen family had just finished eating.

"Please sit, please sit," Ah Woo said. "Leen, please take some of these bowls away!"

At that, a gray-haired woman barreled through the door and began to clear the table of bowls and cups. "Always Leen," she mumbled to herself as she stacked the bowls.

Ah Woo paid no attention to this complaint, but poured Pei a cup of tea. "I'm sorry for all this mess. We've just finished eating."

"Not the family?" Pei let slip.

"Oh no, not in here!" Ah Woo laughed, high and shrill. "I can't imagine Chen tai ever sitting at this table." Her round hand lay flat against the worn, scarred surface.

Pei blushed at her mistake.

"Don't worry," Ah Woo said reassuringly. "You'll soon learn the ways of the household. When I first arrived, I had no idea one family could ever live in such a big house. Why, back home, my entire village could live comfortably here!"

"How many are there in the Chen family?" Pei asked.

Ah Woo sat down. "There are six members of the immediate family, though three of the four children are away at boarding school. Only the youngest, twelve-year-old Ying-ying, is at home right now. But she is a handful all alone! And Chen tai's sister often comes to stay. Let me tell you about the position we need to fill." Ah Woo sat back in her chair as the old servant Leen reached over and cleared away the last of the bowls from the table.

"I . . . I don't have much experience doing domestic work," Pei admitted.

Ah Woo smiled. "Many have come from the silk work, especially now with the Japanese devils swallowing up Canton. Nothing you'll learn here is harder than your life at the silk factory. If you can loosen threads from cocoons and unwind their silk in boiling water, surely you can draw a hot bath or launder a few clothes. Why, when I first came to Hong Kong, I thought I wouldn't last an hour." She shook her head. "It wasn't an easy life. But there's nothing here you can't learn to do within the first week. We've all had to start at the beginning. You've already met Fong, who came here less than a year ago from the silk work."

Pei swallowed the discomfort she'd felt with Fong, and asked, "Are there many servants in this household?"

"Too many! But Leen and I have been here the longest. We're too old for them to kick us out now. Chen seen-san is a very wealthy man, and can afford to have an amah to take care of his family's every need." Ah Woo paused. "I've seen many faces come and go over the years, but usually there are eight or nine servants working here continuously. The three of us live in the house full-time, while the others go home to their own families in the evening."

Pei was astonished at the number of people it took to care for the Chen household. Even at Lin's house in Canton, there were only two old servants who had long been part of their family.

"And would I stay here?" Pei asked.

Ah Woo nodded. "Chen tai is a very busy woman. She's often invited to social events and her cheongsams must be ready and waiting for her. You will be the *saitong,* the wash-and-iron amah. Fong cares for Ying-ying, and Leen is the cook amah. Then there are the two drivers and Wing, the gardener. Two girls come in to clean every week, and I make sure the general running of the household continues smoothly"—Ah Woo smiled—"which is sometimes more difficult than you can imagine!"

Pei nodded, weighing another question. "There's something I need to ask you."

"What is it?"

"I have a younger cousin whom I care for," Pei began, thinking her request might carry more weight if Ji Shen were a family relation. "She has to come with me."

Ah Woo's smile disappeared as she shook her head. "I'm afraid Chen tai won't be happy with the situation."

Pei stood up, feeling the job slip through her fingers. "Then I'm sorry to have taken up your time," she said.

Ah Woo placed both of her plump hands on the table and pushed herself up. "Let me see what I can do," she said. "You wait here." She gestured for Pei to sit back down and finish drinking her tea.

By the time Pei had walked back to Ma-ling's boardinghouse, her head throbbed and her legs felt weak. She stopped in front of the herbalist store downstairs and wondered if he carried the white-flower and snake-tongue-grass tea that Moi used to brew at the girls' house when one of them couldn't sleep. Pei hesitated, then pushed the door open. It was cool and dark inside, the musty aroma of herbs and dried abalone immediately enveloping her. Leaves in muted black, brown, and green, dried orange-red berries, roots, and gnarled branches lay in open wooden barrels. Behind the crowded counter, rows and rows of small drawers stood against the wall. And in one of the dusty jars on the counter, Pei recognized two bear paws floating in a cloudy liquid.

"Hello?" she called out softly. Her voice echoed through the room and back to her. She felt a whisper of wind brush against her neck, and was just about to turn and leave when an old man appeared from behind a curtain.

"Yes, how can I help you?" His slight, wiry build and kind eyes put Pei at ease.

"I need some tea," she said.

"Yes, yes, I have all kinds of tea. Medicinal or for drinking pleasure?"

"To help me sleep." Just saying the word made Pei suddenly weary.

"Ah." He slipped behind the counter and opened several drawers that Pei knew contained his magic. "Here we are," he said, measuring different dark leaves into a white piece of paper. "And just a dash of chrysanthemum. You will sleep like a child." He folded the paper and wrote "Dream Tea" on it in Chinese characters, then pushed the small package across the counter.

"Thank you," Pei said as she paid the herbalist.

"After you've eaten. Before you go to bed," he instructed.

Pei nodded. Then, as she walked out, he added, "If the tea fails, let me know. Every person is different. Fortunately, there are as many teas as there are days of the year."

Outside the shop, Pei found Quan and his rickshaw parked near the doorway of the boardinghouse. Ji Shen stood by the door speaking to him, curling the end of her braid around her fingers. When he heard Pei approaching, Quan turned and blushed.

"Hello, missee, I came by to see if everything was all right." He smiled.

Pei smiled back. "Everything's fine. We're getting settled here."

"Anytime you would like a quick tour of Hong Kong, I'd be glad to take you." He glanced at Ji Shen. "Free of charge, of course."

"I'd like to see Hong Kong," Ji Shen said enthusiastically.

Pei saw the flash of anticipation in their young faces. "Thank you, Quan," she said, reaching out to touch his thin arm. "We'll arrange something very soon."

Quan grinned, then backed away slowly and picked up the wooden handles of his rickshaw. "I'd better go. Anytime—you just ask for Quan and I'll get the message," he said, turning the rickshaw and gliding down the street before they had a chance to say another word.

Ji Shen's excited voice filled the air even before Pei closed the front door behind her. "What happened?"

"Let's go upstairs."

Ji Shen followed her. "Did you get the position?"

Ma-ling greeted her at the top of the stairs. "I hope it went well," she said.

Pei nodded, but led them to the sitting room before she'd say more. In the comfort of the old room she sighed, then looked at the two eager faces before her and forced a smile. "I begin work at the end of the week."

Pei felt a gentle breeze stirring, the first bit of relief she'd felt from the heat since arriving in Hong Kong. She and Ji Shen always left the window open in their small cubicle, despite the drunken voices, loud yet indistinct, and the sudden staccato bursts of music erupting from some Wan Chai bar. The past few nights the air had been so heavy, Pei thoughtthey might suffocate in their sleep. She had hardly slept, her pillow damp from sweat, straining to hear Ji Shen's short breaths keep a steady rhythm.

Tonight, even after she had drunk the herbalist's dream tea, Pei's wandering thoughts kept her awake. The prospect of her move in a few days to the Chen household and her new job as a saitong left her more anxious than excited. She glanced again at Ji Shen, whose pale skin glistened in the darkness as she slept. Pei would never forget the look of disappointment on Ji Shen's face when she found out that only Pei would be moving to the Chen household.

"I'll be good," Ji Shen had pleaded.

"I know you will, but it's not possible," Pei replied. "The Tai tai doesn't have room for both of us."

Ji Shen stared silently, straining against tears. "What will happen to me?" she finally asked, a tinge of fear in her voice.

"You must go to school. You'll stay here with Ma-ling. Just until I can earn enough to get us a place of our own."

Ji Shen had swallowed and nodded. For the rest of the evening, no matter how hard Pei tried to keep the conversation going, a dull haze surrounded them.

What Pei hadn't told Ji Shen and Ma-ling that afternoon was that Chen tai had agreed to let Ji Shen come stay as long as she also worked for her room and board. "Not heavy work. Just some cleaning and running errands," Ah Woo had said eagerly. Pei felt the blood rush to her head. She needed the work and had little choice but to agree—but instead, she found herself saying, "There might be another place she can stay while I work here." Pei was determined that Ji Shen have an education, and Po Shan Road was too far away from any public school. She felt certain that once Ji Shen was settled in school, they could work out a feasible schedule to see each other regularly.

Pei breathed deeply and swallowed the guilt of having lied to Ji Shen, the only family she had in Hong Kong. She watched the flickering lights and shadows dance against the walls, then closed her eyes. "It's a start," she heard Lin's voice whisper in the night—a slight, cooling breeze against her cheek. Before Pei's thoughts wandered further, she was asleep.

The House on Po Shan Road

The early-morning air still carried a hint of freshness. Pei shifted her scant bundle of belongings from one hand to the other and knocked on the back door of the Chen house. This time she was prepared for Fong's coldness, but was instead welcomed by Ah Woo, buttoning the last frog of her white-and-blue-striped tunic.

"Ah, good, good, you've arrived early enough to sit down and eat with us. It will give you chance to meet everyone." Ah Woo pulled Pei into the kitchen. "Let's get you settled first. You re-member Leen."

"Yes," Pei said, swallowing. "I'm happy to see you again."

Leen nodded, then returned to her pot of boiling *jook*. Steam rising from the porridge filled the kitchen with the sweet smell of Pei's childhood.

"This way," Ah Woo said. She led Pei out of the kitchen through a narrow corridor that divided into a number of small rooms. "These are the servants' quarters. My room is here." Ah Woo swung open the door nearest to the kitchen. In it were a narrow cot, a small dresser, and a chair. "Leen's room is across from mine." She pointed to a closed door, then continued down the hall to the last door, at the end of the corridor. "And this will be your room, across from Fong's." Ah Woo pushed the door open and they were greeted by the sharp, scent of mothballs. Ah Woo waved her hand through the stale air and hurried to open the window.

"Thank you," Pei said, entering. The space was modest; still, it was larger than the cubicle she shared with Ji Shen, and would afford her some privacy.

"Why don't you get settled? Then you can join us for breakfast. Don't worry, I'm sure you'll fit right in." Ah Woo closed the door behind her.

In the short time Pei had taken to unpack her few belongings and lay out Lin's silver brush and combs on the chipped surface of the dresser, all the other household servants had gathered around the kitchen table. Pei stopped in the doorway and listened to the quick, sociable voices. She took a deep breath and entered to meet them.

Ah Woo jumped up from her chair and, taking Pei gently by the arm, guided her to the others. "Quiet, quiet. This is Pei. She's our new saitong, and will be staying here with us."

There were soft murmurs of greeting. "You've already met Fong," Ah Woo began, though Fong's sweet smile never gave a hint to her cold greeting the other day. "And this is Wing, who takes care of the garden." He stood up and bowed with a smile, the same old man who had greeted Pei when she arrived looking for Ah Woo. Pei smiled back. "And lastly, this is Lu, our daytime chauffeur." The thin, middle-aged man in a white shirt and dark trousers barely glanced up from his bowl of jook.

"Please sit down." Wing offered Pei a chair.

Throughout breakfast, Ah Woo kept up the conversation and put Pei at ease as she explained the household schedule. "Each day begins right after our breakfast at six-thirty—sometimes before, if the Tai tai rings for one of us. Chen seen-san usually leaves for the office at eight o'clock, and drops Ying-ying off at school, while Chen tai lingers to plan her day. She is often out to lunch and mah-jongg until dinner. After they've had their breakfast, I will introduce you to them."

Pei looked up from her jook with a nervous smile. From the corner of her eye, she saw a faint sneer on Fong's face.

After breakfast, the servants scattered to their respective duties. Ah Woo went upstairs to awaken the Chens, and Fong went to tend to Ying-ying, while the two men hurried out the back door. Pei, left dangling, rose to help Leen collect the bowls and clear the table. Only then, when they were alone in the kitchen, did Leen utter her first words.

"I've been here a long time," she whispered, taking the bowls from Pei. "It's always safest to remain silent."

Pei watched Leen's fluid movements; faint remnants of cooking stained her white tunic. "What do you mean?"

"I watch and listen." Leen filled a kettle with water to boil. "Nothing escapes me. I've been here a long time," she repeated. "For over twenty years. Before that, I worked for Chen seen-san's father. Now, he was a man of great dignity."

"And Chen seen-san?" Pei dared to ask. She quickly cleared the rest of the table and handed Leen the last of the bowls.

Leen shook her head. "Not half the man his baba was."

Pei began to wonder if she should remain silent in order to survive in the Chen household.

"And Chen tai?" Her words slipped out.

Leen's eyes narrowed as she carefully scrutinized Pei from head to toe. Seeming satisfied, she moved closer to Pei and whispered, "Chen tai has led a pampered life, surrounded by those who cater to all her whims. Many times this keeps her from seeing the truth."

"What do you mean?" Pei asked, stepping back.

Leen laughed bitterly. "Not all of us are what we appear. I can see that you are a fast learner. Just watch out. In time, all truths are revealed."

Pei felt Leen's words lie heavy in her stomach. Before anything else was said, Ah Woo came back in through the kitchen door. "Everyone's awakened," she sang out, only to pause when her eyes fell on Pei. "You look pale. Is everything all right?" Ah Woo's smile disappeared as she turned toward Leen.

"Oh, yes," Pei quickly answered.

Leen looked down and busied herself with washing the breakfast bowls.

"At times we aren't as helpful as we should be," Ah Woo snapped.

Leen snickered, then set each washed bowl on the counter with a dull clink.

"Anyway," Ah Woo went on, recovering, "I've told Chen tai that you've arrived, Pei, and she would like to meet you before breakfast."

"Now?"

Ah Woo smiled again and said, "Chen tai has more clothes than half of Hong Kong. The sooner she meets her new saitong, the better."

Pei glanced over at Leen, who carefully lowered two brown eggs into a pot to boil.

Ah Woo quietly pushed the dining room door open, allowing Pei a pause before she met the Chen family. A sweet, strong scent of gardenia filled the air. The dining room was the grandest Pei had ever seen. Not even the one in Lin's childhood home in Canton could compare in size and extravagance. Red and gold and silver flickered everywhere around the room. Against one wall was an enormous rosewood cabinet with glass doors divided into three sections. The two outer cabinets held Chinese ceramic and mosaic vases, while the middle displayed a full silver tea set, with crystal goblets and bowls. Pei wondered how one family could use so many beautiful things.

A round carved-mahogany dining table stood in the middle of the room, atop a soft, thick carpet of deep red with intricate gold scroll designs. Chen seen-san sat at one side in a tall, carved mahogany chair, flipping furiously through a newspaper; Chen tai, across from him, talked to Ying-ying, who sat between them, slowly sipping her milk.

"Excuse us," Pei heard Ah Woo say, "but this is our new saitong, Pei."

Chen tai and Ying-ying immediately looked up from their conversation. Heavier and bigger-boned than Pei had imagined, Chen tai had a smooth, creamy complexion, and wore a jade-green cheongsam of cotton voile, trimmed with black piping. Pei felt as if her feet had sunk too deep into the soft square of carpet and she'd never be able to move. Ah Woo leaned over and gave her a light nudge forward.

"Tso sun, Chen seen-san, Chen tai, sui-je," Pei stuttered her good mornings to them, bowing her head.

Ying-ying laughed and said, "She's so tall!" Her round face gleamed.

"Ssh," Chen tai scolded. "We're happy to have you with us," she said. "I'm sure Ah Woo has explained some of your duties here."

"Yes."

"I have to attend many social functions, and it's important to have my clothing ironed and ready for each event." She squeezed the white linen napkin tighter in her hand.

"Yes," Pei said again, this time in a louder, stronger voice.

The newspaper suddenly lowered with a sharp crackle, and a bald, heavyset man wearing thick, black-rimmed spectacles glanced up at Pei. "Where are you from?" Chen seen-san asked.

Pei felt suddenly hot and sticky; a film of sweat gathered at her temple. "The village of Yung Kee."

"Another silk worker?"

"Yes."

He lifted his glasses and stared intently at Pei for a moment with dark, small eyes. "She appears capable enough," he said, before raising his paper again.

*   *   *

In the quiet of her room that night, Pei fingered the smooth silver handle of Lin's brush and assessed her first day in the Chen household. The scent of mothballs lingered heavily. Unanswered questions flashed through her mind so fast she couldn't hold onto them. Had she made the right decision? How was Ji Shen doing all alone at the boardinghouse? Would Quan remember to take her on a tour of Hong Kong at the end of the week? What did Leen mean when she advised Pei to watch out? The house was so big . . . Chen seen-san's thick black glasses . . . Chen tai's closet . . . So many cheongsams of silk and satin . . . So many rules to learn and follow . . .

The faint whine and clicks of doors opening and closing, followed by the faraway sound of voices, brought Pei back. She stood up and walked quietly to her door to listen, grasping Lin's brush tightly in her hand. Very slowly she opened her door a crack, but saw only darkness.

Chapter Three

1939

Pei

Pei filled the iron with hot coals and pushed down on the cover. It felt heavy and solid as she lifted it upright on the wooden ironing board. The first few months of washing and ironing had been difficult, a never-ending process of filling the washtub with water and heating the coals for the iron. Now, after six months, Pei's back ached constantly and her hands were rough and dry, her fingers cracked and split. Water and steam surrounded her as they had in her early days at the silk factory, soaking cocoons. Only now, Lin wasn't there to help her through the long days.

On her first full day in the Chen household, Ah Woo had sat Pei down and explained the rules she was to follow: "You are never to enter a room in the main part of the house without permission. . . . Never touch any of the Chens' property. . . . You are not to have any personal guests in your room. . . . Bathe regularly and keep yourself presentable. . . . You'll have every other Sunday off." The words came out stilted and formal, and Pei could almost hear Ah Woo breathe a sigh of relief when she had finished her prepared speech.

Pei observed other rules, unspoken, yet just as important. As the saitong, she spent most of her time in the small laundry room off the kitchen, or outside, where she hung the clothes to dry.

Getting along with the other servants in the house came second to keeping the household running smoothly. Ah Woo and Leen did all they could to help Pei settle in. So did Wing, the gardener, who ventured to the backyard on Pei's first morning of washing. "For you," he said, producing a yellow lily from behind his back, while Fong smiled politely from a distance. When they passed each other in the hallway or kitchen, Pei and Fong nodded stiffly to each other, as if there were some great wall between them. "Fong thinks she's better than us," Leen had confided in Pei. "Just because she cares for Ying-ying and spends more time upstairs."

After six months, work in the Chen household had become routine. Every morning Chen tai left the clothes she wanted washed and pressed on a chair next to her bed. While the Chens ate breakfast, Pei hurried up to their rooms and gathered the clothes—silk stockings, undergarments, Chen seen-san's white shirts, which had to be soaked and starched, Ying-ying's school and play clothes. If there was a big social event for Chen tai to attend that evening, she would tell Pei what she wanted washed and pressed the night before. But as often as not, she changed her mind the next day and Pei would have to rush to iron another cheongsam just before Chen tai left the house.

Pei scooped up the clothes, never daring to linger too long in the large, ornate bedroom. "Best to keep your mind on your work," Ah Woo had told Pei her first day. "Those who can't, don't last long here."

Ah Woo needn't have worried. Everything in the Chens' room felt foreign and intimidating, from the antique black lacquer furniture to the mother-of-pearl-inlaid headboard that adorned the massive, unmade bed. Pei feared that if she touched anything, something bad might happen. Only once or twice did she stop in front of Chen tai's opened closet, which extended the entire length of one wall. She'd never seen so many cheongsams before, nor such a multitude of colors, from pale pink to a deep midnight blue. Chen tai had another, smaller closet just to store all her matching shoes and handbags. Pei imagined these came from all the fancy department stores she'd heard about from Ah Woo.

"Down in Central you can buy anything in the world," Ah Woo had said. "It's like some great bazaar where you can see everyone and everything."

"Do you go down to Central often?" Pei asked.

"Only when Chen tai needs my help to carry all her packages. When she shops, she's treated like a queen!" Ah Woo laughed. "As for me, entering one of those stores is like entering a foreign country."

Pei pushed open the small window of the cluttered laundry room next to the kitchen. It had rained the past two days, hard and relentless, but this morning a weak sun shone through the gray clouds. Pei felt a breath of sticky autumn air enter, the damp smell of dirt a sudden reminder of her father's fish ponds. A cold shiver ran up her spine, followed by a small stab of sadness. Since her mother's death more than a year ago, Pei no longer received any letters. She imagined Baba on the farm all by himself now. And while her parents had lost contact with Pei's sister Li years before, Pei often thought of her and wondered if she still lived somewhere near Yung Kee. If so, would they even recognize each other after almost twenty years? Li must have children of her own now—Pei's nieces and nephews. She still clung to the hope of seeing Li again. Over the years the flame sputtered and flashed, but had never burned out.

Swallowing her thoughts, Pei reached for the jar of cream made from the aloe plant and sunflower oil, and rubbed some into her swollen fingers. The first chance she'd had, Pei had gone back down to Wan Chai to see Ji Shen and the old herbalist whose store was under Ma-ling's boardinghouse.

The herbalist had taken Pei's hands in his, examining her dry, cracked fingers, then shaken his head sympathetically and guaranteed the cream would soothe them by the end of the week. "Rub it thoroughly into your hands and fingers once in the morning, and again at night before you go to bed," he'd told her, "and avoid soap and water."

Pei smiled, feeling a tingling sensation from his hands on hers. "But I'll still have to wash and iron every day," she said.

The herbalist squeezed her hands slightly. "It's a shame that such beautiful hands can never rest."

"Will they still heal?"

He gently let go. "They'll heal," he said, "but it will take longer."

With quick and knowing hands, Pei sorted through the morning's laundry. Each time she held one of Chen tai's silk cheongsams in her hands, Pei could hardly believe that it was woven from the same thin, almost invisible threads of silk she'd once reeled onto spools. In her mind's eye she could see the cocoons dancing on the surface of the boiling water as they unraveled. As she stroked the sleek, shiny material, the Yung Kee Silk Factory felt like a lifetime ago. She held the red-and-gold cheongsam up against her stark white tunic and baggy black pants. She couldn't imagine herself wearing something so tight and revealing.

Pei picked up Chen tai's beige lace cheongsam and laid it flat on the ironing board. She waited a few moments longer for the iron to heat up, meanwhile examining the intricate lace handwork of Chen tai's new dress, tailor made like all her dresses for the most auspicious occasions.

Chen tai had surprised Pei that morning by bringing the dress down to the laundry room herself. Her hair was pulled back in a tight chignon and her strong features looked softer without makeup. She was dressed casually, in a blue silk tunic and pants.

"Chen seen-san is being honored by the Hong Kong chamber

of commerce at a very special banquet this evening," she said, handing the dress carefully to Pei.

Then, instead of leaving, she stood solid and imposing in the narrow doorway. From the kitchen came the sharp, scraping noise of Leen sharpening her knives and cleavers.

"Is there something else I can do for you?" Pei cradled the dress gently in her arms. She wished the tiny room weren't so messy.

"No, nothing for now," Chen tai answered. "Only, I wanted to say that you've done a very good job in the past six months."

Pei blushed. "Thank you."

"Keep it up." Chen tai turned to leave. Then she stopped and turned back, her eyes traveling once around the small room. "Perhaps you'd like to come along when I go down to Central next week."

Pei looked up, not believing what she was hearing. That honor was usually given to Ah Woo, who had been a trusted member of the family for so many years. "Yes, I would, thank you," Pei answered, a quick flush heating her cheeks.

Chen tai's gaze softened into a smile. Thin fine lines appeared around her eyes. "I'll let Ah Woo know that you'll be coming with me, then." She turned and left the room before Pei could say anything.

Pei returned to her work. For the rest of the morning, a faint trace of Chen tai's sweet rose fragrance mingled with the hot, dry air of her ironing.

Pei was pleased when Chen tai wore her beige lace cheongsam as planned and left for the banquet on time. Instead of rushing to iron another dress at the last minute, Pei helped Chen tai dress, then extracted a gold evening bag and shoes to match from her smaller closet. Even the usually impassive Chen seen-san was smiling happily when Pei closed the front door behind them.

*   *   *

The kitchen was warm with the garlicky aroma of dinner cooking. Pei was famished by the time she sat down between Fong and Ah Woo, and gratefully received her bowl of rice. Like Moi, Leen was a wonderful cook who prepared at least three or four dishes each night. Most of the time, only the four of them—Pei, Ah Woo, Leen, and Fong—ate dinner together. Wing and Lu went home to their families, while the night chauffeur was usually on duty.

"I see Chen seen-san and Chen tai are off on time tonight," Ah Woo said. "It must be a big banquet they're giving in honor of Chen seen-san."

Leen scraped her chair back and sat down. "He must have donated a great deal of money." She lifted her bowl and pushed some rice into her mouth.

Ah Woo glanced at Leen, then quickly changed the subject. "Pei is going down to Central with Chen tai at the beginning of the week."

Pei looked up at the mention of her name, and saw the quick change of expression on Fong's face. Ah Woo was watching Fong, too.

"Like a zoo down there." Leen picked up a piece of lean pork from a plate in front of her.

Ah Woo laughed. "It's true, another whole world can be found down in Central." She balanced a green bean between her chopsticks.

Fong lowered her rice bowl. "As far as I'm concerned, Central's a much better world," she said, her eyes narrowing as she reached for a piece of steamed fish.

After dinner Pei retired to her room. Once she closed the door on the other women, she felt like herself again. She was exhausted from all the small talk, from constantly keeping up her guard on account of Leen's warning to be careful. Pei sat down and carefully unwound her chignon. She picked up Lin's silver brush and worked the bristles through her hair in long, slow strokes. In these quiet moments she could almost feel Lin there beside her. Tomorrow was her Sunday off, and her heart lightened at the thought of visiting Ji Shen and Ma-ling at the boardinghouse.

Pei had just finished brushing her hair when there was a quick knock at her door. Her heart leaped, and she was surprised to find Fong standing in the doorway holding a small black tin with red roses on it.

"Here, this is for you," Fong said, a slight smile on her full lips. She held out the round tin. "It's just some butterscotch candy. I want to apologize for my unfriendly behavior since you've been here."

"It doesn't matter," Pei answered. She kept the door half-closed between them.

"But it does," Fong continued. "I've been going through some difficult times. I shouldn't have taken it out on you. Please, take this. It would make me feel much better." She pushed the round tin at Pei.

Pei hesitated, then accepted the tin. "Thank you."

Fong smiled, then touched the back of her own head and said, "You have beautiful hair. Much nicer than mine. It's a shame we can't wear it down."

Pei nodded, noting the flecks of gray on the top of Fong's head.

"I hate to start things off badly, especially since we do live and work here together."

"Yes, you're right," Pei said, trying to smile back. It was wise to keep on friendly terms in such close quarters.

"How do you like it here?" Fong asked, peering around the door into Pei's room.

"It's fine," Pei answered. "Thank you for the candy. I hope you sleep well." She slowly began closing the door.

Fong shrugged. "Okay then, we'll visit another time." She

smiled and started to leave, then turned back. "Anytime you need anything, don't hesitate to ask."

"I won't," Pei said.

"Enjoy the butterscotch."

The candy rattled against the hollow tin when Pei lifted it. "I will, thank you." She closed the door and leaned heavily against it, wondering if her being chosen to accompany Chen tai down to Central had anything to do with Fong's sudden change of heart.

Ji Shen

Ji Shen glanced out the window of the sitting room, but saw no sign of Pei walking up the street. Every other Sunday, Pei came to visit at the boardinghouse for a few hours before returning to Po Shan Road. Ji Shen waited anxiously by the window like an angry child. Ever since Pei had gone to work in the Chen household and sent her to Spring Valley, a public school in Wan Chai, Ji Shen had felt something hard and cold growing inside her.

Ji Shen had missed Pei terribly the first few weeks after she'd left. They'd been together ever since she stumbled into the girls' house over a year ago, after the brutal murders of her parents and sister by the Japanese devils in Nanking. Then Lin's death had left them both orphans. Pei became her older sister, the one who eased her nightmares and guided her to their new life in Hong Kong. But now, Ji Shen was alone each night in her small cubicle, wondering how long it would be until she and Pei were together again.

Ma-ling was nice enough, but still a stranger. Ji Shen's only pleasure was that Quan came to visit her a few times a week. In the first week after Pei left, he took her on a tour around Hong Kong. He shyly waited outside by his rickshaw while Ji Shen ran upstairs to tell Ma-ling. Ji-Shen quickly tied a red ribbon at the end of each braid, and pinched her high cheekbones for color.

She ran back down the stairs, then stood behind the lace curtain watching Quan nervously rubbing his hands together as he paced back and forth. Ji Shen took a deep breath to calm herself before she swung the door open.

Quan helped Ji Shen into the rickshaw. "Where would you like to go first?"

Ji Shen didn't know what to say. For a moment she felt as if she were at Spring Valley, in the large, echoing classroom that smelled old, dusty, slightly sour. The day Pei first brought her there, all the curious eyes of her classmates followed her until she sat down on the hard wooden bench.

"Where are you from?" the thin, tired-looking teacher had asked.

Ji Shen sat staring at the old, scratched desk in front of her and slowly answered, "Nan-king, Chen-chiang pro-vince," trying to hide her heavy northern accent, to keep from slurring the hard Cantonese words. Then she heard the muted whispers and the laughter of the girls and boys nudging each other around her.

"What kind of accent is that?"

"Why is she dressed like a servant?"

Ji Shen looked down at the white tunic and black trousers she had worn ever since coming to the girls' house, then at the bright yellow and blue shirts and dresses her classmates wore. She wanted to jump up and run after Pei.

From that day on, Ji Shen felt too old, out of place among her classmates. They made silly, careless conversation and knew nothing about life. Day after day she sat in the airless classroom for Pei's sake. As far as Ji Shen was concerned, she could learn far more by working in a store or restaurant and earning her own money.

"Where would you like to go first?" Quan asked again.

"I don't know," Ji Shen finally answered. "Where do you usually take your customers?"

Quan smiled. "I know a few places," he said, lifting the wooden poles and setting off down the street.

The rest of the day was like a dream. Quan took Ji Shen through Central, where men in dark, serious suits strode from one building to the other, and women glided down the sidewalks in beautiful silk cheongsams or Western dresses and veiled hats. Quan rattled off exotic names—Swire House; Jardine, Matheson; Des Voeux Road, The Gloucester Hotel; King's Theatre—as he and Ji Shen flew past tall, stately buildings like the wind. He finally came to a stop, in front of a large stucco building.

"This is the Central Market," Quan explained, pulling his rickshaw to one side. "You can buy anything here." He helped Ji Shen down and led her through the maze of stalls, where hundreds of merchants sold everything from bok choy and Chinese mustard greens to bananas and mangoes. Pigs and ducks squealed and quacked in open pens. The pungent odors of salt fish and dried blood mixed in the air. Voices sang out, their melody punctuated by the dull thuds of cleavers severing the heads of chickens and fish. Ji Shen saw the many cook amahs dressed in white tunics and black pants, bargaining at stalls as they scurried to buy for their households, and her thoughts drifted back to her own servant's clothes and how they set her apart from everyone else at Spring Valley.

From the Central Market, Quan took Ji Shen down to the Star Ferry building to watch the crowded green-and-white ferries cross the harbor.

"They're all named after stars," Quan explained. They sat on the concrete wall, watching a ferry float smoothly into its berth as Chinese sailors, dressed in blue cotton uniforms, jumped onto the concrete platform to tie the thick ropes before they lowered the wooden ramp for the multitude of passengers to disembark. "That's the *Lone Star*. There's also the *Morning Star, Day Star, Northern Star, Celestial, Shining Star, Silver Star,* and *Meridian*."

Ji Shen remembered the rocking motion beneath her feet when

she rode the ferry down from Canton, which was now under Japanese occupation. "How do you know their names?"

"I've seen the entire fleet of star ferries, every one of them," Quan boasted.

"Do you think we can ride on one someday?" Ji Shen stared at the mixed crowd of people, men and women, young and old, Westerners and Chinese, even Sikh Indians, pushing and pulling as they flowed from the ferry.

"I promise." Quan pointed to another ferry crossing the harbor. "Just choose any star you want, and that's the one we'll take across the harbor."

"The *Shining Star*," Ji Shen said. "Like the one that must have guided us here to Hong Kong."

The door to the sitting room suddenly clicked open. Ji Shen turned from the window to see Ma-ling enter. Sometimes Ma-ling moved so quietly through rooms she was like a puff of air, or a shadow hovering. "Pei should be here any minute now," she said, closing the door behind her.

"Yes," Ji Shen mumbled back. Moments later she heard the downstairs door open and close, the soft tapping of footsteps up the wooden stairs . . . eight, nine, ten, eleven, twelve . . . and then Pei entered, breathless and smiling.

Ji Shen jumped up and hugged her, breathed in the salty smell of sweat and lavender soap. Even her loose-fitting tunic couldn't hide the fact that Pei had lost weight. Ji Shen gave her another squeeze and hung on until she felt Pei pull back.

"How's school?" Pei asked as soon as they settled onto the sofa in the sitting room. Ma-ling had retreated to the kitchen to make some tea.

"Fine." Ji Shen avoided Pei's eyes.

"Have you made some new friends?"

"Not many."

"You will in time." Pei reached for her hand. "Do you like your teacher any better?"

Ji Shen shrugged her shoulders. She felt Pei watching her, waiting for some kind of answer. "She's all right," Ji Shen said, but the words felt hard in her throat. No matter how she hated Spring Valley, she knew how much Pei wanted her to finish school.

Pei's gaze never wavered, though she sat forward and changed the subject. "Oh, yes, I brought you this." She reached into the cloth bag by her feet and pulled out a blue cotton dress with a white Peter Pan collar.

Ji Shen smiled. "Where did you get it?" She saw the flicker of happiness in Pei's face at her interest, and felt bad for acting so spoiled.

"It was given to the Chens' daughter Ying-ying, but it's similar to another dress she already has."

Ji Shen's smile disappeared. "So it's something they've discarded," she said, too sharply. She could feel her pulse quickening in anger, despite her intense desire for the blue dress.

"It's like new," Pei answered, laying the dress flat across her lap.

Ji Shen jumped up. "Did they give it to you, or did you have to beg for it?"

Pei paused. When she spoke, she kept her voice calm. "I worked for it."

Ji Shen stepped back, knowing she'd been wrong to speak as she had. Her eyes blurred. The sight of Pei's raw, red fingers made her heart ache. She wanted to take Pei's hands in hers, heal them with her touch. Instead, Ji Shen reached down for the dress. "I'm sorry, I'm sorry. It's beautiful. I can't wait to wear it to school."

Pei's face softened.

Ma-ling returned to the sitting room with tea. "Song Lee should be here any minute now. I hope you don't mind. She wants to see how you're doing and didn't want to disturb you at the Chens'."

"Of course I don't mind," Pei answered, turning her attention to Ma-ling.

Ji Shen smiled with relief. Song Lee's kindness and happy disposition would distract Pei for a good part of the afternoon. Ji Shen had upset Pei enough for one visit. She didn't want to let slip what she really felt—how she didn't want Pei to leave again, how she hated the thought of returning to the dusty classroom each day, and how terrified she felt, waking up from her nightmares, only to find herself alone in her closet-sized cubicle. Ji Shen walked slowly over to the window and opened it, filling the room with a choir of screeching street voices, blaring horns, and babies' cries.

The Saitong

Pei returned to the Chens' house that evening feeling unsettled. Ji Shen had been distant and quiet the entire afternoon. Pei knew she was hiding something under her flat answers and forced smiles. Their separation had proven more difficult than she expected. All Pei wanted was for Ji Shen to get a good education, so that she would have a better future. But she felt Ji Shen's silence like the sharp edge of a knife, stinging as if Pei were to blame. Even as Ji Shen waved good-bye at the door, clutching the blue cotton dress, Pei grieved for their lost time together.

All the way back to the house, Pei tried to block out Ji Shen's sullenness by recalling Song Lee's visit. By the time the rotund Song Lee had climbed the stairs and fallen onto the sofa next to Pei, Ji Shen had already retreated to a chair by the window.

"And how is it, working for the Chens?" Song Lee asked, breathing heavily.

"It's fine." Pei poured her a cup of tea. "I'm still getting used to everything."

Song Lee smiled. "All the different personalities," she said knowingly.

"Yes, and all the dos and don'ts."

"I've heard the Chens are much better than others." Song Lee took a large swallow of tea, then lowered her voice to a whisper. "There are more horror stories than you can imagine—tiny, filthy rooms, long hours, too little food, beatings; some are even raped by their employers."

Pei nodded, knowing that she should thank the gods for her good fortune. Yet she couldn't help feeling uneasy. "Do you know much about Fong, who takes care of the Chens' daughter Ying-ying? She used to be a silk worker."

Song Lee's tongue flicked out and moistened her lips as she eyed Pei more closely. "Yes. From the Shun-te region. I know who she is. Is there a problem between you?"

"No," Pei answered too quickly. In the moment of silence that passed between them, Song Lee's large, clear eyes never wavered from hers. Pei felt she could trust Song Lee, but didn't want to cause her more problems. "Nothing of importance. I just wondered where she was from."

"There have been rumors. . . ." Song Lee leaned closer. "Some say she was really a grass widow with a young child, and that she abandoned the child when she came to Hong Kong. Others say she was never a silk worker, but just pretends to be as a means of finding work in a good household."

"What do you believe?"

Song Lee fell back against the sofa with a throaty laugh. "I have heard so many stories over the years, I've ceased to believe any of them. I've learned to wait and see what happens instead of taking sides. One way or another, a person's past eventually makes itself known."

Pei hesitated. "What do you mean?"

"Just that we can't run away from what defines our fates.

Who we are and what we believe in grow from the roots of our past, no matter how much we might try to deny it."

From the corner of her eye, Pei saw Ji Shen staring blankly out the window. Would she understand one day why she must stay at the boardinghouse and study now? Pei's thoughts turned to her own past, to Lin and the silk work. If she hadn't been given to the silk work, her life would have taken a very different path. She might have been forced into a marriage in which she had no choice, or, fated not to marry, been left to fend for herself in a world that regarded an unmarried woman as worse than a disease. Pei couldn't imagine what her life would have been without the strength of Auntie Yee, the obstinacy of Moi, the love of Lin.

"I see what you mean," she finally said.

Song Lee's eyes narrowed as she watched Pei closely. "Yes, I can see that you do."

Pei paced back and forth in her room, listening for the first stirrings of the morning—the soft creaking of a door opening, the sharp scrape of Leen's iron kettle against the stone counter. Pei had been up for over an hour, worrying about her trip down to Central with Chen tai. What would they talk about the entire afternoon? What if she said or did the wrong thing? Was she supposed to wait inside or outside the store? Pei put her ear to the door, hoping to catch Ah Woo before the others awoke.

After dinner the night before, Pei had only wanted to retire to her own room, exhausted from her visit with Ji Shen at the boardinghouse. She'd just finished clearing the table when Ah Woo returned from the dining room and whispered, "Chen tai would like to see you," as if it were a secret. Pei could feel Fong and Leen watching her every move, their gazes piercing through the kitchen door as it swung closed behind her.

The Chens had already abandoned the dining room for their living room, with its tall ceiling and large windows overlooking the front garden. Pei had entered the living room just once before, when Ah Woo gave her a tour of the house. Easily three times the size of Lin's Canton house, the room smelled of incense and spices. Pei had never seen so many beautiful objects displayed in one room. It was crowded with rich rosewood furniture, elaborate embroideries, an ornate rug the color of cinnamon and tea leaves, Chinese scroll paintings, and a set of black lacquer screens. There were large and small statues of tigers, lions, and the goddess Kuan Yin, and each tabletop was adorned with vases of inlaid mother-of-pearl and bright cloisonné of red, green, yellow, and gold. Pei wondered how such a vast room could feel so suffocating.

Pei stood in the marble foyer and knocked lightly on the already opened double doors.

"Come in, come in, Pei," Chen tai said, from the far end of the room.

Pei approached Chen tai, being careful not to knock anything down. Chen seen-san and Ying-ying were nowhere in sight. "You wanted to speak to me?"

Chen tai sat against a maroon silk brocade cushion on one of the rosewood chairs. Dressed in an off-white cheongsam, she looked positively regal. "We will go down to Central tomorrow afternoon." She smiled. "You can do some washing in the morning, and leave the rest for the day after."

Pei shuffled from one foot to the other. "Yes, Chen tai," she answered, already warm at the thought of her first trip down to Central.

"We'll leave tomorrow after lunch, then," Chen tai continued. "Tell Ah Woo to have Leen make me something plain—a bowl of jook will do."

Pei nodded, hesitated, then turned to leave just as Chen seen-san walked into the room. Large and stocky, dressed in a dark

Western-style suit, he appeared out of place amid all the delicate Chinese artifacts.

"And just what are you two discussing so seriously?" he asked, speaking more words than Pei had ever heard him say.

Chen tai laughed and waved her husband closer. "Pei is going down to Central with me tomorrow."

Chen seen-san cleared his throat; behind his thick, black glasses, his eyes traced Pei from head to toe and back again. "Can I trust you to keep Chen tai from spending all my hard-earned money?"

Chen tai laughed again, high and shrill.

"Yes." Pei pinched the edge of her cotton tunic.

Chen seen-san roared with laughter, his baldness glistening in the pale light. "I like this one!" He flipped open a black lacquer box and lifted out a cigarette. "Finally, someone to help keep me from going into debt." He brought the cigarette to his lips, lit it, and blew a stream of smoke toward the ceiling.

"I'd like to know who could stop you?" Chen tai waved the smoke away.

"Perhaps Pei will come along with me next time." He snickered and blew smoke in his wife's direction. Then he turned to Pei and asked, "How would you like that?"

Pei held her breath, the words refusing to emerge. She wished Lin were there to take charge, put Chen seen-san in his place with a few simple words—"No, I wouldn't like it," or "I'm too busy for your games." Instead, she breathed out slowly, feeling the heat spread through her body, coloring her face. "I . . ." she began, but before Pei could answer, Chen tai spoke.

"You can go now," Chen tai instructed, her gaze remaining on her husband.

Pei hurried out. She'd never been so happy to return to the safety of the bare, scrubbed kitchen.

*   *   *

In the early-morning light, everything was muted, soft. Pei slipped out of her room, stepped quietly into the kitchen, and ladled some water into the kettle for tea. The house creaked in a long sigh, then settled into stillness. As the water boiled, Ah Woo emerged from her room. "Ah, you're up early," she said, settling down in her chair at the table.

"I couldn't sleep," Pei admitted. She took down another cup and poured Ah Woo some tea.

"There's nothing to worry about," Ah Woo said knowingly. "Central is like everywhere else in Hong Kong: too noisy and crowded."

"What if I make a mistake and upset Chen tai?"

Ah Woo laughed. "And what kind of mistake can you make carrying her packages?" She sipped her tea. "Let me tell you something I've learned over the years. Simply do as Chen tai instructs. She'll tell you, 'Come with me,' 'Wait here,' 'Take these packages,' so there's nothing to worry about. And, oh, yes," Ah Woo added, "never speak unless spoken to first. Chen tai likes to be in charge."

Pei nodded, and finished her tea in one large swallow.

After lunch, Ah Woo walked Chen tai and Pei to the front door; Lu was waiting with the car. From the corner of her eye, Pei saw Fong lingering in the stairwell. "You'll be fine," Ah Woo whispered in Pei's ear just before closing the door behind them.

Pei was terrified. The glare of the hot sun beat down on her. The last time she'd been so close to a car was years ago, during the strike at the Yung Kee silk factory. She remembered the angry voices and the thick crowd parting as Chung's long black car inched through the gate, then flinched at the shock—she could still feel it—of seeing Sui-Ying's lifeless body sprawled on the ground. In the end, they had won shorter working hours, but at the terrible cost of her friend's life.

Now just the thought of riding in the big black metal monster made her stomach turn. Ah Woo had called it the latest-model "Packard." It was as long as two beds, with a roofless front seat that exposed the driver to the sky, while the backseat, where Chen tai sat, was separated from the front by a glass window and covered with a roof. The front grill shone bright silver in the sunlight, and the four black tires had bright white circles on them. Pei hoped she could sit up front in the open air, even if Lu didn't say a word to her the entire trip down to Central.

"You can sit on my other side," Chen tai said, as Lu, dressed in a chauffeur's uniform, with two rows of gold buttons up the front of his black jacket, opened the back door and stepped aside.

"Get in from the other side," she heard Lu's voice command.

Pei hurried around to the other side of the car and reached out to pull on the handle of the shiny black door as she'd just seen Lu do. The door opened with a deep click and swung out toward her. Pei quickly stepped in and pulled the door closed. The tan seats were smooth. They smelled of leather polish and, faintly, of cigarette smoke.

When Chen tai settled into the seat next to her, she brought along the strong scent of gardenia. The slippery sound of her blue silk cheongsam against the leather suddenly made Pei conscious of her own simple tunic and pants. Until that moment, she had never felt out of place wearing them. Pei moved closer to ˌthe door afraid she was taking up too much room. From her purse Chen tai pulled out a flowered fan, flipped it open, and began fanning the thick air in the enclosed space.

"It's hot," she muttered.

Pei wasn't sure if Chen tai was talking to her or not, so she simply stayed quiet, watching closely as Chen tai grabbed a handle on the door and rolled down the window.

"Aren't you hot?" Chen tai turned to Pei and asked. "You can roll down the window if you want."

"Thank you." Pei smiled. She did the same thing with the handle on her side of the door, each revolution bringing the glass window down lower.

When the big car roared to a start, then lurched forward, Pei gripped the door handle, white-knuckled. They pulled out past the iron gates; other houses darted by as they picked up speed. Pei felt as if she were gliding on air. Chen tai snapped open her compact and powdered her nose. For a moment, Pei allowed her body to relax into the soft leather seat.

Central was, as Ah Woo had said, another world. Pei looked back and forth from one side of Des Voeux Road to the other. She was hypnotized by the tall buildings, the double-decker electric trams, the colorful signs, the throngs of people, the ragged beggars, the voices and bells that rang and clanged through the humid heat, the thick, sickening fumes from the cars that crowded the road.

"I'd like you to stop at Lane Crawford's," Chen tai said into a horn-shaped speaker in front of her.

Lu's voice suddenly filled their enclosed space, hollow and distant. "Yes, Chen tai."

Pei sat up in her seat and stared through the window at the back of Lu's head. He leaned over and replaced the horn-shaped speaker without turning back.

"Let's see how much it takes for Chen seen-san to really go into debt, shall we?" Chen tai said, not smiling, staring straight ahead.

Pei made a small sound in response, wincing inwardly at the thought that she was again caught in the middle of the Chens' game.

Lu turned onto a wide, crowded street and coasted to a complete stop in front of a large store with big glass windows.

"The latest styles from London and Paris." Chen tai stepped out of the car before Lu had a chance to open her door for her. Pei sat and waited for Chen tai to tell her what to do next.

"Come along, then," she heard Chen tai call.

Pei quickly got out of the car and hurried after her. Horns

blared at the Packard blocking the road, but Lu ignored them all. More people than Pei had ever seen in one place pushed along the concrete sidewalk. The hum of movement made Pei dizzy as she followed Chen tai through the glass double doors into the cool, quiet Lane Crawford department store. Instantly, Pei was embraced by the soft, hazy lighting, and the sharp, perfumed smell of cosmetics.

"Good afternoon, Chen tai," the saleswomen called as she moved from one department to another, trying on hats, then gloves, then shoes. Chen tai lingered longest in the dress department, caressing a red taffeta evening dress from Paris, only to abruptly let it go, hissing, "Chen seen-san prefers cheongsams."

As the afternoon drifted on, Pei carried more and more packages, stumbling after Chen tai, who never seemed to tire. Waiting in the handbag department, Pei stared down into a glass case where black and brown bags were on display. She wondered what she would put into one of them. She had traveled through life with so few possessions. Pei closed her eyes against the glare of the glass, then opened them. She looked up, and a face across the wide aisle made her heart clench, then beat rapidly. She tried to swallow, but her throat felt dry and sore. That narrow face was so much like Lin's. Pei stared a moment longer, stunned, but when Lin's brother Ho Yung looked over in her direction, she quickly turned away from those dark eyes, Lin's eyes.

"What's the matter?" Chen tai said. "You're as pale as a ghost!"

Pei gathered up all Chen tai's packages, the pulse throbbing at her temple. "I'm fine." She struggled, willing herself to keep moving. For a moment, it was almost as if Lin had returned and were right across the room from her.

Chen tai glanced at her watch. "Well, we'd better be getting back. Lu must be waiting for us in front."

Pei didn't dare look over in the direction of Ho Yung again. She bowed her head low and quickly followed Chen tai back out into the blinding white sunlight.

Chapter Four

1939–40

Pei

Pei awoke just before dawn, a gray light seeping through the window of her small room. She pushed herself deeper down into the bed, wrapped herself tighter in the thin blanket. Since she'd seen Ho Yung at Lane Crawford's, her nights had been restless, punctuated by dreams that left her exhausted in the morning when there was so much work to be done. It was as if some small part of Lin had come alive again, bringing back a dull ache of memories.

Pei stared up at the ceiling, then closed her eyes and tried to sleep. She remembered again her first morning at the girls' house. The biting smell of ammonia. The low hum of voices. She couldn't have been more than eight years old. She'd awakened to see someone staring down at her. "My name is Lin," the girl had said, her face so smooth and delicate compared to Pei's large features. It took little time for Pei to realize that Lin's beauty was second only to her kindness.

Pei opened her eyes and forced the memory away. The house creaked and shifted in the wind. She couldn't help but wonder how Ho Yung might have reacted if she'd dared to approach him that afternoon. "Do you remember me?" she might have asked.

Or she could have said, "Ji Shen and I are managing quite well here in Hong Kong."

A faraway rooster crowed the start of another day. What if Ho Yung hadn't remembered her? Pei grew warm at the thought. She flung off her blanket, her feet touching the cold wood floor as she hurried to the small dresser and carefully pulled open the top drawer. Buried beneath her clothes was the worn envelope that held all her savings. She extracted it and flipped through the bills until she found what she was looking for: Ho Yung's card, with his Hong Kong address printed in careful black lettering.

Each day Pei immersed herself in the monotony of washing and ironing. When it rained she worked in the cluttered laundry room next to the kitchen. But despite the cooler winter weather, Pei preferred to wash in the gray tub out in the backyard. She looked forward to being in the fresh air every morning, and to the occasional visits from the gardener, Wing, who was usually carrying a rake or broom when he sauntered by, just in case Ah Woo or Chen tai should catch him loitering.

"She's in a bad mood today," Wing said that morning, gripping the broom in front of him. He made halfhearted sweeping motions.

"Who?" Pei poured the hot water from the kettle into the washtub.

"Chen tai. Always gets into a mood when Chen seen-san's away on *business*."

Pei pushed a loose strand of hair away from her face, then dropped a pair of Ying-ying's overalls into the hot water. "What do you mean?"

"Everyone knows that Chen seen-san supports another family in Singapore."

Pei jerked her head up. "Even Chen tai?"

Wing nodded. "It's been going on for years now, but everyone pretends otherwise. It's the way of the rich."

"And how many wives do *you* have?"

Wing laughed. "One is more than enough for this poor man!"

Before Pei could say anything else, the back door swung open. Wing quickly began sweeping the stone pathway, just as Ah Woo stepped out.

"What are you doing back here? You know Chen tai wants fresh cut flowers in her room now!" Ah Woo snapped.

"Yes, yes, right away." Wing winked at Pei, then hurried back to the front garden.

"Don't know what I'm going to do with that old man!" Ah Woo continued, her face stern and tired.

Pei scrubbed the overalls. She'd never seen Ah Woo so harried. "Is everything all right?"

Ah Woo paced back and forth, then stopped in front of Pei's washtub. "I guess there's no way to ask you this, but to just come out and ask you."

Pei stopped washing, her hands slippery with soap and water. "What is it?"

"Have you seen Chen tai's pearl necklace?"

"No." Pei dried her hands on her black cotton trousers. "I didn't know she had one. I've never seen it."

"After breakfast, when Chen tai went back to her room, it was gone."

"You don't think I—"

Ah Woo's face softened. "You're the only one who has been in her room this morning."

"To pick up the laundry," Pei said, her voice tight and strained. "Just like every morning!"

"You know I have to ask," Ah Woo continued. "Perhaps Chen tai just misplaced it. She's not herself when Chen seen-san's away." She touched Pei on the arm. "Don't worry, I'm sure the necklace will turn up."

Ah Woo stood there awkwardly for a moment, then mumbled something about Leen and hurried back to the kitchen. When the back door clicked shut behind her, Pei felt a cold breeze graze the back of her neck. The sky turned heavy and gray as she plunged Chen seen-san's white shirt into the washtub and began scrubbing furiously.

That night at dinner, Pei only sipped at her winter-melon soup. She could hardly eat. Everyone was quiet except for Fong, who spoke nonstop about Ying-ying.

"That girl is a monster," Fong said, helping herself to more rice. "I waited, then circled the school four times before I rushed back here to find her in her room. And do you know what she said to me? 'You were late, so I walked home myself.' She is a demon!"

"Ssh!" Ah Woo said. "Watch your tongue if you value your job!"

Leen stood up and spooned more soup into Pei's bowl.

Fong smiled, pushed more rice into her mouth. "It's not my job you should be worrying about," she said, glancing at Pei.

Again Pei couldn't sleep. She lay perfectly still until her every worry was magnified in the darkness. Since the shopping trip to Central a few weeks ago, everything had gone so well. Chen tai had even turned to Pei and said, "We'll go again soon," before she stepped out of the Packard.

Now everything had changed. All day Pei stayed in the laundry room and kitchen, away from the others. But when Chen tai came into the kitchen after dinner looking for Ah Woo, Pei couldn't avoid her cold glare. Afterward, Pei retired to bed early with an upset stomach.

Chen tai's pearl necklace was missing, and how could they not suspect Pei, when she alone entered the Chens' bedroom each morning? Pei kicked away her thin cotton blanket, punched her pillow. She'd never so much as seen Chen tai's necklace, and even if she had, why would she risk her job by taking it? Pei was relieved that she hadn't brought Ji Shen into the house. What if blame had been placed on the girl because she dusted Chen tai's room, or picked up the laundry for Pei? As unhappy as Ji Shen was attending Spring Valley, Pei was at least thankful she was above suspicion at Ma-ling's boardinghouse.

The next afternoon, Ah Woo was waiting for Pei in the kitchen when she carried in the laundry to be ironed. From the pale, severe expression on Ah Woo's face, Pei knew something was very wrong.

"There you are," Ah Woo said, more to herself than to Pei.

"Did you find the necklace?" Pei put down the basket of clothes and sat down.

Ah Woo nodded.

"Where?"

From her lap Ah Woo lifted the black candy tin that Fong had given her. "Is this yours?" she asked.

Pei sat up stiff and straight in her chair, as if she had suddenly awakened from a dream. "Fong gave it to me a few weeks ago."

"Did you ever open it?" Ah Woo pulled off the lid.

"Yes, and I left it on my dresser. It was just butterscotch. I never thought . . ."

Ah Woo shook her head. "Fong told Chen tai she found the pearl necklace in this candy tin in your room. She admits it was wrong of her to go into your room, but she only wanted something sweet to suck on, and then she remembered the candy she'd given you."

Pei stood up, knocking the chair over. "She's lying! It wasn't me! Can't you tell Chen tai the truth!"

Ah Woo looked up at Pei. "It's Fong's word against yours. Even if I know that she's nothing but trouble, she has always known how to keep herself on Chen tai's good side, especially when Chen seen-san's away."

"It wasn't me!" Pei repeated.

"I'm sorry." Ah Woo avoided Pei's eyes. "Chen tai would like you out of the house by tomorrow morning."

"But you must know the truth!"

"It doesn't matter what I know." Ah Woo shook her head, reached out for Pei's hand. "Chen tai won't listen. Fong has really gone too far this time. But she can only play with fire for so long without burning herself." Ah Woo stood up and pushed an envelope toward Pei. "Here's your salary, paid up until the end of the month. I'll make sure Song Lee knows what really happened. And Fong . . . Fong will learn her lesson soon enough. I'm so sorry."

Pei stood helpless, the tears burning behind her eyes. She watched Ah Woo walk out of the kitchen; the door swung closed behind her.

Pei refused to stay in the Chen household until morning. After she'd finished ironing the day's laundry, she packed her few possessions in a cloth sack, determined to walk the two hours back down to Wan Chai. Not all Ah Woo and Leen's pleas could make her stay another night in the same house with Fong, who slyly remained upstairs with Ying-ying.

"Please stay. It will be dark soon," Ah Woo begged, moving to block the door. "You can say good-bye to Wing tomorrow morning before you leave."

"Eat, eat first," Leen insisted, gripping a cleaver in her hand.

Pei glimpsed the ingredients of their dinner already lying on the counter—a dark, slippery catfish ready to be steamed, long stems of green onion, a bundle of bok choy, and sliced black mushrooms.

"No." She swallowed the sourness that had risen to her throat. "Please say good-bye to Wing for me."

Pei lingered a moment in the doorway, trying to smile reassuringly at the two women; then she stepped outside and banged the door closed behind her.

* * *

The large, gated houses of Po Shan Road gradually gave way to smaller houses and taller apartment buildings as Pei walked down the hill. Occasionally a voice rang out in the dark. Pei still couldn't believe Fong would go to such lengths to get rid of her. Had she been planning it ever since she'd given her the tin of candy? Leen had warned her to watch out, and still, Pei had stupidly fallen right into Fong's trap.

With each step she took, Pei grew angrier. Through her blood raced thoughts of revenge, laced with self-pity, and then despair at having to find work elsewhere. She gripped the cloth bag and swung it over her shoulder, thumping it hard against her back. Pei took a deep breath. It would be all right, she told herself. She had put aside some money in the past six months, and she and Ji Shen would be together again. Pei ached for Lin to guide her to safe ground. The cool night air swirled around her, pushing her onward.

Wan Chai bustled at night: the congested tenements, the bars with their flashing signs, the brassy music that blared out of opened doorways. Pei sidestepped crowds of drunken sailors with scantily dressed Chinese women. A loud voice screamed out in a hard, gruff language. A rumble of laughter filled the dense, smoky air. Pei kept walking and didn't dare turn back.

By the time she reached Ma-ling's boardinghouse, it was late. Downstairs, the herbal store was completely dark. She imagined the old herbalist holed up in a back room, sleeping happily amidst his precious remedies. Her own legs suddenly felt weak from the tiredness that spread throughout her body. Pei looked up to see lights still flickering from the windows of Ma-ling's sitting room. Only then did she allow herself to relax.

Song Lee

Song Lee had sensed Fong would be trouble from the first moment they'd met, three years ago. It was all there in the other woman's quick, impatient demeanor and forced smiles. Newly arrived from Shun-te, Fong lived briefly at Ma-ling's boardinghouse. She was anxious to begin her new life in Hong Kong. "I'll take whatever position you can find for me," she'd said, confidently. "I can always move up from there."

Song Lee had sipped her tea and watched the pale young woman, with her prominent square jaw, a sure sign, Song Lee knew, of one who was stubborn and self-centered. And Fong's dark, three-cornered eyes left her with a discomfort she couldn't name. Then Song Lee remembered what her own mother had once told her: "The eyes mirror the heart of a person. An entire life can be seen through them. Love, sorrow, deceit, pain. If you look closely, it's all there." Fong's eyes darted from side to side; she avoided looking directly at Song Lee when she spoke. Her flitting gaze reminded Song Lee of a Siamese cat—intelligent, yet conniving.

She recalled the Siamese owned by the first Tai tai she'd worked for in Hong Kong. One evening, as the cat was being lovingly stroked by the Tai tai, it suddenly jerked around and viciously clawed her, drawing blood and leaving fine red lines that remained on her fleshy arm for weeks. The Tai tai screamed bloody murder and gave the cat to her servants to look after. "The cat can't be trusted," the servants whispered. "It's just lucky we aren't eating it in tonight's stew." When Pei mentioned Fong's name again, Song Lee felt the same mistrust surge through her.

The morning Ah Woo sent her a note saying that Chen tai had let Pei go, Song Lee at once knew the dismissal had something to do with Fong, even before the rest of the characters on the page confirmed her suspicions. Song Lee went to work trying to find Pei a new household immediately before rumors could spread. Hong Kong was a small world, where words sped from one household to the next. Song Lee imagined how stories took on a life of their own, exaggerated with each retelling: "She found herself pregnant, and had to take the necklace in order to get rid of the baby," or "The husband gave it to her to keep quiet about their love affair."

Over the years, Song Lee had heard all the rumors; she knew the awful lengths to which some servants would go to get ahead. She cleared her mind of idle gossip, and learned early on to go directly to the source.

The following afternoon, she went to Ma-ling's boarding house, hoping to learn what had really happened. As December approached, the weather was turning cooler, with a slight breeze that brought relief from the humidity. Song Lee stopped to catch her breath and peered into the crowded herbalist shop, to catch her own reflection in the dark window. Her face had filled out in the past year, the deceitful glow of wealth and serenity that many Tai tais also had when they reached middle age. What Song Lee saw in the mirror wasn't the emaciated face she'd had when she almost died, years ago. Song Lee still cringed at the thought of the excruciating pain that racked her stomach and burned through her intestines until she begged to die. She'd drunk down that soup, tasting just a hint of bitterness, never realizing that each sip brought her closer to death. For days she lingered, until the poison slowly seeped from her body and, to everyone's surprise, she lived.

Pale and drawn, Pei answered the door and led Song Lee up to the sitting room, bleached a pale gray in the weak afternoon sun. "I didn't take it!" Pei said, even before Song Lee sat down. "I've never even seen Chen tai's necklace."

"Why do I feel Fong knows a great deal about Chen tai's necklace?" Song Lee said.

Pei nodded, her lips pressed tightly together.

"I've already begun looking for another household for you," Song Lee said gently. "Before any rumors start." She watched as Pei poured her tea, then leaned over to offer her a plate of almond cookies.

"Why would she do such a thing?" Pei's voice was raw and tight.

Song Lee cleared her throat. "I suppose she felt threatened by you. Especially since Chen tai had taken a liking to you. Ah Woo told me as much in her letter."

"I never did anything to Fong."

"It's nothing new." Song Lee shook her head. "Why, I know of a girl who poisoned another just to get her position. A week went by before she was found out, and then it was only because she was foolish enough to keep the poison hidden among her clothes instead of throwing it away. When she was asked why she hadn't gotten rid of the poison, the girl said she was afraid she'd need to use it again in the future!"

Pei's eyes widened. "Did the other girl live?"

"Just barely," Song Lee answered, and felt a twinge in her stomach. She leaned closer to Pei. "Unfortunately, Fong isn't so simple-minded, and life has gotten too complicated in this big city. At least in the silk villages, we were all working for the same cause. There wasn't this vicious competition for money and rank."

"Who will have me now?" Pei swallowed, fingering a frog on her tunic.

Song Lee smiled. "Don't worry, we'll soon see."

Word of Chen tai's stolen necklace spread even more quickly than Song Lee had imagined. By the end of the month, many of the Chinese households she approached weren't interested in hiring Pei. "Why risk a thief?" they said, or "A bad seed will never blossom into a flower." Even if the rumor was just a rumor, no Chinese household wanted to hire a servant whose past carried even a sliver of bad fortune.

Song Lee spent all her free time making inquiries, putting the word out through other silk sisters. She visited Pei and Ji Shen as much as she could, and often found them in the sitting room, where Pei diligently helped Ji Shen with her homework. Song Lee remained in the doorway, not wanting to disturb them.

"You have to try harder," Pei said, her voice raising in exasperation.

"It doesn't matter how well I do." Ji Shen slapped her book shut. "They'll make fun of me anyway. If it's not my accent, it's my clothes. It won't make any difference if I get the best grades in the class!"

Pei softened. "It does matter. It's what you do for yourself."

Shrugging, Ji Shen looked up to see Song Lee standing in the doorway. "I'll finish this later," she said, gathering up her books and quickly leaving the room.

Song Lee sat down next to Pei, and couldn't help but feel she was interrupting. "Ji Shen's growing up."

"She has a mind of her own," Pei said, frowning.

Song Lee saw tiredness in Pei's eyes, and knew it had to do with the weeks that had gone by with no hint of a new position. "But would you want her to be any other way?" Song Lee gently asked.

"No, you're right. And she has been happier since I've been back," Pei continued, "At least I'm able to spend more time with her."

"She needs someone strong in her life right now. She's lucky to have you," Song Lee said reassuringly.

"Sometimes I'm not so sure I'm the right person," Pei said, her voice strained. "Ji Shen seems to think that my wanting her to get an education is some kind of punishment."

"Nonsense! One day she'll thank you. Just enjoy the time you have off. You'll be busy again soon enough. I promise!"

The following day, Song Lee made a quick stop at Ma-ling's on her way to pick up a new cheongsam for her Tai tai at a seamstress in Wan Chai—she was always careful not to take too much time away from her own duties. As Song Lee left the boardinghouse, Ji Shen was trudging down the street on her way home from school. Song Lee saw something troubled and faraway in the young girl's gaze as she meandered down the sidewalk, swinging her schoolbag back and forth, distancing herself from the crowds with each thrust of her bag. Song Lee smiled and stepped toward Ji Shen, more determined than ever to find Pei a position before the end of another month.

Two weeks later, Song Lee hurried up Ma-ling's narrow wooden stairs. And when Pei came into the sitting room, the older woman was too excited to wait until she'd caught her breath.

"I—found you—a new—household," she said panting.

Pei suddenly came alive, her face widening into a smile. "Where? How?"

"You see," Song Lee continued, "not everyone believes what they hear. They prefer to judge for themselves."

Pei grabbed Song Lee's hand. "Thanks to you."

Song Lee dismissed Pei's gratitude with a quick click of her tongue. "You will go to see her tomorrow morning. She has a large flat on Conduit Road."

"What is this Tai tai's family name?" Pei asked eagerly.

Song Lee hesitated for just a moment. "You haven't been placed in a Chinese household. You'll be working for an Englishwoman named—she sounded it out, clutching the piece of paper tightly in her hand—"Car-o-line Fee-inch."

Lily of the Valley

Pei climbed the stone steps to the second-floor flat and knocked lightly on the door. She brushed away the dust on her white tunic and smoothed back stray hairs. Ever since Song Lee had told her about her new employer, Pei's fears had multiplied and swarmed around her. She'd never been alone in the same room with a white devil before, much less had a conversation with one. She wondered if she should look directly at the woman, or keep her eyes lowered. Should she wait to speak until spoken to? And just how would they understand each other? Pei had asked Song Lee. She'd always thought English sounded loud and harsh.

Song Lee had eased her fears. "The Englishwoman knows how to speak Chinese. She has lived in Hong Kong for many years, so there won't be any communication problems."

Pei persisted. "But what if I say or do the wrong thing without knowing it?"

"Don't worry," Song Lee reassured her. "I'm sure she'll tell you how she likes things done. I've heard the English are set in their ways, but at times much easier to work for than the Chinese are. At least they don't hide what they're really thinking behind false smiles."

Pei sighed wondering which was the lesser of two evils.

Ji Shen was excited to hear that Pei's new position wasn't in a Chinese household. "Maybe I'll be able to go with you," she'd said. "It'll be as good as going to school, learning about a whole new way of life," she'd added, with a sly smile.

"You'll still have to finish school." Pei bit the thread off as she finished sewing Ji Shen's black trousers. "There you are!" Over the years Pei had darned Ji Shen's and her own clothes with such skill, the many mendings were hardly noticeable. The last thing she wanted was to embarrass Ji Shen in front of her classmates.

Ji Shen reached for her trousers. "Anywhere would be better than Spring Valley!"

Pei heard quick, hollow steps approaching the door, and swallowed her fears. Her head was swimming with quick thoughts. She could always say no to the job if she didn't like the Englishwoman, even if doing so meant she might be out of work for another few months. She could stretch her savings if she was careful. And just the thought that she had a choice helped Pei to stay calm.

"Come in, come in," a high, tight voice with a strange accent rang out even before the door was fully opened.

Pei bowed her head and smiled shyly.

"Do come in," the voice repeated. It was sharp and cheerful, as if on the verge of laughter. "We won't get to know each other any better with you standing outside my front door!"

Pei raised her gaze to see a thin, smiling woman with a face full of wrinkles, her gray hair knotted loosely at the top of her head.

"I've come about the—"

"You must be Pei. I'm Caroline Finch. Please, come in." She opened the door wider, reached for Pei's arm, and pulled her gently inside.

Pei had never been in a room quite like this one before. Large and comfortable, it was dark and embracing, with sturdy rose-colored velvet furniture and heavy damask drapes. Crowded bookcases lined one entire wall, and throughout the room, on white embroidered doilies, were glass figurines of all sizes and shapes. There were more glass pieces than Pei had ever seen before.

"I'm a collector of sorts," Mrs. Finch said, following Pei's gaze. "The figurines are from all around the world. The late Mr.

Finch often brought them back to me when I was unable to travel with him."

Pei smiled. "They're very beautiful."

"Dust collectors mostly, but they remind me of other places, other times." Mrs. Finch pointed to an overstuffed armchair. A tray of tea already stood on the table in front of it. "Please, have a seat."

"Thank you." Pei sank down on the edge of the smooth velvet cushion. When Mrs. Finch sat down, a soft scent of lily of the valley rose from her.

"I'm not the type to mince words," Mrs. Finch began. "So tell me, what's all this about you taking a necklace?" She eyed Pei closely.

"I didn't take it," Pei answered flatly, feeling hot as blood flushed her face. She had never expected this Englishwoman to know what had happened in a Chinese household. She'd always felt a world apart from the white devils, with their strange ways and strong odors.

Mrs. Finch watched her for a moment longer. "Hong Kong is a ridiculously small place, after all, with everyone scampering to get ahead. My mother taught me early on to go by my instincts. 'Trust yourself,' she said. 'Then there'll be no one to blame but you!' Somehow, I don't believe you would take the necklace."

Pei lowered her gaze and felt a rush of tears well up behind her eyes. How could this stranger, a white devil, believe her when so many Chinese had already condemned her?

"Tea?" Mrs. Finch poured from a shiny silver pot.

"Shouldn't I do that?" Pei asked, startled. She couldn't imagine Chen tai pouring tea for her.

Mrs. Finch filled a china teacup with red roses on it. "Nonsense! I'm certainly capable of pouring a cup or two of tea."

Pei flinched. "I'm sorry." She clenched her hands tightly in her lap, not knowing what to do next.

Mrs. Finch smiled and handed her a cup. "Don't be frightened. I just want you to know that I'm capable of pouring my own tea, as well as a host of other duties. I don't expect you to cater to my every whim, though you will have to listen to me go on about things." She poured herself a cup of tea and sat back. "I *do* expect you to do the cleaning and some cooking, and to run the daily errands. Everything else, we'll deal with when we come to it. Now, is that acceptable to you? If it isn't, I'd prefer that you speak up now."

Pei grasped the warm teacup in her hands. She'd never been spoken to so directly before. It took a moment before all Mrs. Finch's words sank in. "Yes," Pei answered. "Yes, it is very acceptable."

"Good; then it's settled. Well, you can begin next week if you'd like."

"There's one more thing." Pei turned to Mrs. Finch and looked directly into her green eyes. She'd made a decision: This time, she wouldn't leave Ji Shen behind. "I have a younger cousin who's still in school. She has no one else. She has to come with me."

"Well . . ." Mrs. Finch spooned another lump of sugar into her tea and stirred. "I've rattled around this old apartment for years since Howard passed on. Never needed anyone. Lately, I've wanted to hear the sound of another voice again. Not to mention that I could use help dusting all these bloody figurines. A nuisance, really." Mrs. Finch smiled and sipped from her teacup. "Perhaps it's two voices I need, after all. Bring the child along, then."

Pei cleared her throat, wondering what the English word "bloody" meant, but simply smiled back in relief. The cluttered room felt warm and welcoming. She watched Mrs. Finch reach for the silver teapot, her hand trembling slightly, but refrained from helping her. Only when Mrs. Finch offered her more tea did Pei lift the light, fragile cup toward her.

Chapter Five

1941

Pei

The music that floated from Mrs. Finch's room every morning sounded like a low moan that moved up and down in waves. Pei stood mesmerized outside the door, balancing the heavy silver breakfast tray, and waited for a pause in the music before she knocked and entered. Since Pei had begun working for Mrs. Finch almost a year ago, this had become their morning ritual. Mrs. Finch had tea and toast in bed before she rose and "stepped into a new day," as she'd put it the first morning Pei came to work for her.

"Ah, there you are!" Mrs. Finch raised herself to a sitting position and patted the yellow chenille bedspread next to her. "Bach's Cello Suites," she whispered. "Music for the soul." Mrs. Finch closed her eyes as she listened to the music.

Pei smiled, set the tray down on the bedspread, and flung open the heavy drapes. She tidied up the stacks of records on the desk, then turned back to Mrs. Finch, who squinted and raised her hand against the bright autumn light.

"Twenty years I've lived in Hong Kong, and the only thing I've ever missed about England is the dear old London fog." She laughed. "Just look what this tropical heat has done to my skin!"

"It looks fine to me," Pei said. She opened the rosewood

armoire, pulled out two flower-print cotton dresses on hangers, and held them up. The comforting scent of lily of the valley floated into the room.

Mrs. Finch poured her tea, then looked up. "The one on the left, thank you."

Pei carefully laid the dress on the chair by the door and hung the other up. In the past year she had come to learn the simple habits of her employer. Unlike Chen tai, who had kept Pei on pins and needles with just a look or gesture, Mrs. Finch was kind and straightforward. There were no confusing contradictions in the small household. And it wasn't long before Pei learned to trust that what Mrs. Finch said was what she meant.

"Did Ji Shen get off to school all right?" Mrs. Finch scraped butter across her toast, then dropped a spoonful of marmalade on top.

"Oh, yes."

Pei was grateful that Mrs. Finch and Ji Shen liked each other. At first, she'd struggled with doubt—could Ji Shen live in such a different world? Even the air in the flat seemed to harbor a foreign scent. It was Song Lee who had finally put all her fears to rest. "Ji Shen has already been through so much in her young life," she said. "Do you think adapting to a new household will harm her? The important thing is that she's with you. Besides, I can tell by this woman's large eyes that she has an open heart."

Pei couldn't imagine how difficult things might be if Ji Shen were still as unhappy as she had been a year ago. But they'd settled into their new life at Mrs. Finch's with relative ease, and Ji Shen seemed to like St. Cecilia's much better than Spring Valley School. It was thanks to Mrs. Finch's kindness that Ji Shen was attending St. Cecilia's instead of a public school farther away. Mrs. Finch was a staunch Catholic, and St. Cecilia's had long benefited from her donations and charity work. They weren't about to turn Ji Shen away when she arrived there one morning with Mrs. Finch.

"She's such a bright child," Mrs. Finch said now. "It's a pity Howard and I never had any children of our own. God's will, I suppose."

"You would have been a wonderful mother," Pei offered.

Without answering, Mrs. Finch took a bite of her toast.

Pei would never forget how generous Mrs. Finch had been on the day they arrived. The living room was warm and dark, the drapes still drawn tight against the morning light. Opening them, Mrs. Finch looked down at the street. "Is the young man down there with you?"

Quan had brought them to Conduit Road in his rickshaw.

"Yes; he just wants to make sure we're all right." Pei waved for him to leave.

"Ah, it's nice to know that chivalry is still alive and well."

But then Ji Shen rushed to peek out the window—and knocked over a glass swan. It cracked against the table. "I'm sorry!" Ji Shen cried. "I didn't mean it." She hovered behind Pei.

In the pause that fell before their next words, Pei was sure they would have to return to Ma-ling's. She stood there helpless, holding the two broken pieces in her hands.

But Mrs. Finch surprised them by shaking her head. "Those knickknacks are a nuisance. Well, one less to dust this way. Come along, then, let me show you to your room."

All Pei's second thoughts about working for the Englishwoman began to fade. And then were banished forever when, instead of leading them toward the kitchen quarters as Pei had expected, Mrs. Finch led them down the hall to a good-sized guest room with two single beds, a dresser, and a mirror. Pei couldn't imagine ever sleeping in a room next to Chen tai and Chen seen-san. Only the baby amah would be allowed to stay on the same floor as her employers, much less in a room so close to theirs.

"Here?" Pei exclaimed. "It's so big!"

"It's about time it was used for something other than a storage room for my past exploits as a teacher." Mrs. Finch waved apologetically at a stack of boxes at one side of the room. "It could use some cleaning, though."

Ji Shen looked out the window. "There's a beautiful garden." She smiled, dropping her bag.

Pei whispered, "Thank you."

"Welcome to your new home." Mrs. Finch cleared her throat. "You must be thirsty. What would you both say to some tea?" On her way out of the room, Mrs. Finch gently pushed aside one of the boxes, and the clinking of glass filled the room.

Everything was uncomplicated for Mrs. Finch. Pei's cooking was mediocre at best, but she had no trouble boiling Mrs. Finch's potatoes and frying her piece of meat. Afterward, she prepared rice and a plate of fish and vegetables for herself and Ji Shen. Pei was thankful that Mrs. Finch had to have her food plain and simple. "I'm afraid my days of rich, spicy sauces are over," she often said with a sigh.

The first time Mrs. Finch had showed her how to cook her meals, Pei could barely resist lifting the meat out of the pan before it became too dry and overcooked. "Just leave it," Mrs. Finch directed. "I like my meat cooked all through, just like my mum used to make it!"

It was much more difficult to please Ji Shen, who had eaten Moi's cooking back at the girls' house and found Pei's efforts decidedly less satisfying.

Each morning, Mrs. Finch had taught Pei a few simple words of English, words she might use at the marketplace, names of fruits and vegetables mainly: "ap-ple" and "or-ange," "po-ta-to" and "to-ma-to." Pei was thrilled with each new word that came from her lips. Mrs. Finch had even rummaged through one of her boxes and produced a small blackboard to teach Pei to write the funny-sounding words.

"A lifetime ago I was a teacher," Mrs. Finch explained. "It runs through my veins, but you have my permission to stop me if I get carried away."

Pei never stopped Mrs. Finch. As if she'd been starved, she couldn't seem to learn fast enough. She moved from words to phrases, the new language rolling off her tongue like a song. Not since Lin had taught her to read and write Chinese characters at the girls' house had anyone taken the time to teach her. Pei smiled to think how much fun Lin would have had repeating over and over, "One, two, three ap-ples in the bas-ket."

Sometimes, in the late afternoon, after the flat had been cleaned and dusted, Pei found some spare time to sit with Ji Shen as she finished her homework in the kitchen. These were her few precious free moments before she began preparing dinner. She loved to sit down across from Ji Shen and practice writing her words on the blackboard, the chalk screeching across the surface until Ji Shen couldn't stand it anymore. "I'll finish the rest of my work in the bedroom!" she said, more times than not, gathering her books and stomping off.

Now Mrs. Finch patted the bed next to her. "Sit down for a moment. I want to tell you something."

Pei knew Mrs. Finch's "moments" could easily lead into hours of reminiscing and stories. During Pei's first few months on Conduit Road, Mrs. Finch had recounted her life story. "I was born and raised in Cheltenham, England," she said. "I knew if I didn't find my way to London as soon as I was out of school, I'd marry, live, and die in a small English village."

Pei had listened intently; then, for the first time she began to divulge bits and pieces of her own life to someone outside the sisterhood.

"I thought I would live the rest of my life in Yung Kee doing the silk work," she began, "but it seems that life plays tricks on you."

Mrs. Finch smiled. "For better or worse, I suppose. But at least we were destined to meet."

Pei nodded, a sad stillness running through her. She couldn't help but wish Lin had lived to meet Mrs. Finch. "I had a friend who would have loved talking to you."

"Had?"

"She died in a fire." She realized it was the first time she'd ever said the words aloud.

"I'm sorry; it must have been horrid for you."

Pei suddenly wished she hadn't brought up Lin's death. "Yes," she said, unable to say any more.

"Time heals," Mrs. Finch said gently, then turned toward the window and changed the subject, as if she could read Pei's mind. "Well, it looks as if it'll be another nice day."

Pei removed the breakfast tray and sat down on the yellow chenille bedspread. Mrs. Finch closed her eyes again, opening them when the music ended. "Since the end of summer, there have been rumors," she began, "that the Japanese will eventually make their way to Hong Kong."

Pei nodded grimly. She'd heard the same rumors down at the Central Market, the prating of servants who insisted Hong Kong would be swallowed up by the Japanese even though it was a British colony. Still other servants spoke of the thick layer of fear rising in the households of the Westerners they worked for: "The wife had everything packed and ready to be shipped back to England by the time the husband came home from work!"

During the first few weeks of September 1941, although Pei watched and waited, she saw little change in the carefree, extravagant Hong Kong way of life. She said nothing to Ji Shen, who had barely survived the Nanking massacre, and who still suffered from nightmares about the death and dying she had witnessed. It wasn't fair that she should have to relive the horror.

Without Lin's guidance, Pei wouldn't know where to go if they had to leave Hong Kong. Now, she wondered if she should seek out Ho Yung, who had been so kind to them once before, but then she shyly put the thought to rest.

"Will you be leaving Hong Kong?" Pei asked.

Mrs. Finch smiled. "Oh, no, my dear, I have no intention of leaving. If the Japanese want me out, they are going to have to carry me out of this flat! And I promise you, that won't be an easy task. But in the event that something so awful does happen, I'd just like us to be prepared, that's all. I didn't mean to frighten you."

Pei breathed a quiet sigh of relief. "Yes, of course."

"Bottled water, canned food—we need to stock those kinds of things. You can never be too safe. I don't know how Mr. Finch and I made it through the war back in 1914. London was all but shut down; there was so little food and no fuel. It's the only time I've ever thanked God that we had no small children to worry about."

"Where did you go?"

"Go? We stayed put. London was our home. I was still teaching at the time. Howard hadn't been called to serve because he was already in his forties. He never did feel right about it. Volunteered in every civilian war effort he could. Sometimes, he was out till all hours. I worried about him just as if he were out on the battlefield." Mrs. Finch smiled. "I remember those nights sitting in wait, trying to concentrate on some book by candlelight, while all the time I was wondering when he'd come stumbling back in." Mrs. Finch's voice trailed off. "Only this time, Howard won't be here."

Pei touched Mrs. Finch lightly on her thin wrist. "But Ji Shen and I will be."

"Yes." Mrs. Finch perked up. "And we girls shall prevail, won't we!"

* * *

By the first week of October, Pei had bought dozens of cans of meat and vegetables, sardines, and boxes of crackers. Now she packed everything into a cardboard box and rearranged the pantry. She planned to continue buying a few more cans each week, just in case. As she pushed the box back behind the other dry foods, she suddenly remembered Moi hiding her clay jars of herbs and dried fruit in Auntie Yee's room. Almost three years ago, the Japanese had seized Canton, and most likely Yung Kee, in one clean sweep. Pei hoped Moi had somehow kept herself safe at the girls' house. She pressed her hands to her knees and forced herself to rise. A wave of fear swept over her as she hurried to her room and carried back the jars of dried herbs and fruits Moi had given them to hide among their other supplies.

Ji Shen

A year ago, when Ji Shen first arrived at Mrs. Finch's Conduit Road flat in Quan's rickshaw, she hadn't really known what to expect.

Quan had shown up at Ma-ling's boardinghouse the morning they left. He insisted on taking them to Conduit Road.

"It's too far," Pei protested.

"I've taken white devils all the way up to the Peak," Quan boasted. He flexed his long, thin arms as if to prove his strength.

Ji Shen smiled. "It's very nice of you to think of us."

Quan seemed to take that as a yes; he began loading their few possessions and Moi's jars into a basket behind his rickshaw. "Get in," he said, "and enjoy the ride."

Ma-ling had packed them sweet rice cakes and dried plums, and even the old herbalist emerged from his shop and stood in the doorway to send them off. In the bright sunlight, Ji Shen thought he looked small and fragile as he helped Pei into the rickshaw. Then he smiled and handed Pei a cloth bag, fastened with a piece of blue ribbon.

"It's tea," he said. "The kind that helps you dream."

Ji Shen watched Pei squeeze his hand tightly before letting go. Then, in the rickshaw, sitting next to Pei as they climbed up the paved streets, she felt both happiness and excitement for the first time in months.

Ji Shen never thought she would feel comfortable in a *gwei lo*'s home, but Mrs. Finch was as unlike a "white devil" as she could imagine. The flat was dark and crowded, and Ji Shen had never seen so many objects in one room before. Every table was covered with glass figures. Mrs. Finch hadn't even been angry when Ji Shen accidentally broke a glass swan. From what Ji Shen had heard from Quan, many Chinese Tai tais would have beaten her for less.

"At least most Westerners pay me," Quan told her a few months later. "When they yell 'Sha!' from the doorways of restaurants and hotels, it's a race to see which puller reaches them first. But one time I couldn't get to the Hong Kong Hotel fast enough for one Chinese Tai tai, and she just climbed down from my rickshaw and walked off without paying. When I ran after her, she told the doorman I was bothering her!"

"That's terrible."

"You can't trust anyone out there." Quan shook his head. "But this Englishwoman seems nice enough."

Ji Shen nodded. "Pei likes her a great deal. Mrs. Finch is even teaching her English."

Quan laughed. "From what I've been hearing, she'd probably be better off learning Japanese!"

"Don't say such things!" Ji Shen scolded, her voice harsher than she had expected. She caught herself, realized Quan knew nothing of the murders of her parents and sister by the Japanese devils in Nanking. "It might come true." She clutched the edge of her tunic.

Quan wiped his dirty palms against his trousers. "I won't let anyone hurt you," he said with a shy smile.

Even though Pei said little about the Japanese armies making their way to Hong Kong, Ji Shen's classmates whispered among themselves: It was just a matter of time before the Japanese came. Some of the European families had already left. Now sixteen, Ji Shen felt her past terrors begin to loom large again. Most of the time, she refused to believe anything was going to change—she liked Mrs. Finch and St. Cecilia's, and the uniform dark blue sweater and skirt that made her feel she was no different from any other girl there. And she loved living with Pei again. Not since Ji Shen was a little girl with her own family in Nanking, before the Japanese invasion, had she felt so secure.

Sometimes, Ji Shen found Quan waiting for her when St. Cecilia's let out. He'd be hovering around the front entrance of the pale pink building, craning his neck in search of her. The first few times she'd been excited to see him, but as Ji Shen made more friends, she found herself secretly wishing Quan would stop coming. Each time the final bell rang, her heart skipped a beat as she walked out the door, fearing he'd be there.

"So you really like this school?" Quan asked. He had waved at her when she came out of the building, and there was no way she could avoid him.

"Very much." Ji Shen looked around to see if anyone she knew had seen Quan. He had grown taller and stronger in the past year, but at almost seventeen, he still had his boyish smile and callused hands. He was constantly pulling down on his too-short tunic, and she couldn't help but wish his clothes had grown along with him.

"Who's that?" her friend Phoebe Lee had asked a few weeks ago.

"Just a *sha* who pulled us once," Ji Shen quickly answered. "He recognized me and came over to say hello."

Phoebe wrinkled her nose. "I'd rather he didn't say hello if it were me."

Ji Shen had shrugged and changed the subject.

At least Quan was without his rickshaw today; she assumed he had left it somewhere close by. "You came all this way to ask me something you already know?"

Quan stammered, "I had a fare to run not far from here. I thought I might see you coming out of school."

"Oh, that's nice of you." Ji Shen began walking briskly down the street.

"Are you in a hurry?"

Ji Shen didn't stop. "Yes, I just remembered that I'm supposed to help Pei polish the silver this afternoon."

"I'll come along," Quan said, catching up.

"No, you don't have to. I'm sure you have something more important to do than walk me home." Ji Shen knew her next words were cruel as soon as they'd left her lips: "You'd better get back to your rickshaw."

Quan stopped. "So you'd rather I didn't go with you?" His voice sounded small and tight.

Ji Shen paused for a moment. "Thanks, but I don't have much time today." She smiled, then swung her book bag between them. "Maybe another day. I'll meet you down by the ferries."

Quan's face revealed nothing, even as he shrugged and turned away. Ji Shen imagined he had already lived a lifetime of trying to please people and being rejected. He had told her he'd pulled a rickshaw since he was twelve, when his father had fallen ill and died within a few months. Since then, it had been up to him to support his mother, and younger brother and sister. Ji Shen swallowed her guilt, but it was becoming obvious to her that her new life at St. Cecilia's didn't include him. Why couldn't he understand that? For the first time in her own life, Ji Shen felt well-liked and was eager to learn. The school was bright and clean, and the popular girls included her in their group. There was Mei Wa, whose father was a doctor; Phoebe Lee, who wore lipstick after school; and Janet Teng, who shared her lunch of steamed pork buns with Ji Shen. Sister Margaret, the strictest teacher at St. Cecilia's, even admired her slightly slurred northern accent. Ji Shen just didn't want to lose any of that.

"On Sunday morning," Ji Shen yelled after Quan. "I'll meet you down by the pier."

Quan turned around with a smile. "Ten o'clock!" he yelled back with a wave.

Ji Shen hurried down to Central. She had told Pei she was going to Mei Wa's house to study after school, but she really wanted to buy a copy of "Moonlight Serenade," the latest record by Glenn Miller. Mrs. Finch allowed Ji Shen to use her phonograph for a short time each afternoon. She had two dollars, saved the past two months from her lunch allowance, tucked in the side of her shoe.

Central was busy and crowded. More people came to Hong Kong every day. Once in a while, Ji Shen saw signs of the war with the Japanese in the half hearted advertisements for war bonds, in the sandbags piled in front of tall, important-looking buildings. But as she stepped into the record store, Ji Shen forgot everything but the Glenn Miller record.

The first time she'd heard music coming from a spinning black disk, she thought some ghostly force must be hidden in the fine grooves to make the music emerge.

"How can it be?" she asked.

Mrs. Finch laughed and showed her how the needle picked up a groove and played back what was recorded on it. "It is a little piece of magic," she said. "I remember when Howard first brought this Victrola home. It was just after we'd moved to Hong

Kong back in 1921. He carried in this wonderful box and set up the elegant horn, and with several good turns of the handle, we danced all night to Irving Berlin. Even now, every time I lift the arm and place it on a record, I think I'll turn around and Howard will be waiting for the first dance."

Ji Shen watched the record spinning on the turntable, imagining a young Mrs. Finch and her husband twirling around the room.

"Since then, I've accumulated quite a collection of records." Mrs. Finch looked at the stacks of 78's sitting neatly on the desk. "But I'm rambling. What I wanted to say was that if you'd like to borrow the Victrola for a bit each day, you may. It has brought me great pleasure over the years since Mr. Finch died. Here, you try." Mrs. Finch stepped aside and gestured Ji Shen to pick up the metal arm.

"Thank you." Ji Shen's hand shook as she lifted the slender arm, in which a fine needle was set, then placed it gently on the spinning record. It jumped and skipped a moment before settling into a groove to produce a scratchy, sweet strain of music that filled the air.

By the time Ji Shen returned to the flat, she was hot and tired. She climbed the stone steps and carefully felt for the record that she'd slipped into her schoolbag between her Chinese and history books. By the time Pei caught on that she'd bought yet another new record, it would already be old. Not that she liked to keep secrets from Pei, but in the past month, Pei had become even more careful than usual of every dollar she made. "You never know what the future will bring," she said, never looking Ji Shen in the eyes. The more pessimistic Pei became, the more Ji Shen wanted to go out and spend.

The front door creaked open and Mrs. Finch's familiar sweet scent met Ji Shen.

"How was your day?" Pei's voice was a sudden surprise. Ji

Shen stepped into the cluttered living room to see her dusting the glass figurines.

"Nothing new." Ji Shen shifted from one foot to the other. She cradled her book bag, hoping her record hadn't cracked. Then she would have spent all her lunch money for nothing! She glanced around the room. "Where's Mrs. Finch?"

Pei replaced a glass piece on the table, then flung the cleaning cloth over her shoulder. "She left to have lunch with her friend Mrs. Tate, and to take care of some errands. She took a taxi and said she'd be home by dinner, or else for us to go ahead and eat."

"What are we eating?"

Pei stood up and stretched. "Steamed vegetables and chicken."

Ji Shen shrugged and went into the kitchen to make herself a cup of Ovaltine. Her stomach rumbled. She looked for the tin of biscuits she'd seen in the cabinet the other day and grabbed a handful. Ji Shen ate the crackers hungrily, then drank down her Ovaltine as she waited for Pei to return to her cleaning. Only then would she steal into Mrs. Finch's room and quietly listen to her new record.

Possessions

Caroline Finch stroked the last of her old records, then put them carefully in a sturdy box and taped it closed. Pale late-autumn sunlight streamed through the window, revealing a shower of dust motes in the air. She couldn't believe how much she had collected over the years. As she looked around her cramped flat, she saw glass figurines, needlepoint pillows, teacups . . . the remnants of a past she planned to seal away. By the first week of November, Mrs. Finch had slowly begun packing her things, usually when Pei was out at the market, Ji Shen at school, so she wouldn't worry them.

With each passing day, it became more evident that the Japanese would invade Hong Kong. Since September, when the Japanese had occupied Indochina, the Americans and British had imposed embargoes on all steel and oil exports to Japan. Tensions were running high in the Pacific, and many of Caroline's oldest friends were leaving Hong Kong and returning to England.

They pleaded with her to do the same. "Please, Caroline. You can't stay here alone."

"Hong Kong is my home now. Besides, I'm not alone. I have Pei and Ji Shen with me."

She listened as their voices grew excited and they raised their hands in exasperation, as if talking to a stubborn child.

"Caroline, you must be reasonable. They're servants, not your family."

"Ah, but they are my family." Her voice was calm and certain.

While Mrs. Finch wasn't about to leave her home, it didn't hurt to tidy up. There was no point in letting the old records clutter the room when she barely listened to most of them anymore. It seemed like a lifetime ago that George Gershwin, Rudy Vallee, and Kate Smith had kept her swooning, made her believe that anything was possible. Even now, their songs still evoked memories that stung her heart. She remembered how "You Made Me Love You" had been playing when Howard came home with the news of his promotion. He stood tall and handsome in his dark suit as he announced, "We're off to the colonies, old girl." It took Caroline a moment to realize what Howard was saying: He was being sent to manage the Hong Kong branch of his London bank. Ever since she was a little girl, Hong Kong had seemed like a fairy tale. The days before they were to leave stuffy old England couldn't go by fast enough.

Mrs. Finch patted the box of records and remembered the joy

and excitement as if it were just yesterday. When the steamer made its way into Hong Kong Harbor, dozens of junks and sampans accompanied her ship to the dock. Voices cried out in high, nasal tones. The smell of salt and fish filled the air. Entire families lived on the tiny boats that bobbed along beside the steamer. Clothes hung across cluttered decks to dry, and half-naked babies were strapped across their mothers' backs as the women cooked over steaming black pots. Caroline looked beyond the boats to the tall peak rising dark and majestic from Hong Kong Island. It was the most wonderful sight she'd ever seen.

As soon as Caroline set foot in Hong Kong, she knew she'd found her new home. Howard was just as captivated. For eight years they had lived a charmed life, discovering new aspects of their adopted home. She had refused to follow the example of other English expatriates, who clung together in stuffy clubs and had afternoon tea together as if they'd never left England.

Instead, while Howard was at the bank, Caroline embarked on a rigorous project of learning to speak Cantonese and getting to know the Chinese people. "What a beautiful baby!" she'd once exclaimed in Chinese to a baby amah strolling down the street with a baby in her arms.

The amah wrapped her arms tighter around the baby as if shielding it from her. "No, no!" She shook her head and raised her voice as she backed away. "This boy has the face of a dog! He will have a very hard life."

Only later did Mrs. Finch learn that the baby amah believed the superstition that providence might take away a baby who was too smart or good-looking. Even now, she blushed at all the mistakes she'd made over the years. It didn't take her long to realize that living in another culture was like being a child and learning everything all over again.

In those early years, Caroline liked to linger at the marketplace with her first cook amah, Kuo. The sharp, pungent smell of the live pigs and chickens reached her first, along with the bargaining voices. The buyers haggled over everything, from the dried sausage and the ducks to the fist-sized tiger prawns still twitching in wooden crates. The first time Caroline entered the market, a headless chicken ran around in circles, blood spurting from its neck, only to collapse at her feet.

Kuo shook her head disapprovingly whenever Caroline struck up a conversation with the old fruit-and-vegetable peddler who roamed her street every morning. Each time she heard his high, singsong voice calling out, in Chinese, "Or-anges . . . ba-na-nas . . . or-anges!" Caroline ran down to the front door, buying fruits and vegetables by the bunch in order to keep up the conversation and learn more about how he lived. "He's harmless. Old enough to be my grandfather," she told Kuo, ignoring her glare.

Soon Caroline became friendly with the thin, wiry peddler, whose name was Chang. After a while, he showed up every morning and tapped lightly on her front door, offering her his fruit at bargain prices.

"Two for the price of one!" He held up two oranges in one hand.

"It's a deal," Caroline said, choosing two more oranges from one of the baskets he balanced on a pole across his neck and shoulders.

"How many hours do you work?" she once asked, hoping he understood her broken Cantonese.

Chang shifted the pole across his shoulders. "From day to night," he answered.

"And what about your family?"

A toothless smile flashed proudly across his wrinkled, sun-baked face. "Five children," he said. "Not so many for a man who is almost forty years old. My oldest girl just turned twelve years old, and my youngest son, newly born!"

Caroline was taken aback. In the weeks she had known Chang, she'd assumed he was already an old man, a grandfather with grown children. She looked closer at the deeply lined face, the stubby shadow of beard, and the dark, tired eyes. She was several years older than he was. Caroline's heart skipped a beat as she stepped back into the doorway. It was one thing to chat with an old man; it was another to become too familiar with a man her age or younger! She would never want to cause Howard any embarrassment.

"And you, Tai tai, how many children do you have?" Chang lifted the pole from his neck and gently placing the two baskets of fruit on the ground.

"Oh, we weren't blessed with any children." Caroline looked down at the basket of oranges, then back up at Chang. "I really must go now."

Chang watched her closely. "The Tai tai seems upset this morning."

Caroline paid quickly, blushing. "I'm in a bit of a hurry today," she said, gathering up her oranges. "Well, good-bye, then." She balanced the fruit in her hands as she stepped back into the cool, dark entranceway and hastily closed the door.

Caroline had been careful after that. She would never do anything to jeopardize Howard's career with the bank. They had married late in life, just past her twenty-sixth birthday. Before then, she hadn't met anyone she wanted to marry. Howard had been a bachelor of thirty-two. He was shy and awkward, but his kindness had won her heart. For three decades, theirs was a marriage built on love and friendship.

After Howard had unexpectedly died of a heart attack, almost twelve years ago, Caroline was in a state of shock. His sudden death left her dizzy, as if the room were spinning around her. She needed to hold on to anything that was a reminder of their life together. Caroline couldn't throw away a thing. She wouldn't abandon Howard as he had abandoned her. The first few days after he had died, she turned to the empty space in their bed and placed her cheek on his pillow, breathing in the lingering scent of him. The same ritual continued with his starched white shirts, which still hung in the closet. She wrapped the lifeless sleeves around her neck and imagined herself and her husband dancing together again. A last dance. At fifty-six, she was certain her life had as good as ended.

"You can't keep mourning," friends had told her after six months. "You'll feel much better once you get out."

Mrs. Finch had read somewhere that Chinese women mourned the death of their husbands for three years, dressed from head to toe in black.

"Yes," she agreed, her entire body numb.

"You still have a full life ahead of you," they added. "And when you return to London . . ."

Then, thinking they were being helpful, they packed away Howard's clothes and left her closet half-empty, her life even emptier. Caroline remembered waking up the next morning and turning to Howard's side of the bed. She placed her cheek on his pillow and breathed deeply, smelling nothing but freshly laundered sheets. She turned full-face into the pillow and pressed down hard into it. A simple thought flowed through her mind. *It would be so easy to follow him.* Her heart pounded in her breast, throbbing in her temple like a drumbeat. She held her breath until her lungs felt as if they'd burst. A few minutes longer and it would all be over . . . over . . . over . . .

Caroline jerked upward, gasping for breath like the fish at the marketplace, their bodies flipflopping, reaching for air. She breathed in huge mouthfuls, as if swallowing water for a parched throat. When she had calmed again, she lay back onto her pillow. She had no intention of returning to London, she realized. She dismissed all her servants and began to live life on her own.

Mrs. Finch sighed heavily. She was sixty-eight: her dancing days were over, her legs already stiff and tired from kneeling on the floor. She stacked the few records she listened to these days— Bach, Handel, and Mozart—next to the Victrola. Classical music was still a comfort. She stood up and felt lightheaded, the room spinning around her. Mrs. Finch staggered to her bed and fell heavily onto it.

"Are you all right?"

Mrs. Finch looked up to see Pei standing in the doorway. She smiled at the young woman who had become her closest companion in the past year. "Yes, yes, of course. Nothing youth and beauty wouldn't cure."

Pei quickly propped up her pillows behind her. "Youth and beauty just come with another set of problems."

Mrs. Finch knew Pei was concerned about Ji Shen. In the past few months, the girl's grades had been slipping, and she didn't seem to care about anything but clothes and listening to the latest records. The situation had gotten so bad that Mrs. Finch had taken away Ji Shen's phonograph privileges: "Just until your grades pick up." Ji Shen had simply shrugged and pressed her records tightly against her chest.

"Growing pains. She's seventeen," Mrs. Finch said. "They'll pass."

Pei nodded and sat down at the side of her bed. "What mischief were you making in here?" She pointed to the cardboard boxes on the floor.

"Packing away more of the past. No point in cluttering up the room anymore!"

"Soon I won't recognize this room."

"Maybe later you can help me put those boxes away in the hall closet."

"Of course," Pei said, standing up. "Would you like your tea now?"

Mrs. Finch gently reached for her arm. "Sit awhile."

Pei sat down as she always did, without protest. Mrs. Finch had grown so fond of Pei, so quickly. There was something genuinely good and honest about her. As in her Howard. She also liked Pei's quick intelligence, and her ability to compliment an old lady who talked too much.

"Have you ever lost someone you felt was your entire life?"

Mrs. Finch watched the expression on Pei's face change from surprise to understanding.

"Yes," she answered calmly.

"Do you believe that kind of love ever dies?"

Pei brushed back a strand of her hair and looked squarely into Mrs. Finch's eyes. "No. I believe it lives within you down the most difficult paths in life."

Mrs. Finch smiled and wondered if it was the friend who had died in a fire that Pei was remembering. She had said so little about her past life, offering only tidbits: that she was born in the delta region outside Canton and had grown up doing silk work in the village of Yung Kee.

Mrs. Finch leaned forward. "Yes. But sometimes, we do find others to love and cherish." She looked down at her swollen hands and pulled off her emerald ring with difficulty. "This ring was the first anniversary gift Howard gave me, over forty years ago. I want you to have it." She pushed the ring into Pei's palm.

"Oh, no." Pei pushed it back.

Mrs. Finch persisted. "You are the child I would have hoped to have. You and Ji Shen have given me great joy in the past year. I want you to have something that was a token of the great happiness that Howard and I shared. You deserve no less, my dear."

Pei looked down at the ring, then back at Mrs. Finch. "But I can't . . ."

"Of course you can. Now, how about that tea? I'm parched."

Mrs. Finch eased back against her pillows. As if some great weight had been lifted off her shoulders, she watched Pei hurry out of the room, still clutching the ring in the palm of her hand. Mrs. Finch breathed in the warm, slightly sweet air. It was much easier to let go than she had thought.

1941

Pei

The long, high-ceilinged room was hot and steamy. The faintly sweet scent of cocoons unraveling in boiling water rose up around her. Pei's legs felt numb from the long hours of standing. Her reeling machine whizzed faster and faster, and she rushed to pick up the main threads from the cocoons soaking in the iron basin in front of her. But just as Pei finished reeling the one bunch soaking, she'd look down to see another sink full of cocoons waiting for her. She couldn't keep up, no matter how fast she worked, her fingers scalded by the hot water each time she reached for a thread. Pei glanced up through the steam and spoke to Lin working right beside her, but Pei's voice was lost among the whirling machines that whistled louder and louder. . . .

The high-pitched whistling sound startled Pei awake. For a moment, her hands still grasping at the invisible thread, she couldn't tell where she was. At last she roused herself from her steamy sleep and looked over to see Ji Shen sitting up, wide-eyed, in the bed next to hers.

"What's that noise?" Ji Shen asked, her voice trembling.

The whistling grew louder. "I don't know."

Pei jumped from her bed and glanced out the window, just as a quick shadow shrieked by her toward the stone wall that divided the building behind them from the one next to it. The shell exploded with such a roar Pei thought the entire building would collapse on them. The force of the blast knocked her to the floor. Glass from their window splintered everywhere and Pei felt a sharp sting along her hairline. The entire flat was vibrating. Pei's ears rang and her eyes watered as acrid smoke drifted through the broken panes. She faintly heard Ji Shen's screams through the haze; then she became aware of the muffled sounds of barking dogs, and high, frantic cries from the street. Then Mrs. Finch's voice rose louder yet, calling from her room in a mixture of English and Chinese. "Oh, dear God! Are you girls all right?"

As the smoke cleared, Pei picked herself up off the floor and rushed to Ji Shen, who'd also been knocked down. "Are you all right?"

"Your head?" Ji Shen pointed, as she rubbed her arm.

Lightheaded, Pei tasted the salty, metallic tang of blood that dripped from her temple to the corner of her mouth. "I'm fine," she assured Ji Shen, though her head throbbed. "Let's see about Mrs. Finch."

She grasped Ji Shen's hand and pulled her through the debris to Mrs. Finch's room. The hallway was dark and smoky. Pei's eyes stung as her thoughts flickered back and forth from the shocking to the mundane—the sight of Lin's charred body after the fire, the dark spot she had tried endlessly to rub out of the kitchen floor, the clothes she washed yesterday and hung to dry in the back room . . .

Mrs. Finch met them halfway, wobbling unsteadily to her doorway in a rose-patterned cotton nightgown. "A fine wake-up call," she said, pale and shaken, then added, "Thank God, thank God!" She opened her arms wide as both Pei and Ji Shen rushed into her embrace.

The following morning, after the first all-clear siren sounded, they made their way back to the flat from the nearest bomb shelter, still dazed by the violent events of the night before. Mrs. Finch walked briskly and tried to keep up a cheerful demeanor. "What I wouldn't do for a nice cup of tea," she remarked lightly.

But when they opened the door to the flat Pei heard Mrs. Finch's stunned intake of breath. A smoky veil still lingered in the air. While the building itself was mostly intact, everything in it seemed to have been lifted up and slammed back down again. Windows had been blown out. Glass figurines littered the floor; many were smashed beyond recognition. Paintings and needlepoint pictures that once hung on the wall had been hurled across the room. The heavy furnishings lay toppled.

Mrs. Finch coughed in short sputtering sounds. Pei quickly picked up an overturned chair for her, and patted her back as Ji Shen ran to the kitchen for a glass of water.

When Mrs. Finch had drunk it, Pei cleared her own dry throat and said, "Let me make some tea."

"No, please." Mrs. Finch grasped her arm. "Humor an old lady. Allow me to fetch the tea this time."

Pei and Ji Shen watched as Mrs. Finch stood up and hurried to the kitchen, shattered glass grinding beneath her shoes.

Later that afternoon Mrs. Finch suggested that Pei and Ji Shen move into the living room, which faced the other side of the building, but Pei refused.

"Once we sweep up the glass and pick up the pictures, it will be our room again. We can't run away from our fates."

Instead of arguing, Mrs. Finch relented. "I don't imagine I'll change your mind now that it's made up." She looked pale and tired.

Pei and Ji Shen immediately set to work cleaning their room and putting everything back in order. While Ji Shen held board after board across their blown-out bedroom window, Pei nailed them down until the window was completely covered. When they were done, Pei stood back, her head throbbing from all the pounding.

That night Pei was suddenly awakened by the floor creaking under footsteps. She heard the soft cadence of Ji Shen's even breathing accompanied by another rhythm—shallower and faster. Pei lay still, her heart racing, her eyes darting across the dark room. It took her a few moments to realize that it was Mrs. Finch's thin figure standing so quietly in the doorway.

"Is everything all right?" Pei's voice jumped out in the darkness.

Mrs. Finch took a step forward. "I'm sorry to wake you. I couldn't sleep, and I wanted to check and see if you girls were all right. I was also wondering . . . if you'd ever gotten around to putting by some supplies?"

Pei threw her covers off and in the next moment stood grasping Mrs. Finch's trembling hands in hers.

"Don't worry, I've put aside enough to last us a good month or more," Pei whispered.

Mrs. Finch squeezed Pei's hand tightly as she struggled with her words. "You needn't worry about me. According to rumors I'm afraid the Japanese will probably call me in if it comes to that. If so, I want to make sure there's enough for you and Ji Shen. I'm just glad Howard isn't alive to see how the world has gone mad."

"We're still together," Pei whispered. She wanted to say something more comforting, but in the dark warmth of the room, she simply put her arms around Mrs. Finch, wishing she could protect her forever.

By December 12, Japanese dive-bombers were devastating Central both day and night, while artillery screamed across the harbor from Japanese-occupied Kowloon. Mrs. Finch, Pei, and Ji Shen huddled in the darkness of the rank, crowded bomb shelters. Fires raged through Central and Wan Chai, and Pei prayed to the goddess Kuan Yin that somehow Song Lee, Ma-ling, and Quan were safe from all the destruction. So far, there had been no word from any of them. When the bombs finally stopped long enough for an all-clear siren to wail, the night air was thick and bitter with smoke.

By the end of the second week in December, the blackout was enforced every night, while constant shelling targeted the Central District. Japanese propaganda blasted from the harbor in English, Chinese, and Hindi: "We have come in friendship to free you from British imperialism." Next came the staticky strains of "Home Sweet Home."

When they weren't rushing to a bomb shelter, threading their way through debris and craters that scarred the roads, Mrs. Finch drowned out the constant propaganda by playing her own records. Pei knew this was for the benefit of Ji Shen, who'd grown increasingly quiet, barely saying a word to anyone. School had been canceled and Quan was nowhere to be seen. Every time the high shrill of the air-raid siren went off, she covered her ears with her hands and silently followed Pei to the shelter. Pei wondered what kind of fate would force Ji Shen to endure the trauma she had experienced in Nanking yet again. How many times would she have to relive that nightmare? It seemed so unfair.

Every evening after dinner, Mrs. Finch carefully slipped an old record from its envelope, telling a story with each song she played, helping Pei and Ji Shen forget for a moment that they sat defenseless against the Japanese. Pei watched with gratitude and admiration as Mrs. Finch placed a record lovingly on the Victrola, which had miraculously suffered only minor damage through the bombing of the last week.

"The first time Howard and I tried to dance the Charleston, he threw his back out and had to stay in bed for a week! I don't think there's anything more difficult than a bedridden man. Come on now, let me show you the steps." She placed the needle on the record and tapped her foot to the fast, jumpy beat. "Let's kick up our heels," she said, coaxing Ji Shen to join her.

Ji Shen hesitated, then joined in, alternately kicking up her right leg, then her left, with the beat. Their laughter filled the flat, and for those fleeting moments, Mrs. Finch had convinced Pei and Ji Shen that there wasn't a war going on and that nothing had changed. But at the sudden shriek of the air-raid siren, Ji Shen stopped and covered her ears. They all stood frozen in the middle of Mrs. Finch's room.

Mrs. Finch glanced over at Pei, then shouted above the wail of the siren. "I think they could use a little cheering up in that bloody old shelter this one time!" She stopped the music and quickly disassembled the Victrola, handing each of them a piece. Pei insisted on carrying the heavy base of the phonograph as they hurried toward the shelter.

Voices buzzed through the stale air. Pei caught bits and pieces of their neighbors' low, anxious conversations: "De-capitated . . . Strung up . . . Speared right through . . ."

"What have you got there old girl?" The elderly man calling out as they squeezed through the gathered crowd was Mr. Spencer, a retired British engineer who lived nearby.

"I thought it was about time we had some fun," Mrs. Finch answered.

"There's nothing like music to soothe a savage beast," said Mrs. Finch's friend Mrs. Tate.

They made room in the dimly lit basement as Pei cranked up the Victrola. Glenn Miller sailed through the gloominess and reverberated off the walls.

"I should have taken the gin," a voice piped up.

"And the latest Benny Goodman," Mrs. Tate added.

Just then a nearby explosion shook the room and the needle screeched across the record. Ji Shen screamed and covered her ears. When the dust settled and the explosions had grown distant, Pei got up and put another record on, then watched as Mrs. Finch pulled Ji Shen's hands away from her ears and said, "I believe this was my dance."

Less than a week later, on Christmas Day, 1941, the Japanese took control of Hong Kong, and Pei knew that nothing would ever be the same.

"A Merry Christmas to the gallant British soldiers. You have fought a good fight but now is the time to surrender. If you don't, within twenty-four hours, we'll give you all we've got. A Merry Christmas to the gallant British soldiers."

Mrs. Finch

The Japanese wasted no time in making their presence felt. Right after the takeover, roving bands of soldiers moved through the streets like locusts, breaking into stores in Central and Wan Chai and taking whatever they wanted. They wantonly destroyed all that was left behind. Mrs. Finch and Pei still heard distant gunfire from the Peak: a hopeless defense attempt by the few uncaptured British troops. Soon, the only gunfire came from the Japanese soldiers.

Amongst the general panic and uncertainty, there was an emergency meeting of all the British citizens left in the Conduit Road vicinity, who now numbered fewer than forty-five. It was held at the third-floor apartment of Mr. Spencer, less than a block from where Mrs. Finch lived. She had come to know most of her fellow expatriates well during their long hours spent in bomb shelters. In the dim, musty cellars of houses and apartment buildings, a solidarity emerged, based on fear and fading hope.

"My God, Caroline, have you heard the news?"

Isabel Tate, also a widow, rushed across the living room. Mrs.

Finch watched her quick, nervous movements, thinking Isabel would have been better off returning to London with most of the others.

"Calm down, Isabel." Mrs. Finch took her friend's hand. "What is it?"

"Have you heard? Now the Japanese are beating and murdering people who aren't bowing low enough. Gladys says you have to bow like this." She bowed low toward the ground. "And never make eye contact with them!"

Mrs. Finch tried to remain calm. "It might be an isolated incident," she said, knowing full well that the monstrous atrocities increased every day. "Aren't there other things we could talk about?" She was ready to change the subject.

But Mrs. Tate continued. "They're not only confiscating everything they can get their bloody hands on, but raping nurses and bayoneting doctors." She pulled a handkerchief from her sleeve and wiped the corner of her eye. "What's to become of us?"

Mrs. Finch tried to smile reassuringly, thinking more of Pei and Ji Shen and their vulnerability; she was sick with awareness of what could happen to them when they were outdoors on their own. "What would they want with a couple of old ladies who have one foot already in the grave! We're more of a nuisance to them than anything else."

"Exactly my point. We're dispensable!" Mrs. Tate anxiously turned to complain to another woman who had entered the room.

Mrs. Finch shook her head in sorrow, as the horrible news of Japanese brutalities spread through the room. "Why, they've left the bloated bodies of soldiers and innocent people just lying on the streets as a reminder of their Japanese superiority," Mr. Spencer was saying. "And everywhere, there's the stink of night soil dumped in the gutters!" he went on.

Mrs. Finch thought of how much easier this would all be if Howard were still alive.

A young man named Douglas—Mrs. Finch thought he was a

barrister—suddenly called for their attention. "There's no need to panic. We've been instructed to stay indoors, and to wait for our next orders from the Japanese commander."

Mrs. Finch watched Douglas pace the floor, and thought his voice soothing, perfect for a courtroom or for making these sorts of announcements. Calm and impartial.

"How long do you think that will be?" she asked.

"We're not sure yet." Douglas smiled reassuringly.

"I suppose it depends on when the Japanese call each of us in," she pressed on.

"Exactly," he said, his smile disappearing.

Behind her came the muffled cries from the other women in the room. She swallowed her own fears; they were all in for a bumpy ride.

In the next few days, Mrs. Finch's life changed in more ways than even she could have imagined. All British and Canadian civilians in banking and business positions were methodically rounded up and taken away, kept in overcrowded Kowloon hotels to await internment. Any sign of resistance would result in death, slow or quick depending on the mood of the officer in charge.

Each morning, Mrs. Finch found herself reluctantly picking up *The Hong Kong News,* the only Japanese-English newspaper, and looking down the list of all Hong Kong and British banks. Each name was followed by neat, narrow columns of safety deposit box numbers. Mrs. Finch anxiously scoured her bank's column for her own safety deposit box number, 8949. Like all the other foreigners living in the Hill District, she had been allowed to remain in her home temporarily. But when her box number appeared, she would have to report immediately to the bank and empty out her box for the Japanese authorities. Afterward, she'd be sent off to an internment camp at Stanley Beach.

Day after day, Japanese ships loaded with stolen jewelry, furniture, and even bathroom fixtures sailed back to Japan. Mrs.

Finch was thankful that she'd kept most of her jewelry and personal valuables with her. Only some important papers were in the box.

Mrs. Finch sipped her tea, nervously scanning the row of numbers in front of her. She released a soft sigh of relief when she didn't see hers, but relief turned to anger at the thought of how four simple numbers could irrevocably change her life and the lives of so many others. If she had been younger, she might have tried to make a run for it with Pei and Ji Shen, escaping into the hills of China until all the insanity had ended. But as Hong Kong residents, the girls were safer blending in among the other Chinese, and Mrs. Finch's age had reduced any other thoughts to dreams.

Isabel Tate's safety deposit box numbers had been listed in the paper yesterday. She had stopped off to see Mrs. Finch on her way to the bank, amazingly calm.

"Well, I'm off, then. Don't know what will become of me, but I suppose I'm in God's hands now." She tried to smile and kissed Mrs. Finch on the cheek. "Pray for me."

"You'll be just fine, Isabel." Mrs. Finch held on a little longer. "I'll be joining you soon enough," she whispered.

Isabel nodded.

From the window, she watched Isabel hurry back down the steps to the street, then lift her hand in a quick wave before she disappeared around the corner.

Mrs. Finch sat back in her chair, and wondered if it weren't better to be Isabel and facing her fate instead of endlessly waiting. She crumpled the newspaper and hurried off to her room. She had to do something, and her jewelry and what little money she'd hidden would benefit Pei and Ji Shen the most. Everything else she had decided to burn, rather than let the horrid Japanese get their hands on it. Just as she'd come to this decision, a dull rumbling from somewhere outside caught her attention. It gradually grew louder, and she hurried to the living room to find Pei and Ji Shen staring out the window.

"What *is* that noise?" Mrs. Finch inched her way between the two.

"It's a piano!" Pei pointed down to the street.

"What piano?" Mrs. Finch craned her head to see her neighbors the Wongs, along with their two children, pushing their grand piano up Conduit Road. The wheels reverberated loudly against the uneven pavement. "Dear God, whatever are they doing?"

"They're taking their piano for a walk!" Ji Shen laughed. "Can we go see?"

Mrs. Finch hesitated, then nodded.

They ran downstairs to the street and watched the Wongs push the piano to the end of the street, assisted by a few others who had emerged from their houses to see what was happening.

At the top of the slope, near Fierce Ghost Bridge, Mr. Wong turned around, wiped his forehead, and yelled, "You want it, you devils, you can have it!" Then, as his family stood back, Mr. Wong walked behind the piano and with all his strength, pushed it back down the hill.

For a moment, Mrs. Finch felt as if she were watching a Charlie Chaplin movie. The piano bumped and skittered across the pavement, slowly picking up momentum. The vibration of the keys against the strings made a mournful tune. The piano thundered past them and didn't stop until it had rolled all the way down the slope and off the curve in the road, smashing on the rocks below. The gathered crowd cheered, as Mr. Wong waved his hands above his head in triumph.

Mrs. Finch closed the door behind them. "And now for the big bonfire," she said, irked that Mr. Wong had taken some of the wind out of her sails, then wondered if the entire neighborhood had the same thoughts of destruction.

Pei and Ji Shen stood looking at her with blank faces. "I don't understand," Pei said.

"When I was young," Mrs. Finch explained, "we'd gather around the yard and burn all the rubbish we no longer wanted. A good house cleaning, my mum would say!"

"But what will we burn?" Ji Shen asked.

"Why, just look all around you."

Fire and Ash

With Pei and Ji Shen's reluctant help, Mrs. Finch burned everything they were able to carry. Even her needlepoint pillows and oil paintings found their way into the flames. At first, Pei thought Mrs. Finch was joking, a reaction to the splintering moan of the piano upon the rocks. But when she saw the steel-gray determination in Mrs. Finch's eyes, she argued against the bonfire—to no avail.

"But what if they see the flames? Won't we get into trouble?" Pei asked.

Mrs. Finch smiled. "You and Ji Shen are to be out of here at the first sign of trouble. I'll take all the blame. They can do as they wish with me."

Pei shook her head, arms crossed against her chest. "No, I won't let you. It's asking for trouble." Ji Shen stood silent next to her.

"I'm not looking for your permission," Mrs. Finch said, in a stern teacher's voice. "Just your help."

"It's too dangerous. The flames will attract the Japanese soldiers," Pei pleaded.

Mrs. Finch grasped a chair. "What's another fire, with all the death and destruction around us? For all they know, it's their own soldiers doing the burning! I have to do this. They can drag me away to bloody hell for all I care, but they shan't have my rugs on their floors, or my paintings on their walls. If you won't help me, I'll do it myself!"

Mrs. Finch picked up a chair and slammed it hard onto the floor, again and again and again. Her breathing was labored, but the chair remained intact.

"Please stop!" Pei begged. "I'll help you with anything you want." Her voice quivered with emotion. "But if those Japanese devils dare to show their faces, they'll have to take me along with you."

"Me too," Ji Shen seconded, coming to life again.

Pei tried to keep the fire under control in the courtyard, a black veil of smoke floating up into the sky. For a moment, she closed her eyes against the crackling heat and willed herself not to think of Lin. When she opened them, it was to see dozens of curious neighbors peeking out of their windows. When they realized what the bonfire was for, they cheered, precious possessions rained from their windows onto the fire—a French lace tablecloth, silk shirts, ties, and a leather handbag.

What they couldn't burn, Mrs. Finch left in the flat—the beds, the sofa, the dining room set, her armoire, all stripped and bare except for the essentials. All her jewelry and everything else of value, Mrs. Finch had secreted inside a hidden drawer in her armoire weeks earlier.

"Howard had it specially made," she had told Pei. "Just push this"—she knelt slowly and reached underneath the armoire for a small lever—"and out it pops." The drawer hidden behind the baseboard slid out, empty. Mrs. Finch raised herself back up and leaned close. "I promise you it'll be full the next time you open it."

The final, most difficult possessions for Mrs. Finch to part with were her books, her records, and her beloved Victrola. She set a small stack of books to one side. "I'd like you to have these if you wish," she said to Pei. Pei craned her head and tried to sound out the titles: *Gr-eat Ex-pec-ta-tions* . . . *Ro-meo and Ju-liet* . . . *Ham-let*. Mrs. Finch fingered the base of the phonograph. "And I want you to have this," she said to Ji Shen. "I can't imagine anyone else making better use of it."

The sky was darkening as they put the last books gently into the fire. The flames popped and crackled; the three women's faces were flushed from the heat. Mrs. Finch sighed, then could no longer hold back her tears. "It's like saying good-bye to dear old friends," she whispered.

The next morning the flat felt cold and empty and the biting smell of smoke still drifted in from the courtyard. Pei rubbed her eyes, wiped away a thin film of ash from the kitchen counter, then listened for any movement from Mrs. Finch in the dining room. Ji Shen was in their bedroom, listening to records. With all the schools closed, her days were filled with the low hum of music. But that, Pei knew, would soon come to an abrupt end when Mrs. Finch had to report to the Japanese authorities.

Pei felt a sinking in her stomach every time she thought about Mrs. Finch having to turn herself in. She scrubbed the counter over and over. She'd heard from some other servants that most British civilians were taken to Stanley Camp on the other side of the island. Pei's mind moved to the quick rhythm of her scrubbing. After Mrs. Finch was called in, Pei would have to find a new place for herself and Ji Shen to live; then she'd have to figure out a way to visit Mrs. Finch at Stanley. Since the bombings began, there'd still been no word from Quan or Song Lee. Pei prayed every day that they were somewhere safe. She swallowed her grief. The past year and a half of living and working for Mrs. Finch had brought her great comfort.

Pei paced the kitchen as she waited for Mrs. Finch to read the paper. Outside, the sky looked as if it might rain. She'd left Mrs.

Finch alone with *The Hong Kong News,* as she had every morning since the occupation began. Each day an eternity seemed to pass before some small sign came from the dining room, letting Pei know Mrs. Finch's safety deposit box number wasn't printed. Usually Mrs. Finch gave a sigh of relief, or a low whistle. So far, Pei had heard nothing. She pulled out their box of supplies, Moi's clay jars knocking against one another as she set the bulky box on the kitchen floor. She began dividing the foodstuffs into separate sacks, so they would be easier for her and Ji Shen to carry when the time came. Pei had just finished when Mrs. Finch surprised her in the doorway of the kitchen, the newspaper clutched in her hand.

"It's here," Mrs. Finch said matter-of-factly, steadying herself against the counter.

Pei's heart raced. "Are you sure?"

"Very." Mrs. Finch let the newspaper fall to the floor. She fitted the teakettle and clanked it on the stove to boil. "It might be nice to have one more cup of *po lai* tea before I leave."

Against Mrs. Finch's initial wishes, Pei and Ji Shen decided to accompany her down to the bank. "I don't want you girls walking back alone," she argued.

"You'll need us to help carry your suitcase," Ji Shen answered.

Pei stood before her in silent determination, until Mrs. Finch finally relented. She was allowed to bring with her one suitcase, which she'd had packed and ready for days. "No need for much," she'd said, carefully folding a few sweaters and three of her favorite cotton dresses into the case.

They walked in silence down the nearly empty streets, pockmarked from the constant Japanese shelling. The sky hung heavy and low. The once vibrant streets were battered beyond recognition. Where there had once been trees and houses, now stood empty craters and burnt-out automobiles. As they weaved around downed power lines and the rubble from collapsed buildings, Pei saw for the first time the extent of the damage the Japanese had inflicted on Hong Kong. She felt sick to her stomach as a strong and repulsive smell drifted through the chilly January air and made them all quickly cover their noses. "What is it?" Ji Shen asked.

Pei didn't point out the dead body that festered beside the road, its face no longer recognizable in decomposition. She picked up the pace along a patch of clear road, then slowed down again to avoid a mangled piece of steel and concrete that resembled part of a ship.

Pei spied a servant hurrying down Robinson Road, and was instantly filled with dread. Was Song Lee safely tucked away with her family up on the Peak? Had Ah Woo and Leen survived the bombing? And what of Quan? Dear Quan, who lived and worked on the streets. Pei tried to clear her mind and swallowed the sourness that rose up to her throat.

Once they arrived down in Central, they were surrounded by groups of Japanese soldiers in their drab, ill-fitting uniforms, rifles fitted with bayonets slung across their shoulders.

As they neared the bank, Mrs. Finch turned to Pei and said in one quick breath, "Now, you know where everything is hidden. It all belongs to you and Ji Shen. Take it and take care of yourselves. I'm afraid, my dears, our paths must part now."

"We'll keep it all safe for you. For when this all comes to an end," Pei added.

The sharp sting of cold air surrounded them.

Mrs. Finch smiled. "Of course you will." She leaned over and kissed Ji Shen, then Pei, on each cheek. "We've had a lovely time together. I wouldn't have traded it for anything in the world."

"I'll come to see you as soon as I can," Pei said, her heart racing. *What else am I forgetting to say?* she wondered. Ji Shen stood stone-still next to Pei, squeezing her hand tighter and tighter.

Mrs. Finch nodded.

Long lines of people waited in front of the bank, carrying

suitcases and other belongings, which Pei suspected would be confiscated—dangling cameras, hat boxes, makeup cases. For a moment she wished they would fight back, flinging their possessions at the thin young Japanese soldiers who pushed them along with their bayoneted rifles.

Mrs. Finch reached for her suitcase, gently prying it from Ji Shen's hand. "Please be careful walking back home," she said, her voice breaking. "God be with you both till we meet again." She waved at them to hurry off. "Go!" she commanded, slapping at the air between them.

Pei and Ji Shen barely had time to wave back before Mrs. Finch turned away from them. They watched her walk to the end of the long line, while the rain began to fall as lightly as tears.

The million and more who comprise the Chinese population of Hong Kong and who have been under British Imperialism for over 100 years have now been released. The Japanese army, by its courageous advance, has, in the shortest interval of time, lifted the hundred years of oppression which the Chinese people have suffered.

The Hong Kong News
December 31, 1941

Pei

The soft clattering of rain interrupted the flat's eerie quiet. The humidity of the day before had evolved into heavy gray clouds. With the electricity out, the room appeared dark and deserted. Pei picked up the newspaper that Mrs. Finch had dropped on the floor that morning and ripped it first in half, then into quarters. They would have to leave the flat as soon as possible now that Mrs. Finch was to be interned at Stanley Camp. There was no telling how soon after she was processed the Kempeitai—the Japanese military police—and soldiers would arrive to confiscate the rest of her possessions. Pei almost wished she could stay to see their faces when they kicked in the front door, to find nothing of value left. In the end, they had been outsmarted by an old woman.

Pei had heard rumors that the Kempeitai were cruel and unrelenting when they wanted something. How could someone as good and humane as Mrs. Finch stand up to them?

She hurried into Mrs. Finch's bedroom, where the lingering scent of lily of the valley offered a comfort, yet tempted tears. She knelt down and searched for the lever underneath the armoire, then popped open the hidden drawer just as Mrs. Finch had instructed. Inside, Pei found a cloth bag containing a diamond brooch shaped like a flower, a gold bracelet, a man's gold wedding band, and a pearl necklace. There was also an envelope of Hong Kong dollars, which, since the Japanese occupation, had been greatly devalued. And lying face down underneath the envelope was the blackboard on which she'd learned to read and write in English. Pei picked it up and turned it over. On it, Mrs. Finch had written in large, clear letters, "You will be with me always."

Pei hugged the blackboard tightly against her chest and closed her eyes against tears. When she looked again, the words were smudged, the chalk a dusty veil across her breast.

Pei and Ji Shen had been back at the apartment for less than an hour when a faint creaking caught Pei's attention. She looked up from the extra pocket she was sewing into her tunic. How could the Japanese soldiers be coming so soon? She quietly stood up, her hands shaking as she tossed aside her sewing and reached down for the sturdy piece of driftwood she kept for her protection. She listened, then heard another creak of the floorboards. With the rugs burned in Mrs. Finch's bonfire, the wood floor no longer muffled even the lightest step.

"Ji Shen," Pei whispered. Ji Shen had closed her eyes in exhaustion while Pei sewed. She quietly inched over to Ji Shen's bed, gently pushing her awake, covering her mouth to keep her from saying anything. "There's someone out there," she murmured quietly into Ji Shen's ear. Ji Shen nodded, wide-eyed, before Pei lifted her hand from the girl's lips.

"Soldiers?" Ji Shen's voice trembled.

"I don't know," Pei whispered.

Ji Shen stayed right behind her as they moved cautiously toward the closed door of their bedroom. If only Pei hadn't stopped to sew more pockets into their clothing. They had planned to gather their belongings, then make their way back down to Wan Chai, where they hoped to find Ma-ling still at the boardinghouse, or the old herbalist ensconced in his crowded shop. It was the only place left for them to go.

The floorboards creaked again, careful steps clearly heading toward their room. Pei took a deep breath, then turned around and gestured for Ji Shen to crouch down low behind the bureau. She gripped the piece of wood with both hands, ready to strike whoever entered.

The steps grew closer. Pei heard a quick intake of breath on the other side of the door; then the doorknob gradually turned. She stepped back to allow herself room to swing the driftwood. If the Japanese were to take them in, it wouldn't be without a good fight.

The door opened slowly. Pei pursed her lips and gripped tighter as a dark head appeared. She was poised to swing when a voice whispered, "Pei? Ji Shen?"

Pei froze.

"Ji Shen?" the voice repeated.

"Quan?" Ji Shen rose from behind the bureau.

Pei dropped the piece of driftwood and swung the door wide open to let Quan in. She had never been so happy to see anyone in her life. He brought with him the salty smell of fish and sweat, as she and Ji Shen rushed toward him with open arms.

* * *

"How did you get in?" Pei asked, her heart still racing in surprise as she put the last of their saved water on to boil for tea. She couldn't believe how tall Quan had grown in the past six months.

Quan rubbed his hands together and glanced shyly at Ji Shen. "It wasn't easy. I jimmied that window." He pointed to the rear of the kitchen. "I just wish I'd known you were still here. It would have been much easier to come through the front door."

"Mrs. Finch had to turn herself in this morning," Ji Shen said in a small voice.

"I thought she would have to sooner or later." Quan sipped the hot tea. "They're holding all British and Canadian citizens at the Hong Kong Hotel, then trucking them off to Stanley prison after they've confiscated everything they own."

"Will she be all right?" Pei asked, her voice breaking.

"From all I've heard about Mrs. Finch, I'm certain she will be. The Japanese take greater pleasure in parading foreign bankers up and down the streets, or bashing in the heads of Chinese citizens who walk too near them instead of crossing the street. They have better things to do than harm an old lady," he said quietly.

"We've been hoping you were all right," Ji Shen said.

Quan wiped his hair away from his eyes and said, "It's been rough. The Japanese bastards have destroyed so many areas in Wan Chai and Central with their shelling. For almost a week, it was nearly nonstop. My family and I stayed hidden anywhere it was safe—in basement shelters, mainly. We were hearing explosions in our dreams."

Ji Shen unpacked some biscuits, then sat down next to Quan. "Is your family safe?" she asked.

Quan nodded; he picked up a biscuit and chewed it slowly. "We're living on a sampan with my aunt and uncle down at the harbor. Now it feels safer on the water than on the island. Those stinking soldiers are everywhere!"

Pei poured more tea into their cups and sat down next to Ji Shen. "Have you seen Ma-ling?"

Quan shook his head. "There's been nothing but confusion. I've been back to Wan Chai, but I didn't get to Ma-ling's. As far as I could see everyone has scattered, or is in hiding. As soon as I thought it was safe, I came here to see if you were all right."

Pei took his hand in hers. "Thank you. What should we do now?" she asked, forgetting for a moment that he was only seventeen.

Quan sat up straight in his chair, taking on full responsibility. "It's best if you rest for a few more hours. We can leave just after sunset."

"What about the Japanese soldiers?" Ji Shen asked.

"It'll take them at least a day to process all their prisoners. Besides, it will be safer for us to move through the streets just after dark. I'll take you to the harbor. You can stay with my family on the sampan until you decide what to do."

"Are you sure?" Pei asked. There was no certainty they would find Ma-ling even if they did make it to Wan Chai.

Quan nodded. "It isn't much, but it's as safe a place as any for now."

"Thank you." Pei looked around the large, empty kitchen and felt something hard and cold lodged in her throat.

Ji Shen handed him another biscuit, her hand brushing quickly against his. "Thank you, Quan," she said softly.

It seemed as if Pei had just closed her eyes when she heard Quan's dull thumps against their door. "We have to leave soon," she heard him whisper.

In the gray hour just before nightfall, Pei and Ji Shen gathered the last of their belongings in the same cloth sacks they'd carried all the way from Yung Kee. Pei carefully distributed Mrs. Finch's jewelry among the pockets she'd sewed into their tunics, taped the envelope of money inside the cover of *Great Expectations,* and watched as Ji Shen struggled over which records to take.

"I didn't think it would be so hard to choose," she said, more to herself than to Pei. "I had it figured out, but now I'm so confused again."

Pei thought of all the choices that she'd had to make without Lin since leaving Yung Kee. "It's never easy."

Ji Shen glanced longingly at Mrs. Finch's Victrola. "I guess it'll have to stay."

Pei nodded.

"I should have burned it along with everything else, just like Mrs. Finch!" Ji Shen blurted, her voice shaky.

Then, for the first time since they'd arrived in Hong Kong, Pei saw the frightened young girl who had stumbled into the girls' house over three years ago. She'd never forget how Moi had found Ji Shen drenched and unconscious at their back door. For days, she lay in bed feverish, her feet swollen to twice their normal size by her horrendous flight from Nanking. When Ji Shen finally opened her eyes, it was to see Pei and Lin, and her new home in the silk factory. The story of her family's death only came out weeks later, and her nightmares continued long after. Before they'd left Yung Kee, Pei had promised Ji Shen that they would be safe in Hong Kong. Now she bit her lip at the thought that they were still running from the same Japanese who had chased Ji Shen out of Nanking.

Pei touched Ji Shen's cheek, then hugged her tight. "Sometimes you have to leave things behind in order to go on," she whispered.

"I've never had anything so beautiful before." Ji Shen pulled away and stroked the polished base of the Victrola.

"You will again, I promise."

Ji Shen cleared her throat and nodded sadly, then began packing the rest of her possessions.

Pei quickly checked each room of the flat, pausing just a moment in front of Mrs. Finch's armoire, breathing in the fading scent of lily of the valley. She hoped Mrs. Finch was safe and among friends at the Hong Kong Hotel. Perhaps the Japanese would allow all the women and children to stay there through the occupation. Pei knew this was wishful thinking—but surely not all the Japanese soldiers were barbaric? They had families— wives and children back in Japan—just like everyone else. What would they gain by hurting someone like Mrs. Finch? Pei swallowed the fear that rose to her throat.

Quan and Ji Shen waited for Pei at the front door. They all carried as much as they could. Quan swung the two sacks of food over his shoulder, and bounded down the steps with Ji Shen right behind him. Pei closed the door to Mrs. Finch's flat and locked it securely. The Japanese would most likely just break the door down, but she was determined to make it as difficult for them as she could. Pei sighed, picked up her sack, and followed Quan and Ji Shen out into the cold evening air.

Under a darkening sky, they walked swiftly down Conduit Road to avoid the Japanese checkpoint on Robinson Road. The streets were eerily quiet, with no soldiers in sight. In the semidarkness, the destruction appeared shadowy, unreal. They walked in single file down the hill, avoiding the rubble and potholes in the sidewalks and streets. A rank smell hung in the air from night soil dumped into gutters. Across one street, a car had crashed into a stone wall and remained there, a burnt-out shell. From what Pei could see, it was not unlike the big black Packard she had once ridden in with Chen tai. She cringed again at the sudden, stabbing thought of how Fong had deceived her.

By the time they reached Central, a hazy streetlight flooded the streets. Scattered groups of Japanese soldiers stood on the corners. Pei's heart pounded as she kept her head bowed low and crossed the street with Quan and Ji Shen to avoid them. "It's one thing if they single you out," Quan had instructed; "then it's better to comply. Otherwise, it's best to remain as invisible as you can, and to get out of their sight as fast as possible."

They hurried away, then turned toward the Central Market. Suddenly the street was packed. Long lines of Chinese men, women, and children, six and seven abreast, were already waiting for the market to open early the next morning. The lines seemed to be blocks long.

"What are they waiting for?" Ji Shen asked.

"Rice." Quan kept walking. "The Japanese have set up rice distribution at all the major markets. This one won't open again for ten hours, but they still wait, even though most will have to go home empty-handed, given what little is sold. We're growing hungrier by the day, while our 'liberators' feast on our chickens, squabs, pigs, fruits, and vegetables."

It was scarcely more than a few weeks into the Japanese occupation, but Pei could see its toll in the defeated faces of those waiting in the lines. Each night they had to stand for hours, with nothing to hold on to but the hope of a few grains of rice. Pei held her cloth sack tighter.

They turned down Lai On Lane, still crowded with peddlers behind their makeshift stands, selling everything from champagne and perfume for a pittance, to worn blankets and peanuts at astronomical prices. The atmosphere was strangely similar to the busy hustle before the occupation, though Pei could feel something desperate and anxious charge the air.

Frantic voices rang out, vying for a quick sale.

"Missee! Missee!" a peddler called out. "Just one Hong Kong dollar will buy you this bottle of champagne and make you forget all about the occupation!" He lifted a bottle toward them.

"What is it?" Ji Shen asked, keeping step with Pei who had picked up her pace.

"Sparkling wine," Quan answered. "Something the Tai tais and Seen-sans used to drink in abundance!"

At one of the makeshift stalls, Pei saw scorched, bloodied clothing for sale that must have been picked up from dead bodies in the streets. She shook her head and kept walking. When Ji Shen began to trail behind among the stalls, Pei grabbed her arm and pulled her along.

The harborside was no less crowded. There was no way to

avoid the soldiers who stood on every street corner, stopping people randomly to frighten them for fun.

Quan turned around once and warned Pei and Ji Shen to keep their heads bowed low and simply walk past the soldiers they were unable to dodge. "Follow me," he said, maneuvering them in and out of the crowd.

"You!" a Japanese soldier yelled.

Pei felt her heart pounding. She clutched both the cloth sacks and Ji Shen's arm tighter, willing her legs to keep moving.

"Keep walking," Quan urged them on.

"You stop now!" the voice boomed.

Pei hesitated, her tunic clinging to her sweaty skin, the cloth sack thumping heavily against her back. She felt Ji Shen begin to slow her pace, though Pei didn't dare turn back.

"Walk faster!" Quan's voice rose above the rest.

"On your knees!" the soldier ordered.

She saw Quan turn around and glance back in the direction of the soldiers. His face relaxed and his pace slowed. "It wasn't us."

Pei turned. She saw a group of soldiers hovering over a young Chinese man, who was on his knees bowing low toward the ground. One of the soldiers yelled, "I said, *lower!*" Then he lifted his boot to the back of the man's neck, and drove his face down into the dirt.

By the time they reached the sampan, Pei and Ji Shen were sweaty and exhausted. A raw, fishy smell, mixed with the stink of night soil and oily cooking, filled the air. Pei felt sick to her stomach. Ji Shen wrinkled her nose but remained quiet. Voices echoed from boat to boat as the rows and rows of dimly lighted sampans bobbed side by side.

"It's not much," Quan said.

He helped them both onto the creaking sampan. Pei steadied herself against the swaying. The sampan was larger than many of the other boats, with a bamboo-and-canvas roof covering a good two-thirds of its length. Stacks of wooden buckets were piled at one side. Just then, the canvas flap flipped open and a thin man in his fifties emerged.

"Ah, you, Quan," he said, looking relieved.

"Uncle Wei," Quan said, "my friends need a place to stay for a few days."

The small man eyed them both for a moment, then broke into a toothless grin. "Welcome, welcome to my humble boat for as long as you like."

"Thank you," Pei said.

"Come meet my family." Quan gestured for them to follow.

He flipped up the canvas flaps and Pei and Ji Shen bent over and followed him inside. After a moment, when their eyes adjusted to the dimness of the cramped space, they saw two women and two children sitting on mats and staring up at them. The oily smell of frying fish hung heavy in the air.

"Ma Ma, Auntie Wei, let me introduce Pei and Ji Shen. They are good friends of mine who need a place to stay for a few days."

The boy and girl, who appeared to be no older than six and eight, giggled.

"Quiet," Quan's mother scolded, then said, "Please sit. Would you like some tea? I'm afraid it isn't very fresh."

"Sit, sit," Auntie Wei echoed.

"Yes, thank you," Pei said, loosening the top frog of her tunic.

"And your family?" Quan's mother asked.

"There's just us," Ji Shen said, before Pei had a chance to answer.

"They're looking for some friends living in Wan Chai," Quan put in.

Auntie Wei nodded. "There isn't much room here, but you are both welcome for as long as it takes."

Pei bowed her head, astonished at the generosity of Quan's

relatives, who would take in two strangers when they themselves had so little. "Thank you for your kindness," Pei said.

They sat cross-legged on the rough straw mats while Auntie Wei poured tea into two battered tin cups. As Pei and Ji Shen sipped the tepid, weak tea, they watched the two thin, agile women roll up one side of the canvas panel to throw the dregs of the tea into the harbor. A cooling breeze filtered in and Pei leaned forward to catch a quick glimpse of white moonlight on the dark water.

During the first few weeks of occupation, all the English signs— "Queen's Road," "Kelly and Walsh," "Thomas Cook"—that Pei had practiced sounding out with Mrs. Finch were taken down and replaced with Japanese names. Rumors ran rampant through the colony about the removal of the royal statues from Statue Square to be melted down, while plans were under way for the building of a Japanese victory memorial on the summit of Mount Cameron, above Central.

"They want to call it the Temple of the Divine Wind," Quan scoffed.

"Wait until the wind changes direction!" said Uncle Wei.

Pei listened to all the rumors, though she could see for herself how the once-vibrant city grew more desolate and barren day by day. Cars and buses were quickly confiscated and shipped back to Japan as scrap metal, so transportation came to a standstill. And in the faces of the men and women Pei saw on the streets was the dazed, wide-eyed panic of animals cornered, with nowhere to run.

On the crowded, suffocating sampan, Ji Shen became quieter. She did everything Pei asked, without question. Their words became fewer, replaced by quick glances and soft whispers. Together they quietly endured bouts of motion sickness and sleepless nights;

eight people were crowded into the cramped living quarters. Despite the discomfort, Pei knew she would always be thankful for Quan and his family's kindness. It gave her the precious time to find a new place to live.

Quan's mother Auntie Lu and his Auntie and Uncle Wei were more than generous to Pei and Ji Shen. They treated the refugees like family members. In return, Pei shared the food she'd collected at Conduit Road and gave Quan's family some of her Hong Kong dollars. It wasn't much, but they could still exchange two Hong Kong dollars for one Hong Kong yen. Pei decided she would sell Mrs. Finch's jewelry only as a last resort. And never the emerald ring. She planned to keep the jewelry hidden and return every piece to Mrs. Finch when the occupation was over.

One morning after Pei and Ji Shen had been living on the sampan for two weeks, Quan left earlier than usual. When he returned late that afternoon, Pei looked twice and still couldn't believe her eyes. A red-faced, panting Song Lee was hurrying down the dock to keep up with Quan's long stride.

"Song Lee!" Pei jumped up and knocked over the bucket of clothes she'd been washing.

Song Lee picked up her pace at the sight of Pei. "Pei! Ji Shen!"

Pei quickly leaped from the boat to the dock, followed by Ji Shen.

"I'm so happy to see you," Pei said, throwing her arms around her short, rotund friend.

"Yes, yes," Song Lee repeated, her eyes liquid. "I was praying that you were both all right. We owe our reunion to Quan. He's been asking about me for the past week. It wasn't until one of the silk sisters recognized him as the sha boy that she let me know."

"We've been staying with Quan's family." Ji Shen patted the rough edge of the boat.

"Yes, I can see. And the Englishwoman?"

Pei's face fell. "She surrendered to the Japanese authorities."

Song Lee nodded her head knowingly, then quickly changed the subject. "There's a large group of us sisters living together again in Wan Chai. With all that we've saved working, most of us have rented rooms in a boardinghouse there. After the Japanese takeover, many of us who worked for Chinese families were dismissed. Or we left on our own."

"Have you seen Ma-ling?" Pei asked.

Song Lee shook her head. "What's left of the boardinghouse is deserted."

"What's left?" Ji Shen grabbed on tight to Pei's arm.

"It wasn't the bomb, but the fire afterward."

Pei swallowed, her mouth dry and bitter. *The fire.* Once again she saw Lin's charred body lying motionless on the ground. Pei could still feel the thick waves of heat that had smoldered and risen all around her that day. Lin had suffocated, the life slowly squeezed out of her, the roaring red flames never consuming her body. Had Ma-ling met another fate? And what of the old herbalist?

Many of the silk sisters had returned to Ma-ling's boarding house to find it in blackened ruins, Song Lee told them.

"They returned like bees to honey, only to learn that the hive was gone. I couldn't believe my eyes!" Song Lee shook her head. "Ma-ling hasn't been seen, though one of the sisters saw the old herbalist walking away with all the jars he could manage to carry."

A shiver ran up from the small of Pei's back to the nape of her neck. For days after Lin's death, she kept hoping Lin would wake up, as if from a deep sleep.

Song Lee shook her head. "Poor Ma-ling. I only pray that she didn't suffer."

"Yes," Pei whispered.

Song Lee changed the subject. "I hope you both will come and join us. Each day new sisters arrive. Only a few have stayed with their households, or what's left of them. The Japanese have taken or destroyed whatever they want. I've heard that several wealthy Chinese families are now all living together in one house. The last thing they want is more mouths to feed, so we amahs were immediately sent away."

Pei thought of Ah Woo and Leen and wondered if Chen tai had just as quickly dismissed them. And if so, where were they now? So many names and faces had passed through Pei's life since she'd arrived in Hong Kong five years ago that they blurred in front of her. And even now, when she closed her eyes and searched for solace, she saw Lin.

"Yes," Pei said, "we'd love to join you."

Mrs. Finch

After she had spent hours waiting in line at the bank that morning, Mrs. Finch's turn to go in had finally come. The room she was ushered into was cold and bare. A tall, well-bred Japanese officer stood waiting and greeted her in perfect English. "Welcome, Mrs. Finch; please take a seat."

Her safety-deposit box was brought in by a young soldier and placed on the table in front of them. The officer smiled at her as he snapped open the cover and began to rifle through the contents. But when he discovered only insurance and personal papers, his smile disappeared and his hand slammed down on the table.

"Where is the rest?" he barked.

Instead of keeping her head bowed low, Mrs. Finch looked up and stared him straight in the eyes. "I'm sorry; that's all there is."

"Do you think I'm so stupid as to believe you wouldn't have jewelry? Money? Please don't play a Japanese Imperial Army officer for a fool, Mrs. Finch."

Mrs. Finch removed her watch and her gold wedding band and pushed them across the table toward him. "There, you have everything I own. My departed husband was a very practical man. He didn't believe in spending money on frivolous things."

The Japanese officer paced back and forth, stopped and smiled down at her. "For your sake, I hope you are telling me the truth."

"Why should I do otherwise?" Mrs. Finch pushed herself up from the chair. "If it would make you feel better, please feel free to search me," she said, raising her arms.

The Japanese officer hesitated, then grabbed her watch and ring and motioned to the guard at the door. "Take her away!" he ordered, stepping aside for Mrs. Finch to pass.

From the bank, Mrs. Finch was taken to the Hong Kong Hotel, where she and a hundred or more other British civilians awaited transport to Stanley Camp. The lobby of the hotel was swarming with Indian and Japanese soldiers. *Young enough to be schoolboys,* thought Mrs. Finch as she was herded into the ballroom with the other prisoners. They were perched on their suitcases or sitting slumped against walls, the boredom of waiting etched on their faces.

Mrs. Finch looked around with a heavy heart. The once-grand ballroom was now just a faded shell, meticulously stripped of everything from light fixtures to furniture. Most likely, all the furnishings had been shipped back to Japan. Deep gashes and dark holes scarred the walls and ceiling wherever she looked.

Even in ruins, the ballroom brought back memories. When they'd first arrived in Hong Kong, she and Howard had often come here. Mrs. Finch remembered the orchestra playing "A Little Bit of Heaven" as they danced under the crystal chandeliers and gilded ceiling. Now she grieved to see how such a beautiful room could be so shamelessly destroyed.

Mrs. Finch saw several familiar faces, including that of the young barrister named Douglas who had directed their meetings on Conduit Road. He caught her gaze and hurried over to her.

"Let me take that for you, Mrs. Finch," he said, removing the deadweight of her suitcase. "I hope they've treated you well."

Mrs. Finch suddenly felt tired, her hand weak from gripping the handle of her suitcase so tightly. "As well as can be expected for a prisoner of war!"

"Come over here." He led her away from the open doors to a quiet corner. "We have orders to keep the doors open at all times. The soldiers barge in at all hours, with their bayonets raised for effect. One minute they want us all standing; the next, we're commanded to sit. It's a circus, but not all that frightful, as the hours wear on." For just a moment, his crooked smile reminded her of a young Howard.

"Have you seen Mrs. Tate?" she asked.

Douglas nodded. "She has been transported to Stanley, evidently." He turned and scanned the room. "I don't see anyone else from Conduit Road, but I'm sure we'll meet up again soon. You must be parched. Let me see if I can get you some water."

Mrs. Finch watched the young man walk away. She leaned back against the wall, then slowly sat down on the floor. Only when she was finally able to relax did she realize how every muscle in her body ached. The room spun slowly around her. Mrs. Finch closed her eyes against the loathing she felt for these men she didn't even know. She tried to focus, instead, on the happiness she'd had with Pei and Ji Shen. They'd become her only family, and the fear of losing them was far greater than any other horror the Japanese could inflict upon her.

Mrs. Finch opened her eyes with a start.

"I'm sorry if I woke you," Douglas said, leaning over with a cup of tepid water. "It's not exactly afternoon tea, but it's all I could find."

She smiled. "You're very kind."

Douglas sat down next to her. "Keeps me out of mischief."

Mrs. Finch was grateful for the company, even if they said few words to each other after that. Just the warmth of another body next to hers seemed to ease her fears, make her feel less lonely amidst the dull murmur of voices.

The next morning they were herded into the back of military trucks for the hour's journey to Stanley, a quiet, sleepy beach resort. Back in 1937, it had acquired a certain notoriety with the building of a new prison. The peninsula itself lay between the waters of Stanley Bay to the west and Tai Tam Wan in the east. Douglas had told Mrs. Finch that he'd heard their camp wouldn't be in the prison itself, but spread across the grounds and out-buildings and the nearby St. Stephen's College, an Anglican in-stitution. She'd let out a sigh of relief. All night she had imagined herself in a striped uniform, with a ball and chain fastened to her ankle. At least nearby was the fishing village of Stanley, which fronted the white sands of Stanley Beach and had always been a calm refuge from the noise of Hong Kong.

Though they couldn't see anything from the covered trucks, Mrs. Finch saw in her mind's eye the tall mountains and green trees, and felt the sharp curves in the road, which would take them past the Repulse Bay Hotel. All its solitude had been shat-tered less than three weeks ago, just days before the Japanese occupation on Christmas Day, when close to two hundred civilians at the hotel were taken prisoner by the Japanese. Rumors circu-lated that over fifty British soldiers and civilians had been tied up and perched at the edge of a cliff, then methodically shot to death. One by one, bodies tumbled over the rocks and into the sea. Mrs. Finch could scarcely believe that such a beautiful place was now tainted with blood.

In better times, she and Howard had often had tea at the hotel. They'd sat on white wicker chairs on the long veranda overlooking the beach, the twirling fans and string orchestra accompanying the constant buzz of the room. It was a place Mrs. Finch had always loved. Without the frantic pace of Central, Repulse Bay and Stanley reminded her of a small English village by the sea, a quainter, quieter place of the past. It was the one aspect of British colonial life that Mrs. Finch cherished.

As they bumped along the road, Douglas leaned over and said, "Do you think they'd let us take a quick dip in the ocean?"

Mrs. Finch laughed out loud. "Now, wouldn't that be a treat!" She sat back and breathed deeply, certain she could smell the sea.

When the truck slowed, Mrs. Finch heard the long whine of a gate opening, then closing behind them. The truck came to a full stop. Quick, harsh-sounding Japanese words were spoken before the canvas flaps suddenly flipped open and a blinding sunlight filled the back of her truck. With bayonets raised, the Japanese soldiers ordered them out, then lined them up under the warm sun. Mrs. Finch heard the lapping water of the nearby beach and smelled the salt-tinged air; she wished for the cooler weather of the day before. The sun's heat burned against her back; her cotton dress was sticky with perspiration. Her legs felt heavy, and her stomach growled from hunger. All they'd been given to eat both morning and night was two bowls of watery rice gruel. It seemed an eternity before the stocky Japanese officer in charge of the prison came out to inspect his new shipment of prisoners.

"Keep your heads bowed. Eyes to the ground!" a guard reminded them.

"Welcome, welcome," the officer said. A younger soldier next to him was translating. The officer clasped his hands behind his back as he strolled back and forth in front of them. "You are the fortunate guests of the Imperial Japanese Army. We wish you no harm, but you must understand the rigors of war. In order to ensure your safety during the difficult transitional days ahead, we will house you here."

Mrs. Finch felt lightheaded, the heat swirling around her like a cloud of flies. She glanced up and beyond the Japanese officer to see a handful of young Chinese boys hawking what looked like chocolate bars. They peered through the barbed-wire fence, yelling out something that she couldn't understand, until they were chased away by some Japanese guards.

"For your benefit, we will try to make your stay here a comfortable one. . . ." the officer went on.

Mrs. Finch shaded her eyes against the glare of the sun, a soft buzzing in her ears.

"You will be well fed . . . well taken care of. . . ."

His voice slowed and grew fainter. The ground began to spin beneath her feet and Mrs. Finch reached forward, grabbing at the warm air. Then everything before her eyes turned to shadows and disappeared into blackness.

When Mrs. Finch came to, she was on a wobbly canvas cot. She sat up and tried to recall what had happened. Propped up on her elbows, she looked around the small, cramped room. It was dingy and musty smelling, furnished with a few wooden crates and three other cots, side by side. Squashed bedbugs made red-brown streaks along the rough, whitewashed walls.

"Not exactly the Peninsula, is it?" a familiar voice said.

Mrs. Finch turned to see Isabel Tate walking toward her, carrying a tin cup. "Isabel," she said, her head throbbing, her words sounding thick and rubbery.

"I'm glad to see you're up. You gave us quite a scare when they carried you in. Here, take a sip." Mrs. Tate handed her the cup.

"Did I faint?"

Mrs. Tate nodded. "All a bit frightful," she said, patting Mrs. Finch's hand. "You'll be fine."

Mrs. Finch took a mouthful of what she expected to be water, but instead was brandy. She choked it down.

Mrs. Tate whispered, "It's black-market. We keep it hidden. For medicinal purposes."

"Where is everyone?" she asked.

"They're outside trying to get some exercise or waiting in some queue. Also, Griffith has called everyone in our block together for a meeting."

"Who's Griffith?"

"You could say he's the acting governor of Stanley Camp." Mrs. Tate laughed. "It's not much, but it's home." She waved her arm around the cramped room.

"Where are we?" Mrs. Finch asked.

"We're in the blocks known as the old Indian Quarters. Most of the Indian guards who used to work at Stanley prison used to be housed here. We've been divided into two main groups: the flats associated with Stanley Prison and the others belonging to St. Stephen's College." Isabel sat down heavily on the cot next to hers. "There are also the Married Quarters, the Master's House, where most of the single men reside, the Main Blocks, which house the Americans and so on. There are about three thousand of us cramped into these buildings."

"Dear God."

Isabel leaned close. "You haven't seen anything yet. Sometimes thirty-five people share a two-room flat and one bathroom. You can imagine the queues every morning. There are four of us women who share this room. I managed to get you assigned here. It was good luck I saw the truck arrive and went to sneak a peek. Rather than take you to our small infirmary, I had them carry you in here."

"Thank you."

"It's not quite as awful as it sounds." Isabel smiled. "If it weren't for the overcrowded space, bad food, barbed wire, and Japanese guards, you'd think colonial Britain still reigned."

Mrs. Finch smiled. Isabel looked and acted so unlike the frightened woman who'd come to their meetings just after the occupation began. "You seem so different."

"I've had little choice," Mrs. Tate replied. "Either I remain afraid of my own shadow, or I make do with the cards that were dealt me. It's a strange thing, Caroline. It wasn't until I simply gave up everything that I suddenly felt free."

"I know just what you mean." Mrs. Finch lay slowly back down on the wobbly cot, the bit of brandy warming her all over.

As the days passed, Mrs. Finch fell into the slow, difficult rhythm of camp life. She took long walks around the camp when she could, happy to discover, near the Indian Quarters, a wonderful spot that gave her an unobstructed view of Stanley Beach through the trees and barbed-wire fence. Whenever she could, Mrs. Finch found her way there, "A Little Bit of Heaven" playing over and over in her head as she gazed out at the blue sea, imagining the warm, white sand between her bare toes.

The Japanese shelling and bombing had damaged most of the buildings on the campgrounds. Most of the flats were devoid of furniture, except for cots crammed in next to each other. Prisoners without cots slept on the cold stone floors. Their daily meals were two cups of rice, sometimes supplemented by poor-quality vegetables—stale pumpkin or watery spinach. Her thoughts often turned to Pei and Ji Shen. Thank goodness Pei had stockpiled food. She could only hope they were safely tucked away somewhere and would make it through the occupation. She longed for a visit from them, not knowing if it was even possible.

True to Isabel Tate's words, despite their living conditions, the internees' social life remained quite on a par with what they had once had in Hong Kong. Even incarcerated, they complained about the British government and the lack of servants. They formed committees, put on plays, and held card games, which diligently broke for afternoon tea, even if tea consisted only of lukewarm water and hard biscuits bought on the black market.

The young Chinese hawkers she'd seen lingering outside the barbed-wire fence the day she arrived were their most vital link to the outside world. Every few days they sold goods by the east fence, overlooking Tai Tam Wan. Occasionally, the Japanese guards chased the hawkers away, but usually they turned a blind eye to all the bargaining in order to appease the prisoners.

"Chocolate bars! Biscuits!" the vendors yelled, hands and merchandise sliding between the barbed wire.

"I bring any kind of cigarettes you want!" another voice cried.

While Mrs. Finch had left all her worldly possessions to Pei and Ji Shen, other prisoners had had the presence of mind to smuggle in money and jewelry, taped to their bodies, cleverly sewn into clothes, or buried within their children's stuffed animals. When their money ran out, the Chinese hawkers accepted IOUs, trusting that the British citizens wouldn't go back on their word when the occupation came to an end. Magazines and bars of soap, sold at three times their worth, were still readily snapped up. Mrs. Finch shook her head and marveled at the Chinese loyalty to the British colonials. On many occasions since she had moved to Hong Kong, she'd found herself embarrassed by her countrymen's superior British attitude and rudeness toward the Chinese. The British could learn so much from the Chinese people, if they just opened their eyes.

After her first few months in camp, Mrs. Finch saw how inconveniences had to be tolerated and tempers controlled. Even among the woman and children, baby blankets and bars of soap were readily stolen once their owner's head was turned. Basic necessities, such as a hot bath or a good night's sleep, once taken for granted, were now something longed for. With thousands of men, women, and children crammed into the buildings, bathing was an all-day affair of waiting in long lines only to have a few minutes under a rusty shower head, where barely enough cold water dripped to make the wait worthwhile. In the back of a storage room, Mrs. Finch found an old wooden bucket that held enough water to take a sponge bath or wash her hair. Usually the bucket was rotated among the women in their building, so that everyone had the luxury of using it.

On a hot and humid afternoon in July, with tempers particularly on edge, a cold bath was the only way to cool off. A woman who usually kept to herself confronted Mrs. Finch and demanded the bucket right away.

"You'll have to wait your turn, just like the rest of us," Mrs. Finch said calmly.

"I want it right now!" she barked, barring the doorway to the bathroom.

Mrs. Finch simply said, "Well, my dear, it's not yours to want."

"I said, *now*!" The woman, lunged forward, slapped Mrs. Finch hard across the face, and grabbed the bucket.

Before Mrs. Finch had time to react, Isabel Tate came to her rescue. "Now, just who do you think you are, her Royal Highness the Queen? Well, I think not." She slapped the woman back across the face, seized the bucket, and returned it to Mrs. Finch.

"Here you are, Caroline," she said, returning to her place in line, as the rest of the group cheered her on.

Mrs. Finch felt a hot sting across her cheek, her stomach churning at the thought of how many times she'd seen a Japanese soldier slap a prisoner in just the same way.

On other days, a numbness would set in among the prisoners, an awful awareness that this was not a game. Electricity and water were turned on and off without warning, and during the winter of 1942–43 the cold winds from the bay kept them awake all night with icy feet and chilblains. Rumors circulated among the women, whispers of the torture and beating of men accused of espionage or of trying to escape. Dysentery and malaria began to take lives in their cramped quarters. By the beginning of 1943, Mrs. Finch saw the rows of makeshift gravestones multiply in the cemetery overlooking Stanley Bay.

One October morning, shouting abruptly awakened them. Heart pounding and feet numb, Mrs. Finch rose from her cot and peered out the window. In the pale light, she could just make out a group of Japanese soldiers dragging several men out the camp gate in the direction of the beach.

"What is going on?" Mrs. Tate whispered.

"They're taking some men down to the beach." Mrs. Finch massaged her feet, trying to get the circulation flowing again, then hurried to dress.

"Where are you going?"

"I want to see what's going on. Don't worry, go back to sleep. I'll be right back."

"Over my dead body. I'm going with you." Mrs. Tate rose quietly from her cot and quickly dressed.

Groans came from the other cots as the door creaked open and they stepped out into the morning air. They closed the door quietly behind them, then caught the quick movement of a guard making his rounds and froze. When the guard disappeared and it was safe again, Mrs. Finch sighed with relief.

"This way," Mrs. Finch said, stealing behind their building and across to the next. From her favorite spot, they had a clear view of the beach.

"Look!" Mrs. Tate pointed down to the open beach.

The soldiers pushed the six internees out onto the sand. All of the prisoners had their hands bound behind their backs. They stumbled forward and were made to kneel on the sand with their heads bowed. A soldier stood straight beside each prisoner like a dark guardian, hand poised on the shaft of his sword.

Mrs. Finch pressed closer to the barbed wire, noting how the prisoners were evenly spaced three feet apart. Seagulls squawked and circled overhead. "What are they doing?" she whispered.

An answer came before either woman said another word. As the sky brightened into morning, a glint of sunlight caught the swords as they swung down and beheaded one prisoner after the other. Mrs. Finch thought she heard a man cry out, *"Wait!"* before the sharp edge of the sword silenced his voice forever.

Mrs. Finch stood stunned, her thumb pressing into the sharp

point of the barbed wire, drawing blood. A quick sting followed by a dull throb. For months after, every time Mrs. Finch closed her eyes she saw again the perfect arc of the sword as it rose up and swung down, cleanly separating each head from its body. The thick silence suddenly broken by the shrieking seagulls and her own voice crying out, *"Wait!"*

Another Life

The room Pei and Ji Shen had rented at the boardinghouse in Wan Chai in February 1942 reminded Pei of the one she'd shared with Lin at the sisters' house in Yung Kee. It was just as plain and bare, with two beds, a dresser, and walls the color of pale sand. Pei imagined the walls must have been white at one time, yellowed over the years. Sometimes Pei would turn around in the small room expecting to see Lin standing there, as if they had met only yesterday instead of a lifetime ago. The Lin she saw in her mind was still young and beautiful, though at thirty-two, Pei was almost the same age as Lin had been when she died.

Pei smiled to herself, thinking how life sometimes brought you right back to the same place. Here she was living again in a house with other silk sisters. Since the silk work had diminished and the Japanese had sent most of her sisters fleeing to Hong Kong and elsewhere, their lives were constantly in flux. And here they were once more, needing to find a structure for their everyday lives, despite all the difficulties of the Japanese occupation.

But now, instead of the silk work or domestic work, Pei and Ji Shen had to take whatever employment they could find to pay the rent. She hid Mrs. Finch's jewelry behind the dresser, still determined not to sell a single piece. While her other sisters washed clothes or did light housework, Pei made most of her money by sewing and mending for anyone who came to her, a skill she'd learned from her mother. There had been so few luxuries in her childhood; her mother, Yu-sung, had spent endless hours at night mending her daughters' two sets of clothing, hoping to make them last another season before they were outgrown or worn through. There had never been enough time for rich, colorful embroideries like those Pei had seen hanging in the Chen household. As little girls, she and her sister Li had been taught by their mother to read, write, and sew. "To read and write will help you understand life," she'd said. "To sew and mend will help you to survive it."

Pei had quickly gained a reputation as an expert invisible mender, unraveling precious silk thread from a seam or hem and using it to repair a rip or hole. Sometimes she'd close her eyes and once again see the long silk filaments of the cocoons disentangle in the hot water, then wind tightly up onto a spool. As in the silk work, she'd take the hidden threads and let them perform their magic. She could repair a motheaten hole or a tear so well that the garment looked new again. While others marveled at her handiwork, Pei thought it only natural to follow the tight weave of the material.

Thanks to word of mouth, her business grew with each day. Since the occupation had brought all overseas commerce to a standstill, many of the Hong Kong Tai tais her silk sisters had once worked for now brought their treasured cheongsams to Pei to be mended or altered.

Ji Shen ran errands and took whatever small cleaning jobs she could find, mysteriously returning once or twice a week with cans of potted meat and even a few fresh vegetables. Pei knew that, like Quan, Ji Shen was dealing on the black market.

Just the other evening, Luling, one of her sisters also living at the boardinghouse, had said, "If it's not the Japanese, then it's the Triads you have to be afraid of on the streets. I've heard the Triads will cut off a person's arm or leg if they catch him stealing from them."

Daily the fear grew in Pei, growling louder than the emptiness in her stomach. But every time she tried to talk with her, Ji Shen shrugged and said, "There's nothing to worry about; I know what I'm doing."

With the severe rice rationing imposed by the Japanese, people had to scramble to keep their stomachs full. Since the beginning of the occupation, waiting in line had become a way of life in Hong Kong. From sunrise to sunset, everyone lined up for a multitude of reasons—to obtain a small ration of rice, to exchange Hong Kong dollars into Hong Kong yen, to barter for a few wilted vegetables. But at the end of the day, most would still go home without enough to fill their family's stomachs.

Despite her fears about Ji Shen's involvement, Pei also knew that the black market was essential in keeping people in Hong Kong alive. Even the scarcest fruits and vegetables could be readily had, although at astronomical prices. Men, women, and even children produced goods to sell and trade, cautiously bartering and bargaining in the streets, or through peddlers who set up their rickety stalls in the marketplace.

From the time they had lived on the sampan, Pei suspected Quan kept a hand in the black market. While Uncle Wei fished off the boat, Quan disappeared for hours each morning and returned with canned food and biscuits. Once, he even brought home a chicken.

"Where did you get this?" Auntie Lu had asked. Pei watched her squat low and begin to clean the bird; brown feathers fluttered gently through the air.

"Why does it matter as long as our stomachs are full tonight?" He grinned triumphantly.

"Guilt lies heavy in the stomach," she had said, and then hurried to pull the rest of the feathers from the bird. "Just be careful," she said in a softer voice.

They had quickly cooked and eaten the chicken before their neighbors on the other boats realized they had something other than watery rice jook for dinner.

Since their move to Wan Chai, Ji Shen, now eighteen, had grown even further away from Pei. Pei understood all the horror, the ups and downs of Ji Shen's years in Yung Kee and then Hong Kong. Her heart ached for all the losses Ji Shen had suffered in her young life—robbed of her family and childhood, fleeing from place to place.

But even in their most difficult times, Pei recalled the thirteen-year-old girl who had held her hand after Lin's death. She heard again the soothing words that came from Ji Shen's lips when all she wanted to do was close her eyes and die along with Lin. "You must live. For me," Ji Shen had whispered, as if she'd known just what Pei was thinking. The words floated to Pei on the smoky breeze.

When classes began again after the first few months of the occupation, Ji Shen had adamantly refused to return to school. Pei tried to encourage her, but had not wanted to force her. Each school meant another difficult change for her—Spring Valley, St. Cecilia's, and now a new one in Wan Chai.

"But what will you do instead?" Pei asked. "Your education is the most important thing."

"It's more important that we survive," Ji Shen quickly answered. "I'll go back later, after the war. Right now I can wash or clean or even sell things like everyone else, until I find something better."

"What do you have to sell?" Pei argued. "The Triads"—the gangs that ran the black market—"are dangerous." And what about the Japanese soldiers lurking everywhere? It's not safe for you."

"The Triads are only one part of the black market. Quan deals in it, and he's not involved with the Triads. He'll show me what to do. He has kept his family well fed. The Triads won't even notice me."

"Quan's a young man, and the streets are dangerous." Pei shook her head. "You're a young woman."

Pei stepped back and saw the truth of her statement. Ji Shen had grown into a pretty young woman. She stood half a head shorter than Pei and was delicate and small-boned, with fair, smooth skin and mischievous dark brown eyes.

"I'll stick close to Quan. I promise." Ji Shen wrapped her arms around Pei and kissed her on the cheek. "Everyone is out there trying to survive. Just let me try until I can find something else to do. If it doesn't work, I'll go back to school."

At the time, with their day-to-day living conditions so uncertain, Pei couldn't argue further. By the time they were safely settled into the boardinghouse, Ji Shen seemed to have plans of her own.

Pei's only solace was that Quan was also on the streets.

"Don't worry, I'll look after her," he reassured Pei. She studied the young man she had chosen over the other sha pullers. What a lucky choice she had made.

"What does she do all day?" Pei asked.

Quan smiled shyly. "What we all do, just try to get through another day buying and selling what we can."

"But what do you and Ji Shen have to sell?"

"You'd be surprised how easy it is." Quan explained: "You wait in line for a couple of cups of rice, then barter the rice for a few cans of meat, a can of meat for powdered milk, and so on. Throw in a couple of mangoes snatched from a tree and you may even get a chicken." He stood up quickly and stretched his long, muscular limbs, toughened by the years of pulling a rickshaw.

Pei knew this was a simplified explanation of something much more complicated. How fast could a tree grow fruit? What if there was no more rice to be distributed? Even the term "black market" signified something dark and dangerous. Through Luling, Pei had learned more about the Triads, a large organization of secret societies that ran almost all of the black market, supplying the goods for huge profits, while those who worked for them received a small cut. That would leave those not involved with the Triads in a real minority.

"Is that all?" she asked.

Quan shrugged. "Just about."

Pei eyed him closely. "I see."

The next morning, after Pei was sure Ji Shen had gone off with Quan, she found herself walking down the Wan Chai streets, hoping to catch a glimpse of the black market at work. The morning air was still relatively fresh, not yet thick with the oily odors of a long day of hot sun. Instead of hurrying down the street trying to avoid Japanese soldiers, Pei closely watched all the movements around her. As if she'd been blind, she saw life anew. Men and women, who appeared harmless, lingered in the streets or in doorways. They made swift deals—goods and money were exchanged and slipped into pockets as the flow of life continued. Sometimes children were even used as lookouts for Japanese soldiers coming down the street. Pei watched the dizzy display of commerce and couldn't imagine Quan and Ji Shen being part of it all. She started back toward the boardinghouse with more questions than answers, though she was surprised at how efficient and organized the buying and selling appeared from afar.

For now Pei had no choice but to keep quiet and watch for any signs of trouble. Although the very idea of the black market left a bitter taste in her mouth, she would have to trust Quan to take care of Ji Shen.

Her thoughts were broken by clamorous voices down the street and the sudden scattering of boys, chased closely by Japanese soldiers. Heart pounding, Pei slipped down a narrow street to be out of their way. She leaned against a wall and drew in a deep, biting breath. The boys would surely disappear into Wan Chai's myriad streets and alleys before the soldiers knew where they'd gone. Would Ji Shen have to run down the same alleys? Would she be able to find her way out again?

"Perhaps you've come for more dream tea?" a voice suddenly inquired.

Pei turned quickly around, pursuing the familiar voice. Even before she saw him tucked away in the shadows of a doorway, she knew it was the old herbalist.

Pei

Pei hurried down a narrow Wan Chai street, with Ji Shen rushing to keep up. Ever since Pei had told her they were going to visit Mrs. Finch at Stanley Camp, Ji Shen had regained her spirit. All night, questions floated through the air of their small room at the boardinghouse. Ji Shen was filled with a joy and innocence Pei hadn't heard in a long time. "Do you think we'll be able to find her?" Ji Shen asked. And "Do you think she'll look the same?"

As if good fortune were smiling down on Pei, first she'd discovered the old herbalist alive and living with his nephew a few blocks from them in Wan Chai, then she discovered a way to visit Mrs. Finch. While she was standing in line for rice distribution at the Central Market, she'd overheard a large, boisterous woman say that her husband drove the Red Cross medical van to Stanley Camp. Pei stepped closer and smiled. Her mind raced: How could she make a deal that would take her and Ji Shen out to Stanley to see Mrs. Finch?

"How often does he go?" Pei asked.

The woman eyed Pei up and down. "He goes once a month and brings supplies to the prisoners at St. Stephen's College hospital there. Why?"

"I was just wondering if he might take a passenger or two out to Stanley."

"To the village?"

Pei nodded, thinking it might be safer.

The woman smiled. "Well, I wouldn't put it past my husband's good nature to help someone out." Her foot tapped lightly against the pavement. "Of course, it is a great risk to take. . . ."

"He would be greatly compensated," Pei quickly added. "Would fifty Hong Kong yen make it worth his while?" Her mending business was doing well, and she'd put a little money away. Fifty yen seemed a reasonable sum; it would buy some fruit and vegetables or other necessities.

The woman looked down at the ground in thought, then back at Pei. "Let's say one hundred would."

Pei had finally bargained her down to eighty Hong Kong yen, promising to give the woman's husband half on the arranged morning and the other half after they'd returned to Hong Kong. They set a date and time to meet. All the way back to the boardinghouse, Pei was floating on air.

Early the next afternoon, the summer air warm and humid, Pei and Ji Shen dashed down the street. The Wan Chai streets were bustling with people searching for food and bargaining in doorways for black-market goods. Pei and Ji Shen walked past one beer hall after another: the dark, dingy entrances were filled with Japanese soldiers in the company of Chinese, Russian, and Eurasian prostitutes. Filipino musicians played "I Can't Give You Anything but Love, Baby" in every bar. Pei was glad the Japanese soldiers had something to do instead of loitering in the streets and harassing innocent Chinese.

Pei slowed down when she glimpsed a group of Japanese soldiers down the street. "Be careful," she said, pulling Ji Shen into a doorway. Avoiding contact with the Japanese patrols had become a daring game she and Ji Shen played as the occupation dragged on. They'd weave in and out of doorways to keep from having to stop and bow.

By the time they reached Central, it was nearly one o'clock. When a large, shiny car came screeching down a narrow street, the crowds fanned out and disappeared, or turned and bowed low to the passing vehicle. The flag of the Rising Sun fluttered from the car, as it did on all the cars left in Hong Kong. Other flags denoted the rank and title of the officer inside.

Pei turned her back so as not to have to bow at the passing car. "I think the medical van is supposed to be waiting over there." She pointed to the corner.

Ji Shen nodded, adjusting the cloth bag she carried over her shoulder. It held some items Mrs. Finch might need most—soap, powdered milk, a box of crackers, and a can of sardines Pei had saved from her Conduit Road supply. "I can't wait to see Mrs. Finch again."

Pei smiled. "Neither can I."

It had been nearly a year since Pei had watched Mrs. Finch, calm and strong as always, walk away from them and surrender to the Japanese authorities. What Pei hadn't told Ji Shen was how afraid she was that Mrs. Finch might no longer be the same person they'd come to love. Since the beginning of the occupation, Pei had witnessed countless acts of brutality. Men and women were slapped and beaten, made to grovel and eat dirt for no more than an errant look, or for wearing the wrong color. The Japanese would stop at nothing to break a person. And Mrs. Finch was just the kind of person who might try to challenge their authority.

Pei had voiced her fears about Mrs. Finch only once, just days after they'd moved onto the sampan. She had asked Quan, "Do you think Mrs. Finch will survive the internment camp?" Precious grains of rice sifted through her fingers as she washed their small allotment in a wooden bucket.

He shrugged and looked away, then stood up and threw the

fishing net over the side of the sampan. "There's always hope," he answered. But his eyes avoided hers.

Pei's heart had raced. There had to be more than hope, she'd thought to herself. Mrs. Finch was still strong and healthy, and if she just avoided confrontations she'd be able to survive, to start a new life after the occupation. Pei had shoved her hand deeper into the bucket, her knuckles scraping the bottom.

Just then a white van with a bright-red cross painted on its side turned the corner and slowed down. "There he is!" Pei said, picking up her pace.

Mr. Ma, the driver of the van, was short and slender, the opposite of his big-boned wife. He jumped out of the van, pocketed the money Pei handed him, and opened the back door for the women. "It'll be safer if you ride in the back," he said.

Pei leaned forward and strained to peer out through the grimy front window. They sat between boxes that rattled and clinked as the van bumped along the cratered streets. Ji Shen peeked into a box and pulled out a brown bottle filled with clear liquid, with the dark letters "A-L-C-O-H-O-L" on the label. Pei motioned for her to put it back, just before Mr. Ma turned around and smiled at them.

When the van paused, a long black car pulled alongside. Pei's heart skipped a beat when she recognized the woman sitting next to the Japanese officer in the backseat. She craned her head to get a better view. She looked harder, once . . . twice . . . The woman was older and heavily made up, but she was Fong.

The black car roared ahead. It wasn't until the van finally left the city and began rounding the mountain curves that Pei loosened her grip on the door handle, her head still spinning at the sight of Fong.

* * *

Stanley village was teeming with people. Had it not been for the Japanese soldiers who patrolled the area, Pei would have thought the place had somehow gone untouched by the war. Song Lee had cautioned her to be careful, and not to draw attention to herself as she made her way to the prison camp. "Those devils have eyes in the back of their heads," she warned.

Pei arranged to meet Mr. Ma at the van in a few hours. Then she and Ji Shen followed the dirt path that led along the cliffs to the camp. The sun was warm against the top of her head and the rush and roar of the waves below were mesmerizing.

Ahead of her was a group of young boys; an old man in the village had told her to follow them. "They sell to the prisoners," he said, sucking air from his pipe. "They'll lead you right to the camp."

Pei and Ji Shen followed the boys, just far enough back to hear their low chatter. As the path gradually descended, she could see the camp in front of her, dominated on one side by the concrete walls of Stanley Prison. From a distance it looked relatively harmless. The barbed-wire fence wrapped the large compound like a neat package. Several three-story buildings were flanked by smaller bungalows. Pei's heart beat faster. Which building was Mrs. Finch staying in? Would she be able to find her? She and Ji Shen hurried to keep up with the group of boys, watching to see how they made contact with the prisoners.

At the bottom of the path, instead of taking the dirt road that led to the front gate, the boys moved, silently now, in the other direction. Behind one of the tall buildings ahead, Pei saw a group of prisoners gathered by the fence to wait. They greeted the boys like old friends, reaching through the barbed wire to wave them forward.

"Did you get the cigarettes?" she heard one man ask, as the boys began pulling goods from the cloth bags they carried.

"That's a good lad."

"Ah, soap!" a woman exclaimed.

Pei looked from face to face for Mrs. Finch.

"What have you got there, honey?" a woman asked Ji Shen, who turned to Pei for help.

"Mrs. Finch?" Pei said.

"Who?"

"Mrs. Finch!" she said, louder this time. "Caroline Finch."

"She's looking for Caroline," another voice piped up. "Anyone seen Caroline?"

"I think she's still inside the Indian Quarters. One of you lads go fetch Caroline Finch," a woman commanded a group of English boys, who were in the midst of lively bargaining for chocolate bars.

"Three chocolate bars for this pen!" A boy waved a green pen in the air, then passed it through the fence toward reaching hands.

A Chinese boy examined the pen and turned it over slowly in his hands. "I'll give you two chocolate bars for it."

"It's a deal!" The English boy reached through the fence and grabbed the chocolate. "Thanks, mate—bring more at the end of the week."

Watching the transaction, Pei couldn't help but wonder if the boys would ever talk and laugh in the same way once the internment was over. She waited nervously while one of the English boys finally ran off, then returned to say that Mrs. Finch would be there shortly. She and Ji Shen stood aside from the bartering voices and waving hands. Then, in the distance, she saw Mrs. Finch limping toward them.

"There she is!" Ji Shen pointed.

The way Mrs. Finch's flowered print dress hung from her body made it painfully obvious that she had lost weight. It took her only a moment to realize who was standing by the fence. She broke into a smile and paused to smooth her dress, then hurried over.

"Dear God, is it really you?"

Pei pressed closer to the barbed wire. She reached through the fence and tightly grasped Mrs. Finch's hand.

"It's so wonderful to see you. We wanted to come sooner, but we didn't know how we could. There hasn't been any transportation out this way."

"However *did* you get here?"

Ji Shen swung the cloth bag down. "Pei arranged a ride on the medical van."

"That's my girl!" Mrs. Finch said. She smoothed back her hair. "I must look a mess."

"You look wonderful," Ji Shen said quickly.

"And you lie very well." Mrs. Finch laughed. "How have you two been?"

"We're fine," Pei answered. "We were staying with Quan's family after you left, but now we have a room of our own in Wan Chai. Song Lee and other silk sisters are also living there." Her words came out in one overflowing waterfall.

"Thank God. I've been worrying about you both, though I should have known you'd do just fine." She gave Pei's hand a hard squeeze.

Pei let go long enough to pick up the cloth bag and slip it through the barbed wire. "A few things we thought you might need."

"Bless your heart." Mrs. Finch peeked inside. "I'll throw a party in your honor."

"You've lost weight," Pei couldn't help but say aloud.

"Bloody white rice and little else, though I've regained my girlish figure. Don't worry, we've just planted a garden. There should be more to eat in the days to come. Are you both getting enough to eat?"

Pei nodded. "We would have never gotten by without the money you gave us. At enormous prices, you can get whatever you want."

"Ah, I see Hong Kong has survived without us."

"Just barely," Ji Shen whispered.

"We'll bring you more next month," Pei said. "Is there anything you need? I'll find a way to get it."

Mrs. Finch smiled. "Just seeing you both again is all I need."

"We have to go, Caroline," another woman interrupted. "The soldiers will be patrolling this area any moment now."

Mrs. Finch grabbed Pei's and Ji Shen's hands. "You can't know what your visit means to me. You behave yourself," she said to Ji Shen, "and I might teach you to waltz when I get out of here!"

Pei held onto Mrs. Finch's thin hand as a rush of words moved through her mind, but all she could say was "We'll be back to visit next month."

Mrs. Finch backed away slowly, clutching the cloth bag, her eyes filling with tears. "I love you both."

Pei and Ji Shen stood and watched until Mrs. Finch turned around again and waved one last time before she disappeared behind the building. In the distance Pei could hear gruff Japanese voices sending a shiver through her body. She and Ji Shen stood a moment longer in the blazing sun before following the group of boys up the dirt path and back to Stanley village.

Ji Shen

Ji Shen sat in the doorway of the boardinghouse and waited for Quan. For the past six months, he'd picked her up every morning; together, they walked to the Central Market or down to the harbor, the most profitable areas to buy and sell. Only if Quan accompanied Ji Shen would Pei agree to let her go. Ji Shen felt a flush of anger rise up in her. Lately, it seemed as if Pei and all her rules were suffocating her.

A hint of wind brought some relief from the relentless heat. After an unusually cold winter, the oppressive summer heat slowed everything to a standstill. As the occupation headed into its third year, even the few Japanese soldiers who still patrolled the streets appeared tired and faded. Ji Shen could only hope Mrs. Finch was doing all right and finding more relief by the ocean. Ji Shen anxiously awaited their next visit, which wouldn't be for another ten days.

"You and your young man would make much more money if you worked for Lock," a voice broke into her thoughts.

Ji Shen raised her hand and shaded her eyes against the sun. Standing before her was a woman in her forties, whom Ji Shen recognized as a regular peddler on the streets.

"Who's Lock?" Ji Shen asked.

"My name is Ling." She smiled widely, exposing crooked teeth. "And Lock's a businessman I work for. He supplies all the goods and gives you a cut of each product you sell for him. Half the work is already done!"

Ling usually had an entire box of canned meat against the paltry few cans Ji Shen and Quan were able to barter for. When she'd once asked Quan where the woman had gotten all her stock, he had answered curtly, "It's not a part of the black market you want to enter."

"Lock's willing to help anyone who's honest and hard-working," the woman added.

Ji Shen stood up, her cotton trousers sticky against her legs. She was tired of just getting by. She looked quickly around for any sign of Quan, then moved to the side, allowing the woman to step into the shade of the doorway.

"Tell me more," Ji Shen demanded.

Ji Shen clutched Lock's address in her hand. He lived no more than four blocks from their boardinghouse, yet when she turned onto his street, it felt stark and foreign. The bombed-out shell of an apartment building still stood as a reminder of the heavy damage caused by the Japanese bombings. The sidewalk buckled and rose to a small peak; a group of laughing children ran up one side and down the other. During the two years of occupation, the Japanese government had done little to help Hong Kong recover from the devastation its armies had inflicted. Each day Ji Shen saw the city grow sadder and poorer, as everyone struggled harder to survive.

Ji Shen glanced again at the address, then hurried up the stairs of an old stucco building. Lock's apartment was on the third floor and down the hall, according to Ling. Ji Shen's heart raced as she knocked on the door and waited. Nervousness and guilt lay heavy in the pit of her stomach. She had lied to Quan—told him she wasn't feeling well and would stay in today. If only he hadn't reacted so kindly, she might have felt better. He had reached out and touched her forehead with the palm of his hand. When he pulled his coolness away, she felt a sudden loss.

"Do you need anything?" His voice was serious and full of concern.

She shook her head. Her mouth felt dry and bitter from the lie.

"I'll be by tomorrow. Try to get some rest, and you'll feel better."

Ji Shen watched Quan walk away and wanted to call him back, wanted him to go with her to Lock's apartment. But a voice inside her said, *No, don't. He'll never let you go.*

The door pulled open with a jerk. A young man with closely cropped hair and bad skin eyed her up and down. "What do you want?" he asked bluntly.

"I'm here to see Lock," she managed to squeeze out. "I was sent by Ling."

His eyes lingered on her a moment longer before he stepped aside and let her in. The shades were pulled down, but once her eyes adjusted to the dimness of the room, she saw it was crowded with boxes.

"Wait here," the man said, leaving her standing amidst the sea of boxes.

Another door opened and closed. Ji Shen heard voices before the door opened again and a second man approached her. He moved straight to the window and gave the shade a quick tug, so that it wound up with a snap.

"I'm Lock. You wanted to see me?" he asked.

Ji Shen had thought he'd be an older man, but in the sudden light of the room, she saw that Lock was only in his thirties. He had a thin mustache and his dark hair was neatly combed to the side. He was of medium height and weight, and wore an expensive-looking double-breasted suit. His sweet cologne filled the air and made her dizzy. Ji Shen wanted to turn and run out of the apartment, but instead forced herself to speak: "Ling sent me. She said you were willing to help anyone who was willing to work. Well, I want to work."

Lock smiled and watched her intently for a moment. "Yes; yes, I can see that you do. You look like a young woman I can trust."

Ji Shen gathered her courage. "Ling said you would supply the goods for me to sell."

Lock smiled. "As you see, I can supply you with as much as you can sell. You'll get part of the profit from whatever is sold. The more you sell, the more money you'll make. It's just that simple."

"Yes," Ji Shen agreed. *Yes,* she thought, *just that simple.* If she worked for Lock, she and Pei could eventually move from the boardinghouse and not worry about putting away every cent. And she'd be able to buy another Victrola for the day when Mrs. Finch was released from Stanley Camp. This was the first good thing to happen in a long time.

"Then let's give you a try." Lock smiled again. He stepped closer and extended his hand. "A business deal should be sealed with a handshake."

Ji Shen looked down at Lock's pale, delicate hand. She raised her hand and felt it quickly taken into his, a strong, smooth grip closing around hers.

During her first few days working for Lock, Ji Shen saw more than a dozen people stream in and out of his Wan Chai apartment, among them a woman she learned was named Lan Wai. Though they were the same age, Lan Wai appeared years older. She was thin, with a red silk scarf tied around her neck and deep lines already evident across her forehead. Her eyes appeared weary, as if she'd seen a great deal in her twenty years. While most of the people coming and going were street peddlers working for Lock, others were serious-looking men who spoke in low tones. Lock obviously went out of his way to please these visitors.

"Who are they?" Ji Shen had asked Lan Wai.

"They're from the Triads. Lock works for them, and we work for Lock."

Ji Shen grew warm and uncomfortable at the mention of the Triads. She wanted to ask more, but refrained; the explanation must be simple enough. Lock was the middleman, shielding them from all the difficulties of the business. She bought and sold, bringing her proceeds back to Lock, who in turn passed them on to the Triads. Everyone came away with a small profit. It was best for her to keep as invisible as possible, to keep her mouth shut and her eyes open.

Lock had sent Lan Wai out with her to "teach Ji Shen the business," as he said. Lan Wai's story unfolded as they carried a box of potted meat out to sell near the Central Market. She told Ji Shen she'd been living on the streets since she was ten years old.

"I just turned around one day at the marketplace and my mother had disappeared," Lan Wai said matter-of-factly, "along with my younger brother, Nai. I guess she was only able to feed one of us, and he was going to be the one."

Lan Wai looked around the crowded street, then pointed to

a corner directly across from them. "Always make sure there's plenty of street access in case any Japanese soldiers give you trouble. And never carry so much that you can't grab it all and run."

Ji Shen nodded. "What did you do after your mother left you?"

Lan Wai put down the box and took out a can of meat. "Never take out more than one can at a time," she said, then returned to her story. "I started to cry, but no one paid much attention to me, so I just started walking, hoping I could somehow find my mother and brother. I never found them, but an old woman took pity on me and gave me a blanket and a few scraps to eat every night."

A thin Chinese man with a shaved head wandered over and asked, "How much?" He pointed a bony finger at the can.

"Five Hong Kong dollars or three Hong Kong yen," Lan Wai snapped, not looking directly at him.

"It's too much," the man answered.

Lan Wai held the can up to his face. "It's made of good ingredients and will fill your stomach much more than what the others will sell you. See, feel how heavy." She thrust the can into his hand.

The man balanced it on his palm. "I only have two Hong Kong yen."

Lan Wai hesitated: she looked down at the ground and then up again. "Okay, just this once. Just for you." She smiled.

Ji Shen watched as the man slowly walked away, gripping the can tightly. She wondered how many mouths would be fed from that one can.

"Don't you ever feel sorry for—"

"You can't," Lan Wai snapped, before Ji Shen could finish her sentence. But then she relaxed into a smile again. "For all we know, he'll turn around and sell it for a profit."

Ji Shen shrugged. "Yes, I see," she said, leaning over and extracting one can from the box.

Later, when they had sold the entire box of potted meat, Ji Shen grinned victoriously. "It wasn't so hard."

"It gets even easier," Lan Wai said. "You did well."

Ji Shen felt a warm rush of friendship toward the skinny young woman walking beside her. Lan Wai was the opposite of her rich, spoiled classmates at St. Cecilia's, and Ji Shen could feel in her the same simple trust she'd felt with Quan.

"My parents and sister were killed by the Japanese," she suddenly blurted out.

Lan Wai shook her head sadly. "I'm sorry. My mother gave me this scarf. I keep hoping she'll see it one day and remember me," she said, touching it. "So I guess that makes us both orphans then. At least you don't have to look into the face of every woman you see on the street, wondering if she might be your mother."

"At least," Ji Shen repeated.

By the end of the week, Ji Shen knew she could no longer keep her new job a secret from Quan. She had run out of excuses and she knew Quan was suspicious. All night she tossed and turned, trying not to awaken Pei. The next morning she waited for Quan and quickly asked him to take a walk with her.

"Is everything all right?" he asked.

Ji Shen nodded. "I wanted to tell you that I've gone to work for someone else for a while," she finally said, not daring to look up at him. "Just until I put some money aside."

Quan stopped. "Who?"

"His name is Lock."

In the breath of silence that followed, Ji Shen looked up and saw how angry Quan was—a reddish flush had colored his face and he stared at her in disbelief.

"How can you be so stupid?" he asked. "Don't you know that once you get mixed up with the Triads, you can never get out? Lock would sell his own family for the right price!"

A sudden, hard anger rose up inside Ji Shen, a quick pulse

that throbbed at her temple. How dare he speak to her like that? He would never be anything but a sha boy. He didn't know a good opportunity even when it was dangling in front of him. She was tired of him always watching over her, always knowing what was best for her.

It had only been a week and already Lock taught her what to buy and sell, how to be a survivor like he was. He allowed her to be who she wanted to be.

"It's none of your business what I do!" Ji Shen felt a hot rush of tears push up from behind her eyes. "It's my life to live."

Ji Shen heard the low grunt of Quan's disapproval, and clasped her hands tightly behind her back. She stared down at his callused hands. They were the one feature that she would always know him by. His hands revealed his whole character—that he was a hard worker, someone dependable and honest. Why couldn't he just be happy for her? Quan meant more to Ji Shen than he knew; he would always be her first friend in Hong Kong, and the brother she never had.

"You don't know what you want," Quan argued. "You're just blinded by all his flash!"

Ji Shen breathed in slowly and tried to tell herself it was just Quan's anger or jealousy speaking. What Quan couldn't understand was that Lock had to be ruthless on the streets, or else he'd have been "swallowed up a long time ago," as he'd told her the other day. Lock had had a difficult life—he'd been on the streets since he was twelve, and also raised a younger brother and sister.

"What about Pei?" Quan's voice was tight, yet calmer. "Do you think she'd want you involved with the Triads?"

Ji Shen took her time answering; her throat was so dry she could hardly swallow. As smart and generous as Lock was, she knew Pei would never approve of her being with someone who was so much older, and who had Triad connections.

"It's my life," Ji Shen finally said, unable to meet Quan's gaze.

The Gathering

Song Lee moved quickly around the sitting room, opening the window and arranging the chairs so that there'd be enough room for all the sisters she expected to attend the meeting. It was the first large gathering they'd had since the occupation began. Most of their meetings had been confined to the small groups of sisters who lived in various boardinghouses around Wan Chai. Everyday problems of survival took precedence. How to earn money and obtain enough food dominated the discussions at each house, and the women quickly fell back into the old system of support they'd had at the sisters' house. While many of the sisters had saved money during their years as amahs, most washed, ironed, or cleaned to stay afloat, and a few dabbled in the black market or took out small loans from the sisterhood. Song Lee was always proud of the fact that she'd kept the sisterhood's money safely hidden, and had never deposited it into a bank as others had suggested. If she had, all would have been lost to the Japanese devils, and many of her sisters might not have gotten by without help.

At least once a month Song Lee tried to attend the meetings at other houses, so that everyone would be kept up-to-date. Especially now, her sisters went about their lives as quietly as possible. The last thing she and the others wanted was to call any attention to what was left of their sisterhood.

Song Lee lit the thin sticks of incense before the statue of Kuan Yin and prayed that the meeting would go smoothly. Her sisters had been her family for more years than she could remember, and now she would have to tell them that there wasn't enough money left to make any more loans for the duration of the occupation. Song Lee refused to go into the sisters' retirement fund until there was no choice. For now, they could cook, clean, iron, or shovel night soil to keep going.

Sometimes, Song Lee couldn't believe the power of her words. Her sisters always listened in rapt attention and did as she said. As a child, Song Lee had kept her words hidden away, afraid they would somehow change the life around her. As an adult, she wanted nothing more.

She breathed in the pungent scent of the burning incense, which never failed to fill her with the bittersweet memory of her own lonely childhood and of the one person who still visited her in dreams. She wondered how life would have changed if she'd only spoken out then. There had been moments in her life that still stung and swelled under her skin. But over the years, Song Lee embraced each memory, allowed it to return to her with a dull ache or a flicker of happiness.

A year after seven-year-old Song Lee had been given to the silk work, an eight-year-old girl named Ching Lui entered the girls' house. Ching Lui was everything Song Lee wasn't—beautiful, brave, outspoken, and stubborn. For the next six years of her life, she was Song Lee's best friend, and the closest she'd ever had to a real sister.

On warm summer nights, Ching Lui would often dare Song Lee to quietly slip out of the girls' house and go down to the river with her. Song Lee still remembered the suffocating heat and the rich smell of the damp, red earth, the sharp surprise of the cool water against her warm skin, her toes sinking into the soft muddy bottom.

"I dare you," Ching Lui whispered from her bed next to Song Lee's.

"We can't," she whispered back. "We'll get punished if we're caught." It was always the same argument between them.

She saw Ching Lui's shadow rise up from her bed. "Then we won't get caught."

Song Lee hesitated. "I don't know."

Ching Lui leaned close to her. "You're always afraid at first; then you end up having a great time. Come on." She pulled Song Lee's hand.

Song Lee pulled her hand back. She immediately missed her friend's touch, but for once Song Lee didn't move to follow. She had stubbornly decided to stand her ground. The rhythmic breathing of the other girls floated through the long room as she watched Ching Lui quietly walk toward the door. Song Lee sat up in bed, but still didn't make a move to follow.

Ching Lui reached the door at the far end of the room and waved once again for Song Lee to come along. In that moment of darkness, Song Lee wanted to tell her friend not to go, but Ching Lui's impetuous nature kept her silent. Instead, Song Lee lay back down on her bed and didn't look up again until she heard the soft click of the door closing.

In her mind's eye, Song Lee saw Ching Lui stealing down the stairs and out the front door, then across the field to the river where she would drop her nightclothes on the bank and run straight into the cool water. A secret longing rose in Song Lee.

She waited up all night for Ching Lui to return. And when she didn't, it was Song Lee who found her lying lifeless on the bank of the river in the red dirt.

Ching Lui had slipped on the way down to the water hitting her head on a rock. When they brought her back to the girls' house, Song Lee wouldn't go near the body. *I should have said something. I should have gone with her*: an endless lament that turned over and over in her mind. Thoughts of death seem too foreign and far away at thirteen years old. She kept waiting for Ching Lui to return and tell her it was all a joke.

For two days incense filled the girls' house, until Song Lee felt as if she would suffocate. On the second night, before Ching Lui's body was taken away by her family, Song Lee had almost fallen asleep when the overpowering smell of incense filled the room and she felt a sudden warmth beside her. "You were right to stay," a voice whispered. Song Lee lay frozen in her bed.

When she was finally able to turn her head, she was alone in her bed. All that lingered on her pillow was a faint scent of incense.

Song Lee heard voices from the stairwell and wondered if Pei and Ji Shen would be attending the meeting. Lately, she sensed, they were going through a difficult time. Ji Shen was just as willful as Ching Lui. She saw life as it was in the heat of the moment, rather than in the years it took to cultivate and shape it. Song Lee had been trying to smooth the ground between Pei and Ji Shen by involving them in the sisters' meetings.

"Come tonight," she'd asked Pei again that morning at breakfast.

"I'll try," Pei answered, noncommittal. Her spoon skimmed the top of her watery jook.

"It would be a nice change for you and Ji Shen," Song Lee added.

Pei hesitated, then said, "I don't think Ji Shen will be able to make it."

"These are difficult years for all of us, not to mention someone as impressionable as Ji Shen," Song Lee gently said. "Everything will fall into its place. One step at a time."

Pei looked up. The worry she'd been holding in suddenly appeared in the fine lines around her eyes. "Thank you," she said.

Song Lee wanted to say more, but refrained. Over the years she'd kept the peace by remaining one step away, never becoming so close that she couldn't see beyond what was right in front of her.

There was a brisk knock on the door and Luling excitedly announced the arrival of their sisters. Song Lee could hear the voices and laughter filling the stairwell, moving toward her like a flock of birds. She turned back toward Kuan Yin and closed her eyes for a moment, the sweet incense calming her.

Chapter Nine

1945

Pei

A slant of morning sun warmed the room as Pei folded the last of their laundry and placed it neatly in the battered bureau. Soon they were to meet Mr. Ma.

Pei was totally at ease with Ji Shen now only during their visits to Stanley Camp. Mrs. Finch met them at the back fence the first Thursday of every month. Every month for the past year and a half they'd religiously bought a ride from Mr. Ma. He now knew them well enough to give them coconut candy and allow Pei to sit up front with him: "You see much better from up here."

Ji Shen never seemed to grow tired of the cramped, bumpy ride to Stanley. During these trips, Pei felt that Ji Shen was once again the young girl she knew so well, with gentle ease and a quick smile.

"Do you think Mrs. Finch will like this?" Ji Shen asked, pulling out a can of sausages from the cloth bag that lay heavily on her bed.

Pei heard the dull thud of other items shifting in the bag. "I can't imagine she wouldn't." She wanted to give her a hug.

Ji Shen grinned. "I was lucky enough to get her a can of peas this time, too."

Pei refrained from being too enthusiastic about Ji Shen's dealings, though she knew the black market had become a necessity of life in Hong Kong and was glad that Ji Shen's surprises always lifted Mrs. Finch's spirits. Every month Ji Shen packed Mrs. Finch food and essentials. Sometimes she had just cans of potted meat and crackers, but in other months she could happily put together several cans of sardines, liver pâté, a package of bread, and even a small box of peppermints, as if she were preparing for a party.

"Did you tell Song Lee we won't be here for the rest of the day?" Pei closed the drawer.

"I'm going right now," Ji Shen answered.

Pei nodded. "Hurry—Mr. Ma won't like having to wait too long for us."

She watched Ji Shen swing open the door and bound down the stairs of the boardinghouse. Pei stood in the warmth of the sunlight wishing every day could be so simple.

With every passing month, as they drove through the city to Stanley, Hong Kong's decline under Japanese occupation grew more pronounced. In three and a half years, the occupiers had given Japanese names to streets, hotels, and restaurants, but had done little to improve Hong Kong. The van still had to maneuver carefully through the torn-up streets, while buildings bombed, shelled, and burned during the early fighting remained in disrepair. Food and fuel were always in short supply, and as the occupation dragged on, it was clear the Japanese would not be lifting Hong Kong out of its destitution, but pushing it down further. The streets were still desolate, but at least, in the past year, there'd been fewer and fewer Japanese patrols. All the while, the Chinese had simply found ways to survive.

Most Hong Kong Chinese had learned to coexist with the Japanese aggressors with as little bloodshed as possible. They banded together, bartered with and stole from each other, and did whatever it took to keep going in the face of the fading Japanese dominance.

June was stifling. Pei and Ji Shen were sweating by the time they came in sight of the arid, colorless camp. Pei prayed that Mrs. Finch was feeling better. She'd looked so pale and thin last month; her words had been brief and labored. All Pei wanted was for the occupation to end so that Mrs. Finch could regain her health.

A group of internees was already gathered at the barbed-wire fence, writing IOUs to the hawkers, who now did most of their selling in the mornings before the day became too hot. She imagined the sales were now more charity than business, since she couldn't see the boys ever being able to collect on all the IOUs.

Pei worried about how Mrs. Finch was holding up in the heat. The overcrowded buildings must be stifling at night after baking in the sun all day. Mrs. Finch had reassured Pei visit after visit that she'd seen the camp doctor, but each month she appeared weaker.

The day before, Pei had stopped by the old herbalist and told him of Mrs. Finch's shortness of breath and swollen ankles. He shook his head. "I lost so much in the fire. This will have to do." He sprinkled equal amounts of dark leaves and small dry branches from various jars onto white pieces of paper, then folded them into individual packets. Pei noticed the combination was different from the last herbs she'd brought to Mrs. Finch. "Tell her this one is ginseng tea. It will be less foreign to her then."

Pei nodded gratefully.

"She must drink all of it," the old herbalist instructed. "A bowl every day for the next ten days, or it's of no use!"

They hurried down the path, the heat of the sun pushing against them.

"I don't see Mrs. Finch," Ji Shen said.

Pei squinted hard against the bright glare. "It's better she isn't waiting out in the sun."

"There she is!" Ji Shen pointed toward the redbrick building.

Mrs. Finch walked slowly toward them. Pei waved, her hand pausing in midair when she saw her friend's even thinner frame and the new hesitation in her step. Pei's heart ached to see how Mrs. Finch was wilting with each passing month.

"How are you?" Pei called, trying to smile.

Mrs. Finch waved. "I'm fine." She smiled as she approached. "It's just that the heat has made my ankles swell a bit."

Pei pressed closer. "You look a bit pale."

Even the flowers on Mrs. Finch's dress had faded from much washing. "Just the heat. Nothing to be concerned about." Mrs. Finch wiped her forehead with a handkerchief.

Ji Shen swung the bag down from her shoulder. "Look what we've brought you!" She pulled out a can and slipped it through the barbed wire.

"My God, peas! And to think I always refused to eat them as a child. Now they're as good as gold!" She laughed and grasped Ji Shen's hand. "Thank you, my dear."

"Try to stay out of the sun as much as possible," Pei continued. "And drink this ginseng tea." She handed Mrs. Finch the bag of white packets she'd gotten from the old herbalist. "Just let it steep in hot water for a little while. Promise me you'll drink a bowl every day. It'll give you more strength."

Mrs. Finch reached for the herbs and nodded. "Don't worry so. You're acting as old as I am! Now, what news do you have to tell me?"

"The Japanese don't know what to do with us anymore," Ji Shen volunteered. "They've been in Hong Kong for over three years now and have yet to turn us into their little Tokyo. Nothing has changed, except that Hong Kong is still a shambles and they're losing their hold all over the Pacific."

Mrs. Finch looked relieved. "Now that's good news. An end to this occupation!"

"And we'll be back together again," Ji Shen added.

"I'm afraid there won't be much to go back to." Mrs. Finch looked wistful.

"My mending business is doing well. We'll start all over," Pei said. "You'll be out of here before you know it. . . ." She felt a sudden emptiness swallow the rest of her words.

"Until then, what a treat!" Mrs. Finch cradled the tea and canned goods against her chest. "And just wait until I get you on the dance floor," she teased Ji Shen.

"I can't wait," Ji Shen responded. Neither of them mentioned the Victrola.

"Please, stay inside today if you can," Pei said.

Mrs. Finch nodded. She put down her goods, then reached through the barbed wire and took their hands. "Promise me you'll always take care of each other."

"Don't worry about us," Ji Shen said.

Pei held tightly onto Mrs. Finch's hand; she didn't want to let go. "We'll be back next month. Just make sure you drink the tea every day, and try to rest."

"You both have meant more to me than I can say." Mrs. Finch gave Pei's hand one last squeeze.

The finality of Mrs. Finch's mood and words alarmed Pei. "You took us in when no one else would."

Mrs. Finch laughed. "And never regretted it for a moment." Then she looked at them long and hard. "Just remember that life is made up of change. We can't run away from it."

"You'll be able to move right into the boardinghouse with us," Ji Shen said.

Pei swallowed. "We'll take it a month at a time," she said softly.

"Yes, a month at a time," Mrs. Finch repeated.

Mrs. Finch stood longer than usual watching them climb up

the dirt path. When Pei looked back, she was still standing by the fence, gazing up at them as if they were a sky full of stars.

Mrs. Finch

Since the beginning of the year, Mrs. Finch had been making one excuse after another to her friends: "I'm fine, I just ate something that disagreed with me," or "You go on ahead and start the game, I didn't sleep well last night."

It didn't take long before Isabel Tate realized her illness was serious and persuaded her to go to the hospital for a checkup.

The pills they'd given her for her heart did little good. Most of the useful medicines were confiscated or destroyed by the Japanese. "We can calm diarrhea, bandage a cut, or give you aspirin for a headache." The young British camp doctor shook his head sorrowfully. "But we have little else to offer you. Even our monthly supply of calamine lotion, alcohol, and bandages lasts barely two weeks."

"No need to apologize." Mrs. Finch tried to smile and put the doctor at ease. "I'll try to accept each day as a gift."

She thought of how lovely it been just that morning, how clear and in focus the colors of the sea and mountains appeared to her. They seemed close enough to touch. How could she be dying when everything felt so alive and real?

"If you don't strain yourself and get plenty of rest, who can tell, you may even see the end of this war!" The doctor took her trembling hand in his.

Mrs. Finch ate less and less each day; she felt as if a tight band were pressing against her chest, making it hard to swallow. The only time she made any real effort to eat was after a visit with

Pei and Ji Shen. Mrs. Finch could almost see her own deterioration in Pei's dark eyes, and in the edge of fear that traced her voice as she pleaded with her to take care. Caroline had wanted to tell the girls that life was coming to an end for her, that even her love for them couldn't stop her tired heart from failing. So many times the words lingered on the tip of her tongue, before she would swallow them back down again. They had enough to worry about.

So Mrs. Finch lived her life carefully, taking nothing for granted. She wondered why wisdom came so late in life, when there was so little time left to enjoy the gifts of knowledge and acceptance. She'd had a good marriage and a full life. Her one wish was for a few more years to spend with Pei and Ji Shen. But for the most part, it had been a grand life and she had lived each day on her own terms.

Mrs. Finch shared her peas and sausages with Mrs. Tate and a few other women she played gin rummy with every Wednesday afternoon. The food was a welcome supplement to their three daily meals of rice, turnips, shallots, and weak tea. They had so successfully created a regular schedule for themselves that their routine in camp wasn't much different from their lives in free Hong Kong. After three and a half years at Stanley Camp, the British Empire remained alive and well behind the barbed-wire fence. During that time, fewer than a hundred and thirty prisoners out of three thousand had died, mainly of untreated illnesses. The rest of the sick and worn prisoners bickered among themselves and dreamed of soft beds and proper bathing facilities of their own.

"I'd die to have some tender asparagus tips right now!" Mrs. Tate said, wiping her forehead with a handkerchief.

Lately, they had found that talking about the food they missed offered a strangely satisfying substitute for actually eating it.

Louise Powell put down her cards, pulled at the front of her dress, and fanned herself. "A rare, juicy piece of beefsteak, smothered with onions, is what I'd want."

Mrs. Finch laughed. "A well-done chop with some hot mustard on the side and a baked potato drowned in sour cream. Bread pudding for dessert."

"And an ice-cold gin and tonic!" Mrs. Tate added.

"Why not champagne?" Mrs. Powell suggested.

Mrs. Tate threw down her cards. "Yes, why not? I do love a bit of the bubbly!"

Mrs. Finch laughed again, glad for a sweet moment in these increasingly difficult days when she'd felt herself losing control of her body. Lately, she'd found just the act of breathing more difficult; it was accompanied by a grasping discomfort in her neck and shoulders. Each day Mrs. Finch needed to rest for longer periods. The heat of summer pulled her down. Lying on the uncomfortable cot, she was reminded of her own mother's slowing down by a wicked spell of rheumatism. "My limbs are turning against me," she'd said over and over.

"Well, that's enough for me," Mrs. Finch said, pushing herself up from the makeshift table they'd put together of scrap board.

"Are you all right, Caroline?" Isabel stared hard at her. She knew the entire story, but respected her friend's wish to do things her way. She rose from her chair. "Have you been taking the aspirin they gave you at the infirmary?"

"I'm fine." Mrs. Finch smiled reassuringly, sucking in the warm air and trying to catch her breath. "Please, go on with the game; I'll just have a little rest and return in a bit."

She held herself steady and moved with assurance, turning back once to see Isabel's worried gaze follow her down the short hall into their cramped bedroom.

Mrs. Finch lay down on the soft cot, thumping hard against the wood frame, her bones sharp against the sagging canvas. She longed for her own bed on Conduit Road and the soft feather pillows of her London childhood. She couldn't imagine that there was much left of the life she'd once known.

"Gin!" she faintly heard Mrs. Powell's cheerful voice pipe up.

"Not again, Louise!" Isabel's watery voice floated from the other side of the room.

Mrs. Finch smiled, closed her eyes against the rapid beating of her heart. Quick flashes of memory flickered through her mind—the glass figurines, warm bread pudding, Howard's white shirts, the Victrola spinning round and round, Pei clutching the cloth bag. It seemed so strange to think that one could experience so many different lives in a lifetime. Mrs. Finch opened her eyes, felt a gripping pain in her chest that gradually lessened as she lay still. She suddenly heard Howard's hearty laughter, his voice saying, "You're thinking too hard, old girl."

Thinking of tall, kind Howard with each throbbing beat . . . thinking of Pei and Ji Shen's smiling faces on the other side of the barbed wire fence . . . thinking how everything felt as if it were slowing down, condensing into a dark, cool vacuum—then simply stopping.

Goddess of the Sea

Pei and Ji Shen hurried down the path toward Stanley Camp. The already-warm July morning left them hot and sweaty, but the sea air felt less sticky than the hot, crowded streets of Central and Wan Chai. Pei inhaled and tried to relax. For weeks after their last visit, she'd felt uneasy, worried that she'd forgotten to say something more to Mrs. Finch when they parted last month. She couldn't forget the sight of her standing at the fence and gazing up at them as they left.

"It's cooler here." Ji Shen's voice roused Pei from her thoughts.

Pei smiled. "Yes, the weather should be much more bearable now for Mrs. Finch."

She craned her neck to see as they waited by the fence. As always, a crowd had gathered to buy and barter from the boy hawkers.

Pei stepped away from the crowd and waited.

"Where is she?" Ji Shen asked.

Pei's stomach clenched. "I don't know. She should be here by now." She searched the now familiar faces of the prisoners. "Have you seen Mrs. Finch?" she asked.

Their eyes avoided hers. One man mumbled something about Mrs. Tate coming to talk with them. Pei's heart raced and she felt Ji Shen lean closer.

"Do you think she's all right?" Ji Shen asked.

"I hope so. Maybe she just needs to rest."

Pei strained to see if anyone was coming from the redbrick building where Mrs. Finch lived. In the distance Mrs. Tate rounded the corner and hurried toward them. As she drew closer, the look on her face told Pei the terrible answer to Ji Shen's question.

"I'm sorry, girls." Mrs. Tate swallowed, her voice breaking, a Chinese word or two, mixed with her English, emerging in staccato. "Caroline passed away. Almost a month ago. There was nothing the doctor here could do for her. It was heart failure. Caroline was a pillar of strength. She accepted her fate and went peacefully. I'm so sorry. I know how close you were to her."

"A month ago," Ji Shen echoed.

Pei took hold of Ji Shen's arm, her own legs weak at the news. "Where is she now?" Pei heard herself ask, enunciating each English word clearly.

Mrs. Tate pointed at the cemetery on the other side of the grounds. "They let several of us go along to say a few words before they buried her."

Pei bit her lip to hold back her tears. *It's not fair*, she thought. Mrs. Finch had made it so far. The occupation was almost over.

It was rumored on the street that the Japanese were losing the war. Signs of their defeat were everywhere. Japanese soldiers no longer waited on street corners to harass the Chinese. *The Hong Kong News*, once a means for the Japanese to boast of their victories, now sounded shallow and whiny. News of German defeats peppered the columns, even if Japanese troops supposedly remained victorious. For the past month, Chinese people had relaxed; now they lingered freely in the streets to bargain and socialize.

Surely it would be only a matter of months before all the prisoners were released. All Pei's hope evaporated in the heat. Mrs. Finch deserved so much more than a quick prison burial.

"Do you think we might go there?" Pei asked. Her throat suddenly felt so raw and dry, it hurt to swallow.

Mrs. Tate smiled tiredly. "I don't think it would be very wise. There are guards everywhere. Perhaps you can see her grave from outside the fence?"

Pei felt Ji Shen pull on her sleeve.

"I'm so sorry to have to tell you this. Caroline was a lovely person." Mrs. Tate's fingers touched the fence. "She thought the world of you both."

"We thought the world of her," Pei whispered, then turned away, unable to say another word.

She and Ji Shen walked across the hilly path to the cemetery in a daze. Neither of them spoke. Pei wanted to say something to make Ji Shen feel better, but she couldn't find the right words. Mrs. Finch's sudden absence left a sharp emptiness inside her that she hadn't felt since Lin's death. Why did everyone she loved leave her without saying good-bye? As a child, she'd lost her mother and her sister Li, then lovely Lin, and now Mrs. Finch. Pei felt a burning behind her eyes, and the tears streamed slowly down her cheeks.

As they approached the low-walled cemetery, Pei led Ji Shen boldly forward, daring the Japanese guards at the prison to stop them. She was tired of being afraid, of keeping invisible, of dodging soldiers in dark, dank alleys. But even if the soldiers saw them on the outskirts of the cemetery, leaning over the barbed wire fence to look for the grave of Mrs. Finch, no one came to disturb them. There were rows and rows of unmarked graves, and Pei couldn't help but wonder how many families would never know what had happened to their loved ones. Then, in the third row right, she saw the name Caroline Finch, scrawled in black letters on a piece of broken board. Pei supposed that Mrs. Tate had quickly marked the grave before she and the others were herded back to the camp. "Thank you," she heard herself say into the air.

The mounded earth was higher than the bone-dry dirt of the other graves. Pei turned around and saw the ocean, a view she knew Mrs. Finch would have appreciated. "Not a bad place to close my tired eyes," she heard Mrs. Finch say. At least Tin Hau, the goddess of the sea, would protect her here. A cooling sea-salted wind blew in their direction as Pei and Ji Shen kowtowed three times from the other side of the fence. Then they remained silent, staring. Ji Shen stood stiff and stoic, but Pei kicked at the dirt in front of her and fought back more tears.

Chapter Ten

1945

Pei

After Mrs. Finch's death in July, Ji Shen withdrew even further, while Pei began to notice something new and more disturbing in her behavior. It was as if Ji Shen had become a hostile stranger. When Ji Shen was at the boardinghouse, she spoke very little, but stared off into the distance as if in a trance. Her heavy silence made Pei feel uneasy, and though Pei hated to admit it, she was almost relieved when Ji Shen went out.

Usually, Ji Shen left the boardinghouse early in the morning and returned at dinnertime, bringing with her a variety of canned vegetables and meats, which she shared with all the sisters. She gave little explanation other than "I was out with friends." When Pei pressed further, she grew snappish: "Why can't you believe that I was out with Quan and my other friends? There's nothing for you to worry about. I'm not a baby anymore!"

At almost twenty, Ji Shen was indeed no longer a child, though Pei thought she acted like one. Pei felt her own anger simmering just below the surface, but she held her tongue and took comfort in the thought that at least the Japanese had grown conspicuous by their absence in the past months. A sense of spirit had returned to the Chinese as rumors of Japanese surrender continued to spread through the streets.

* * *

During the first days of August, Ji Shen came home to the boardinghouse with a man Pei had never seen before. As Ji Shen rushed up to the sitting room for the purse she'd forgotten, he stood waiting at the bottom of the stairs.

"Who is he?" Pei asked.

Ji Shen avoided her eyes. "Just a friend."

"Won't you ask your friend up?"

Ji Shen grabbed her bag. "We're in a hurry," she answered, looking flushed. "He's very busy. Maybe another time. I promise." Ji Shen smiled nervously, then hurried out of the sitting room and down the stairs.

Pei glanced out the sitting room window and glimpsed Ji Shen's friend. He was older and well-dressed, with neatly combed hair and a dark mustache. He turned back once, so that Pei saw his narrow eyes squint against the sun. Then he walked quickly down the street, while Ji Shen ran behind him in order to keep up.

On a sudden impulse, Pei ran down the stairs and found herself following Ji Shen and her friend toward Central. The crowds thickened as she pushed her way down the street in pursuit. It was obvious from the way Ji Shen was behaving that something was terribly wrong. Everything about her seemed secretive and volatile. Ji Shen was either out or feeling ill and sequestering herself in their room, refusing to talk. When she did return home—always late in the evening—she paced like a trapped and desperate animal.

Now, even though she knew it was wrong to follow Ji Shen and the man, Pei couldn't stop. She had to know what was going on, and she had a strong suspicion that Ji Shen's friend had everything to do with her difficult behavior and Quan's absence from their lives.

* * *

A crowd of people had just emerged from the King's Theatre when Pei reached Queen's Road in Central. She quickly glanced at the faces that swarmed and buzzed around her, hoping Ji Shen was one of them. Pei remembered reading that the Japanese had restored the theaters to full use not long after the occupation began; they ran mostly Japanese propaganda movies. Many of the wealthier Chinese families had wasted no time in reclaiming this small detail of their former lifestyle.

"Pei!"

Pei turned her head toward the male voice that unexpectedly called out her name.

"Pei, is that you?" The voice again, closer, until she felt someone's hand touch her arm. "It's me, Ho Yung."

Pei stepped back, away from his touch, in order to see his face more clearly. In the bright sunlight, Ho Yung's dark eyes looked so much like Lin's. Next to him stood a young woman and another couple, who seemed impatient to leave.

"Ho Yung?"

"Yes—Lin's brother, remember?"

"Yes . . . of course," Pei stammered. How could she ever forget Ho Yung? After Lin's death, he had comforted her and arranged for their safe passage to Hong Kong. Pei could still see him standing on the dock waving to them as she and Ji Shen boarded the ferry. In the six years since she'd seen him at Lane Crawford's, he had aged. Still, there were the unmistakable characteristics that he and Lin shared—the thin lips and dark, round eyes. She swallowed and tried to find the right words to say to him.

"How have you and Ji Shen been?"

"We're fine," Pei answered.

She lifted her hand up against the bright sunlight and saw Ho Yung glance uncomfortably toward his friends. They were all well dressed in dark suits or silk cheongsams.

"How is your family?" She raised her voice against the flurry of noise.

Ho Yung stepped away from the woman standing next to him and moved closer to Pei. "They're as well as can be, considering the occupation. My brother, Ho Chee, and his wife are the parents of two daughters. My mother has been ill in the past few years and is bedridden."

"I'm sorry," Pei said, at once struck by the sudden, sharp memory of the last time she'd seen Wong tai. The hard glare of hate still stung.

"I've often wondered how you and Ji Shen were doing."

Pei looked away. "We've managed to get by."

Ho Yung searched for words. "You look well." The young woman in a silk cheongsam tugged at his arm.

"I'd better be going," Pei said quickly. "I'm supposed to meet Ji Shen."

Ho Yung pulled a card from his pocket. "Please, take my card, and if you ever need anything, don't hesitate to look for me. Perhaps we can meet for tea?"

"Yes, thank you." Pei reached for the card and slipped it into her pocket. "I should go now."

"Yes, of course," Ho Yung said, gently releasing the woman's grip from his arm. "I hope we'll see each other soon."

Pei nodded, then hurried away from King's Theatre, too em-barrassed to stop. Her heart was racing. She must look a mess in her old tunic and pants, among the bright silk dresses. She rushed down the street and pushed everything away—even Ho Yung's serious dark eyes, whose gaze was too much like Lin's.

The bombings of Hiroshima and Nagasaki in early August left no doubt that a Japanese surrender was imminent. Pei could feel the rhythm of the streets humming again.

The following week Ji Shen was late coming home. It was long after dinner and she still hadn't returned. Pei glanced out the window and sighed heavily. "Where can she be?" she asked, more of herself than of the other women in the room. The image of Ji Shen's friend lingered heavily in her mind.

"Ji Shen can take care of herself. Besides, there have been rumors that Hirohito will surrender before the end of the week. Everyone is already out celebrating." Song Lee tried to be reassuring, though her voice was cautious and measured.

"It's almost dark," Pei added. Distant crackling noises sputtered through the night air.

"Ji Shen's probably with her friends," Luling said. "She hasn't needed any of our company for a long time."

Song Lee pulled Pei away from the window. "Don't listen to her. Luling has forgotten what it's like to be young."

Luling snickered.

Song Lee leaned closer. "Quan will look after her."

"It's her other friends I worry about," Pei said.

"I'm sure Ji Shen will have a good explanation," Song Lee added.

Pei sat down and continued sewing, though her fingers were stiff and her stitches too conspicuous. The memory of Ji Shen running after her friend returned again. She bit off the thread and took apart what she'd just sewn. "No more of this!" she said aloud. She grimaced, stood up, and set down the blue cheongsam she was mending, though it was supposed to be ready the next morning. "I'm going out to look for her."

Song Lee followed her to the door. "Wait a little longer. I'm sure she's just late talking with her friends. The occupation is all but over! Everything will be easier then."

"I wish it could be so simple," she sighed.

"Anyway," Song Lee continued, "where do you propose to start looking at this hour?"

"Quan told me they often go to Central, near the theaters, where the best deals can be made."

"But it's almost dark. I'll go with you."

Pei turned and held out her arm to stop Song Lee from following her into the street. She touched the older woman's shoulder to reassure her. "Don't worry, I'll be fine. There are lots of people out tonight." She gestured at the crowds. "If Ji Shen returns, make sure she stays put. I won't be long."

The night air had a smoky flavor, as if something were burning. In the near distance Pei heard quick popping noises that she hoped were firecrackers and not gunfire. She immediately felt something was different. There was an excitement in the atmosphere. A string of popping firecrackers twisted and snaked in front of her. The streets of Wan Chai were bustling as people gathered in the streets. There were no Japanese soldiers in sight.

Someone had turned a radio up loud, and through the static, the calm voice of Emperor Hirohito silenced the crowds as he surrendered to the world. A sudden roar of voices filled the air. A young man grabbed Pei and spun her around before rejoicing with the next person he saw. Groups of Chinese gathered in doorways or stood in the streets, while others ripped down any signs they could reach that bore Japanese names. A Japanese flag burned to cheers from the crowd. Pei raised her arms and cheered along with them.

In the smoke-filled air, music played nearby, horns and cymbals resounding through the night. Groups of young people were laughing and dancing in the streets. Happiness washed over Pei as she continued toward Central. The occupation was finally over. Ji Shen must have known it and stayed out celebrating with Quan and her other friends. Pei took a deep breath, still angry, yet also relieved.

Poor and rich alike were in the streets, cotton tunics and silk cheongsams together, laughing and celebrating the end of the occupation. Pei wondered how long it would take them to forget the long, gaunt years of humiliation and starvation, and all the loved ones who were no longer alive. If only Mrs. Finch could have lived to see this day. Pei missed her more than ever. She paused, only to hear Mrs. Finch's words return: "Life is made up of change. You can't run away from it."

The rapid popping of firecrackers and heavy clouds of smoke filled the air around her. The smoke made Pei's eyes burn and water; tears streamed down her face.

Ji Shen

Ji Shen had indeed been out celebrating the end of the occupation. The smoke from her friends' firecrackers cleared only long enough for another string to be set off. She was so caught up in the revelry with Lan Wai that she hadn't even realized Lock had disappeared.

"Don't worry," Lan Wai said. "He'll show up again, he always does."

"Where did he go?" Ji Shen asked.

Lan Wai shrugged. "Come on, don't worry about him."

Ji Shen felt a twinge in her stomach. "No, I'd better get back. Pei will be worried sick."

She hurried back to the boardinghouse, then hesitated and turned down the street toward Lock's apartment. Many of the street vendors stayed there. "We're just like one big family," he said. "Most of us lost our real families a long time ago."

The wooden stairs creaked as she climbed them. The shadowy thresholds looked dark and menacing. All she wanted was to be with Lock, to tell him she was pregnant with his child. He would have a real family of his own again. Lock would smile and wrap his arms around her happily at the news that he'd soon have an heir . . . or, at worst, he would be dismayed, but gladly take responsibility for his child.

Ji Shen found the spare key she'd seen Lock hide above the doorjamb and slid it into the keyhole, then slowly turned the knob. She entered quietly and waited for her eyes to adjust to the dim light before she negotiated the maze of boxes. Reaching his room, she inched the door open. The room was hot and stuffy, the air tinged with sleep and sweat. She slowly made out objects in the cluttered space—boxes of canned meat, liquor, and cigarettes stacked to one side, clothes on the floor, Lock's long body unmoving under a muted green blanket. Ji Shen smiled, then blushed, as she entertained the idea of slipping under the covers with Lock. Not until she moved closer to the bed did Ji Shen realize there was another body entwined with his. The long black hair of a woman was draped over his arms. She grew warm all over and abruptly felt sick to her stomach. It was as if she'd been suddenly kicked, the air knocked out of her. Ji Shen lurched forward. With an unexpected heave, she vomited on Lock's bed.

"Who's there?" his dazed voice rang out.

Ji Shen's heart raced. She gulped for air against her dizziness as she stumbled toward the door. She heard the muffled scream of the woman, but Ji Shen was already out of the apartment and down the stairs before Lock had time to slip on his pants.

Ji Shen walked back to the boardinghouse, knowing Pei must be beyond worry. She felt numb to everything. She prayed to the gods that it was just a bad dream, that she hadn't seen Lock lying with another woman. She stilled her trembling hands. Tomorrow he would welcome her and their child with soft whispers. . . . But the thought vanished in the dead of night, and Ji Shen began to cry. A few distant firecrackers still crackled through the night air, but the littered streets were largely deserted; almost everyone had gone home to sleep. Tomorrow the streets would be filled again, and all of Hong Kong would be celebrating the end to the Japanese occupation. How could she have been so stupid? Everyone had warned her. Ji Shen looked up at the moon that washed the streets with an eerie pale light. It was as if time were suspended somewhere between day and night, between truth and lies.

From a doorway, a strange man in tattered clothing, reeking of urine and alcohol, stepped out of the shadows. "Drink a little!" he spat out, and offered her the large green bottle he clutched tightly in one hand. Ji Shen dodged him. Her heart pounded in her chest; how would she find the right words to tell Pei she was sorry for everything? Ji Shen couldn't remain silent much longer about the baby growing inside her. She wished Mrs. Finch were still alive to soften the blow, to ease her fears and make everything all right.

"Please, Pei, can't you understand?" The words she'd rehearsed so many times as she walked home came tumbling out into the dark, empty street. An urgent murmur. "I thought I loved him and he loved me. I knew he was someone you wouldn't approve of, but I loved him anyway. And now I'm carrying his child. If it weren't for Lock, we would have never had enough food to carry us through the occupation."

Lock had mesmerized Ji Shen from the beginning. He was everything Quan wasn't—older, smooth-talking, self-assured. There were men and women working for him who hung on his every word and would do anything he asked. But Lock called Ji Shen his little lost swan, and he had chosen her, taken her under his wing, and helped guide her through the intricacies of the black market.

"I would never hurt you," he had whispered to her the first time he made love to her. "Haven't I always shown you the way? Just relax and let me take care of you now."

Ji Shen had never expected it to be that way with a man. The only time she'd seen Lock lose control was when he was inside her. Although the weight of his body on top of her pinned her down, for the first time in her life Ji Shen felt as if she were the one in command.

"Please, Pei, can't you understand?" she asked again.

The street was dark and empty: a sharp popping echoed in the distance.

Lan Wai had been the only one she could confide in. Everything had been so difficult between Pei and Ji Shen, it seemed the words just froze before they could be said. With Lan Wai, everything was understood.

"How do you feel?" Lan Wai had asked the other morning, seeing how pale she was.

Ji Shen looked up, surprised. In the past few months, ever since she'd become closer to Lock, Lan Wai had kept her distance. "I'm having a hard time keeping anything down today."

She could barely swallow the strong *po lai* tea Song Lee liked to drink every morning.

Lan Wai took a deep breath. "It was like that for me, too." She glanced at Ji Shen. "Sometimes dry biscuits help."

"Thank you," Ji Shen said. Her eyes met Lan Wai's in surprise, then quickly pulled away.

All day Lan Wai stayed close to Ji Shen and offered bits of advice. "It's important to drink plenty of water," she said, or "Later on you'll want to stay off your feet as much as you can." She glanced over at Lock across the room. "Don't ever let him tell you otherwise."

"What happened to your baby?" Ji Shen found the courage to ask.

Lan Wai hesitated, then said, "She died of sickness."

"I'm sorry." Ji Shen reached for the young woman's hand.

Lan Wai shrugged. "I suppose it's all for the best. This isn't a life to raise a child in," she said, and pulled her hand slowly away.

Ji Shen opened the front door of the boardinghouse and winced as it creaked loudly. She tiptoed up the stairs, but went into the sitting room instead of going directly to the room she shared with

Pei. A few more stolen moments alone might give her the courage to face Pei.

Pei's voice startled her. "You're late."

Ji Shen's heart raced as she turned to see the shadow of Pei sitting by the window. "You're still awake?"

"What did you expect?" Pei's voice was low and tired. "Didn't you think I would worry?"

Ji Shen stepped closer. "I'm so sorry. Everyone was out celebrating the end of the occupation and I'm afraid I lost track of the time." She suddenly wanted to hug Pei to show her how sorry she was.

Pei leaned forward. "It seems you've lost track of many things lately."

"Yes," Ji Shen agreed. She'd never seen Pei like this before, so distant and reserved, like a stranger. "I'm sorry," she said again.

"It's late. I'm tired." Pei rose from the chair. "I just wanted to make sure you were safely back home. We'll talk more in the morning." Not looking at Ji Shen, Pei walked past her without saying another word.

"Please," Ji Shen pleaded, her voice small and frightened. "I need to talk to you."

Simple Words

Forgiveness was a soothing balm, a cool breeze of relief. Pei finished mending last night's cheongsam while Ji Shen slept late into the morning upstairs. It was the calm, unhurried sleep of a child, not a soon-to-be mother. Last night Ji Shen's words had spilled over. She couldn't stop talking, until Pei stepped forward to take the quivering girl into her arms. "Everything will be all right," she whispered, smelling fear and sweat. "I won't let anything happen to either of you."

Song Lee poured herself another cup of tea and sat down across from Pei. "I knew Ji Shen would have to tell you soon that she was pregnant," she confessed. "I could read her movements as if they were characters on a page."

Pei looked up from her mending. "And you didn't say anything?"

Song Lee cleared her throat and continued in a calm voice. "I knew you would find out sooner or later. It was better for me to stay out of it."

"Was I so blind?" Pei shook her head.

Song Lee smiled kindly. "Sometimes a person is too close to see the truth."

"I should have paid closer attention, but what with all Ji Shen's growing pains, then Mrs. Finch's death and the mending business . . ."

"In the end, it doesn't matter what words are said or unsaid." Song Lee sipped her tea. "Life's mistakes are made whether you can see them or not. What counts is how we learn to live with them."

Pei nodded.

"And what of the father?" Song Lee asked.

Pei sighed. "It doesn't seem as if he has any intention of taking responsibility. Ji Shen found him with another woman."

"The dirty dog!" Song Lee said under her breath.

Pei paused in her mending and looked her friend in the eye. "From what I know, it might be best if she were rid of him."

"Whatever happens from this moment on, we're all part of Ji Shen's family here, and we will welcome this child," Song Lee said.

Pei continued with her work. Her needle and thread slipped

in and out of the material with ease. After so many difficult months, she felt as if the heaviness had been lifted from her shoulders.

In the days after peace came, Pei saw most of the silk sisters return to work as domestic servants. Song Lee and her committees had organized more meetings in the last month to help situate them. While some returned to their old households, many were placed in new positions, whose number increased each week with the growing prosperity of the colony. The interruption in their normal life was over, and Hong Kong again offered her sisters a means of sustenance.

Before long, the boardinghouse was nearly empty of Pei's sisters. Pei herself was wondering if she might start a seamstress business of her own. Her skills as an invisible mender had continued to grow through the occupation. Hong Kong Tai tais were anxious for their old and new dresses to be ready for them now that the round of parties had begun again. Pei dreamed of opening a small shop in Wan Chai, near the boardinghouse, so she wouldn't be far from Ji Shen and the baby when it came. She hadn't told Song Lee yet, but she had no intention of returning to the false smiles and difficult personalities that came along with working in a big house with a new Tai tai and Seen-san.

It was a bittersweet time for Pei. Just after the Japanese surrender in September of 1945, the Japanese soldiers withdrew and the British civilians interned at Stanley were officially released. But most of the ex-prisoners stayed on at the camp for a month or more, for lack of transport and housing.

Meanwhile, Ji Shen was having a difficult pregnancy. Ever since she told Pei about the baby, she felt so nauseated she stayed in bed each morning, barely able to speak.

With Song Lee watching Ji Shen, Pei caught a ride with Mr. Ma out to Stanley in mid-October. She felt a burning need to visit Mrs. Finch's grave and see Stanley Camp one last time.

As they drove through the Hong Kong streets, Pei saw how rapidly the city had regained some of its former glory. After the British government had regained possession of the island, they immediately set to work repairing all the destruction done during the three years and eight months of Japanese occupation. Within a month of their return, the rubble had been cleared and the pockmarked streets were temporarily patched with gravel and tar. The boarded-up windows of businesses, Pei saw, had been re-placed with plate glass. Even a few electric trolley lines, quickly repaired, were running again.

Every now and then a car came lumbering down the road, and Mr. Ma would swing abruptly to the side, but cars were still scarce. The streets, though, bustled with Chinese entrepreneurs who raced to rebuild the businesses stalled during the occupation.

The entire ride flitted by like a dream, filled with the soft touch of the approaching ocean and the sweet smells of the cooler, fresher air. Pei sat back and tried to remember the last time she'd felt so light and happy.

A truckload of British soldiers stood by the front gates of Stanley Camp. Most prisoners had already been transferred back to Hong Kong. The camp felt deserted. Pei tried to imagine how it must have felt to be held captive for so long. How many others, along with Mrs. Finch, had died during their long imprisonment?

Pei climbed the dirt path to the cemetery. Only four months had passed since Mrs. Finch died, and already her grave looked as if it'd been there for years. "If only you could have stayed with us a little while longer," Pei whispered as she touched the wooden marker, fingering the fading black letters of her name. She wished Mrs. Finch were alive to help her with Ji Shen's pregnancy. How would they ever be able to take care of a baby and still go out and make a living? A sudden warm breeze stirred. Pei looked up at the bright glint of the sun, which awakened the sudden memory of Mrs. Finch's jewelry, taped behind the dresser. She had expected to give it back to Mrs. Finch when the occupation was over. Now that she was gone, Pei knew exactly how Mrs. Finch would want her to use it. It might even be enough for her to open a small seamstress shop while they waited for the baby's birth. Another gust of wind blew, and Pei could almost swear she heard Mrs. Finch's voice say, "That's my girl."

Pei glanced down at Ho Yung's card to make sure it matched the address on the rusty gate. Now that she had the means, she needed someone with the resourcefulness to help her rent a shop. The house was old and large, not unlike Lin's old house in Canton that Pei had visited so many years ago. Its square brown walls were in need of paint, and the bushes were unkempt and overgrown.

Pei stood at the front door. She had no idea what she would say to Ho Yung if he was home. She had spoken to him only once in all these years, and had barely known him before Lin died, but he was the only one she could turn to. She lifted the knocker and let it fall hard several times against the door. There wasn't a moment in the past eight years that Pei hadn't wished Lin were still with her, guiding them with her strength. It felt just like yesterday that they returned to Lin's home in Canton. Once again Pei felt the cold fear of leaving Yung Kee and being in Lin's childhood home for the first time.

"Yes, yes," a voice boomed from behind the door.

Pei took a step back as the door swung open and an older, thinner Mui stood before her. For a moment Pei didn't know what to say to Lin's childhood servant.

"We aren't hiring anyone today!" Mui snapped, taking Pei for one of the many men and women who went from house to house looking for a day's work.

"I'm not looking for work," Pei quickly said. "I was wondering if Wong seen-san was in."

Mui stopped at the sound of her voice. She stepped closer to scrutinize Pei, squinting. Then, as if drawing from deep down in her memory, Mui said, "You came with Lin."

Pei nodded.

"Yes, the tall one who made her so happy. Come in, come in." Mui took Pei's hand and pulled her into the cool, dark entrance.

"Is Wong seen-san at home?" Pei asked again.

"Come this way." Mui led Pei into a large sitting room, devoid of any furniture but a few wooden chairs. "The Japanese devils came. Took everything. You wait here." Before Pei could say anything else, Mui quickly disappeared.

Pei wandered over to the fireplace and the small picture frames perched on the mantel. They were the only objects left in the room. Everything else had been stripped to the hardwood floors. Only from so close up did Pei see that the grainy photos showed Lin and her brothers as small children—their spirits frozen in black and white. Pei stared hard at one photo of Lin standing by herself, already beautiful in a light-colored Western-style dress. She must have been no older than ten or eleven when the photo was taken, a few years before she joined the silk work. Pei felt the tears well at the sight of the young Lin, who appeared so alive.

"Pei?" Ho Yung's voice filled the empty room.

Pei swung quickly around, looking first at Ho Yung, then down at the floor so he wouldn't see that she was crying.

"Are you all right?" he asked, walking over to her.

Pei nodded embarrassed. "Yes," she said. "It's just . . ."

"The photos," he finished.

Pei looked up at Ho Yung and tried to smile. "I've never seen a photo of her before." She cleared her throat. "She was so beautiful, even as a child."

"Lin resembled our mother from the day she was born"—

Ho Yung touched the photo—"but she had my father's heart and strength. She had the best of each of our parents, only to die so young. It still seems so unfair."

Pei turned away and wiped her tears with the sleeve of her tunic.

"I'm so sorry," Ho Yung quickly added. "I didn't mean to upset you. Please sit."

Pei sat down just as Mui returned with a tray of tea. The old woman mumbled something and smiled as she handed Pei a cup; then she left the room.

"Is everything all right?" Ho Yung asked, watching Pei closely.

"I've come to ask you a favor." She didn't dare look him in the eyes.

"Anything."

Pei sipped her tea, then said in one breath, "I need your help in starting a business."

Ho Yung's face turned serious. "What kind of business were you thinking about?"

"A small seamstress shop. I have some jewelry to sell, and I'd like to find a location in Wan Chai."

"What do you know about running a business?" Ho Yung questioned.

Pei realized she knew nothing, apart from what she'd been doing in a small way for the past two years. She wavered, thinking that this project might be more complicated than she had hoped.

"I already have a steady flow of customers," she said finally. "Many of the Tai tais feel I do good work. I just need a place to open a shop and expand the business I already have."

Ho Yung began to pace the sitting room. "I don't know very much about the sewing business," he began.

Pei quickly stood and put down her cup. Ho Yung had no reason to take the time to help her just because she asked. He must be busy with his own family's investments and obligations.

"I'm sorry to have bothered you," she said. "I know the

occupation has been difficult for all of us. Please forgive me for disturbing you. It was a foolish idea."

Ho Yung stopped short. "No, not foolish at all. Please, let me finish. What I meant to say was that it may take a short while for us to get the right location, but I'd be happy to help you find a place, and I'll talk with my brother about investing in your shop."

Pei didn't know what to say. In just a breath's time his simple words had changed her life. She smiled shyly at Ho Yung, her gaze moving beyond him to the photo of Lin on the mantel.

Song Lee

Song Lee walked briskly back to the boardinghouse, laden with bags of herbs, bean sprouts, bok choy, and fresh Chinese mustard greens. In another bag were oranges, apple-pears, and starfruit. After so many years of so little, food was once again fresh and abundant. The streets were vibrant and alive. Song Lee was glad to think that Ji Shen would soon give birth to a new life in a much better world. The sudden thought struck her of all the fancy black-market food Ji Shen had brought home for them just before the occupation ended. She'd surprised them with a multitude of exotic canned foods with strange-sounding foreign names—cans of garlicky "es-car-got" or musty-smelling "truf-fles."

"The snails were imported from France," Ji Shen had said, quickly swallowing another one.

Too fast to taste anything, Song Lee thought.

"It's interesting." Pei chewed slowly.

Song Lee spat the chewy snail out into her bowl. "Tastes like rubber," she'd said. "Tomorrow I'll bring home dinner!"

Song Lee had taken care of filling their stomachs since the occupation ended. She made it her personal mission to find the best deals she could each day. "Bean sprouts and radishes for half the price of yesterday!" she yelled triumphantly when she returned with something good from the market. "Tomorrow, old man Fu says he'll have long beans if I arrive early!"

Pei laughed. "You're getting to be as good as Ji Shen."

"Better," Song Lee retorted. "At least I bring home food we can eat!"

With Ji Shen's difficult pregnancy and the work of starting up her own seamstress business, Pei had her hands full, Song Lee knew. The small daily details swelled and seemed to grow. Tears filled Pei's eyes the evening Song Lee took her aside and simply told her, "I'm staying until the baby comes." There would be plenty of time to return to work for her old employer after the baby was born. Meanwhile, cooking had become just one of Song Lee's many household tasks.

Song Lee pushed open the front door of the boardinghouse and slowly climbed the stairs, breathing heavily by the time she reached the landing. A soft buzz of voices came from Pei and Ji Shen's room. Song Lee smiled. Over the months, as Ji Shen's stomach grew round and hard and she stayed away from the black market, Song Lee heard their words grow easier and softer, melting the thick silence that once lay between them. She could see the relief on Pei's face, the ready smile and new light behind her eyes.

At forty-eight years old, Song Lee had a family in Pei and Ji Shen for the first time since Ching Lui and the sisterhood. Her life within the sisterhood had provided for her for almost twenty-five years, until one morning she woke up knowing, the way she knew a body needed food and water to survive, that she had to leave.

"Why did you leave the sisterhood?" Pei had once asked her.

"Because I simply couldn't stay any longer." Song Lee struggled for an answer. "I always felt I belonged elsewhere." She knew this wasn't really an answer.

"And have you found that 'elsewhere'?"

Song Lee smiled. "I think so," she said, though she knew "elsewhere" wasn't so much Hong Kong, as it was now Pei and Ji Shen.

She'd picked up so many skills along the road of life—silk reeling, domestic work, organizing her sisters, reading faces, and now taking care of Pei and Ji Shen. But Song Lee had never expected that she would finally be part of a family so late in her life; that a tall, hardworking woman, a sometimes difficult young one, and a coming baby could fill her days with such happiness.

Song Lee brought the food to the kitchen, and quickly took out the white packets of herbs for twelve *ti bo* tea. The old herbalist had meticulously wrapped them separately. She put water on to boil, then sat down to wait. What Song Lee didn't dare tell Pei was how worried she was about Ji Shen. From the beginning it had been a hard pregnancy, and lately Song Lee saw a pale color in the area between Ji Shen's eyes: a diminishing of her energy. The tea would renew her strength and help her blood circulate. Song Lee would work her magic as quietly as possible; there was no point in worrying Pei. When the water boiled, she sprinkled the herbs into a pot, let it steep to just the right shade of dark brown, as the old herbalist had instructed, then carefully carried the bowl on a tray to join the two women.

Pei

After months of morning sickness, Ji Shen woke up feeling better. Pei saw the flush of pink in her cheeks and reminded herself to thank Song Lee and the old herbalist for their miracle tea. Just last week, Song Lee had said triumphantly that Ji Shen was graduating from twelve *ti bo* tea to thirteen *ti bo* tea now that she was past her sixth month.

"I'm hungry," Ji Shen said, her belly rising as she arched her back in a stretch. "I never thought I would be hungry again."

"Go get something to eat," Pei urged her. "I'll be there shortly." She watched Ji Shen step lightly out the door.

Pei pulled out the cloth bag that contained Mrs. Finch's jewelry and poured the contents onto her bed, where they glistened in the sunlight. It was hard to believe that such simple objects, shaped of metal, stone, and pearls, would be able to finance her new business. She held up each piece—the diamond brooch, the gold bracelet, and the gold wedding band, along with the emerald ring she hoped to keep. Last, Pei picked up the pearl necklace and let the lustrous pearls slip between her fingers like water. Pei felt the love and strength of Mrs. Finch in each one of them.

Ho Yung was supposed to arrive at any moment. They'd finally found the perfect location for her seamstress shop, within walking distance of the boardinghouse. Before the occupation it had been a fish shop, and the salty, tart smell reminded Pei of her father's fishponds. The strong fishy odors were long ingrained in the dull-colored walls and plank floor. Pei felt dizzy at first, only to realize it wasn't out of fear or unhappiness, but out of a strange comfort in returning to a place she once knew well—her own childhood. The downstairs was no larger than the sitting room, but there was also an upstairs where she could work undisturbed, with tall windows and plenty of light. After all the dark, dank stores they'd seen, Pei was certain that this was the right one. They could paint the walls and replace the wood floor. She'd tossed and turned all night, knowing Ho Yung would be talking to the owner that morning.

A quick knock on the door, and Song Lee told her Ho Yung was waiting in the sitting room. Pei gathered the jewelry back into the bag, hoping he had brought her good news. It was strange to think how two swift words like "yes" and "no" could change a life. She braced herself for whatever the answer would be. Pei felt the weight of the jewelry in her hand, then hurried to the sitting room.

Ji Shen's voice could be heard from the kitchen, followed by light laughter. Ho Yung stood staring out the window. He turned around when he heard her come in, and she saw a hint of Lin again. Then, by the calm smile on his face, Pei knew the shop was hers.

Pei's business doubled within the first few months after her mending shop opened in 1946. Word-of-mouth business flowed in and out, the only evidence of the shop's presence being a faded sign that bore a threaded needle in green and Chinese characters in red: "Moth holes, rips, splits, cuts, slashes, tears, and burns— fabric made new."

Most days Ji Shen was at the shop helping. After nearly six months of morning sickness, she felt fine again and had settled comfortably into her last three months of pregnancy. Sitting on a tall stool behind the counter, she greeted customers and collected and tagged cheongsams, Western dresses, trousers, even silk stockings, which soon piled up on Pei's worktable upstairs waiting to be mended.

The tiny bell on the door jingled constantly. Opening and closing, letting in the incessant street noises—high, nasal voices and honking horns. From upstairs Pei could hear it all—a chorus that floated up to her sewing room.

One morning, though, when she stood up and stretched, then went downstairs to get more thread, she suddenly realized how quiet it had become. Her heart skipped a beat. Where was the soft hum of Ji Shen helping a customer? "Torn? Moth-eaten? Don't worry, it will be just like new," Ji Shen would reassure them, beaming as she listened intently to the history of how each garment was acquired. "This dress once belonged to my mother," one woman recounted, near tears. Or "This tie is of the finest Italian silk," a man might brag. Pei smiled to herself when she heard these things. Ji Shen was quickly gaining the patience needed to be a good mother.

Halfway down the stairs Pei saw why everything had come to a standstill: A man stood talking quietly to Ji Shen. For a moment, she was frightened to think that the long, solid figure belonged to the baby's father, that he had finally come to his senses and returned to claim his rights. Pei trod heavily on the next step, and the young man looked up. Only then did she realize he was Quan.

"Quan!" Pei hurried down the stairs and welcomed him with a hug. From the corner of her eye, she saw Ji Shen slide off her stool, stand there rooted and unmoving. Quan had grown tall and had filled out in the past year. No longer the skinny sha boy, he looked handsome and grown-up in a clean, white shirt and dark trousers.

"Where have you been?" Pei asked, stepping back and taking a good look.

Quan grinned. "I've been working on a fishing boat over by the island of Lantau," he answered. "Uncle Wei helped me get the job before the occupation ended. Things were getting too difficult here." He shifted from foot to foot and glanced over at Ji Shen.

"How is your family?" Pei asked.

"Everyone is fine. My brother is the sha boy now."

"We worried about you," Pei said softly. Even if Ji Shen hadn't discussed Quan's whereabouts, Pei always suspected his sudden disappearance had to do with Ji Shen's involvement with the baby's father.

"My mother heard that you'd opened a shop," Quan said, changing the subject. "I've been wanting to visit."

"It keeps a roof over our heads."

"Looks as if business is good." He gestured to a pile of clothes awaiting Pei's mending.

"Yes," Pei said, remembering the thread she'd come down for. "I have some work to finish up. Stay and talk to Ji Shen, then come back with us to the boardinghouse for dinner. You can tell me all about your fishing career then."

Quan nodded shyly.

At the top of the stairs, Pei peered down to see Ji Shen once again talking quietly to Quan, her hands folded lightly over the full moon of her stomach.

Pei usually closed the shop around six each evening and walked slowly back to the boardinghouse with Ji Shen, where Song Lee had dinner waiting for them. That night, she quickly finished mending a pair of silk stockings, then decided to close the shop a half-hour early.

As if Song Lee knew they were bringing Quan home, she had prepared soup, rice, pork with lotus roots, and chicken with long beans. The usually quiet boardinghouse took on a festive air. Quan ate heartily long after all the women had put down their chopsticks. "You don't know how sick I am of eating fish," he said, finally putting down his bowl.

Ji Shen laughed. "I can see."

Quan blushed.

"Nonsense, he's a growing young man. He should eat!" Song Lee filled his bowl again with rice.

Pei hadn't seen Ji Shen so happy in a long time, smiling and teasing. When Quan leaned forward and reached out for his rice bowl, Pei also noticed how little difference there was between a sha boy's hand and a fisherman's hand—they had the same large-knuckled strength. Quan had moved gracefully from the secrets of the streets to the secrets of the sea.

When they'd finished dinner, Quan left to spend some time with his family, promising to return soon. Still in a joyful mood, Pei and Ji Shen adjourned to the sitting room with Song Lee. Pei sat by the window, and as was her habit, began some mending—a cheongsam, tonight—that would be picked up the next morning. She threaded a needle with silver-gray, a wise and calm color. There was always too much work now not to do it late into most evenings. More than once, Song Lee had told her to employ an assistant, but Pei had shrugged off the suggestion. Her business was just getting on its feet, and every cent was needed. Not to mention that very soon there would be one more mouth to feed.

Ji Shen waddled back and forth, her small frame still slim except for her belly, where the baby rode high and round. Song Lee had said to herself over and over again, "The baby sits high, so it should be a boy."

Ji Shen suddenly turned to them from the window and said, "I've been thinking of names."

"For the baby?" Song Lee asked.

Ji Shen laughed. "For the shop."

Pei looked up from her mending. "We've been doing all right without one."

"Ho Yung thinks it's bad business not to have a name," Ji Shen continued. "How will people identify us?"

Pei smiled and continued to sew. Ho Yung came to the shop at least once or twice a week with a new idea to improve business: chairs for customers to sit on while they waited, flowers to brighten up the counter, ways to make each customer feel important.

"Let them chose the shade of thread they want you to use," he said one afternoon, fingering a flat of threads in a rainbow of colors.

Pei remembered stopping for a moment at Ho Yung's idea. She always felt that each color had a personality, a language all its own. After so many years of reeling the pale white threads of the cocoons, and salvaging hidden threads during the occupation, it was a pleasure to have such a multitude of colors to work with.

Perhaps some kind of dialogue with her customers was important. That, and a name.

"The Invisible Thread," Song Lee suddenly suggested.

"The Needle and Thread!" was Ji Shen's idea.

It didn't take Pei long to agree on one. The Invisible Thread, it would be. She liked the sound of it. Simple and clear.

"And now what about a name for the baby?" Song Lee continued.

By the smile on Song Lee's face, Pei knew her friend was pleased that they'd chosen a name for her shop so quickly. She saw it as a good omen, like so much else lately.

"I was thinking if the baby's a girl, we should call her Lin," Ji Shen said.

Pei was startled to hear Lin's name ring so calmly through the room. "She would be honored," Pei said, mostly to herself and not looking up from her sewing. She'd have to get used to saying the name aloud every day again. But how could the child be anything but fortunate in carrying the name of her beloved Lin?

"And if it's a boy?" Pei finally looked up and asked.

"I'd like him to have a prosperous name. My father's name was Gong."

" 'Gong' means bright," Song Lee said. "A good name for a boy. It's important to start a child off right in the world. His name will define who he is in this life."

"It's a good name," Pei seconded. Both of them were. She held the dress she'd been mending up to the light, barely able to tell where it had been ripped.

Two days later, Ji Shen's water broke. Pei held her hand tightly, although Ji Shen's nails dug into her skin with each new spasm of pain. It was going to be a long labor; hours had already passed since her first contraction. They were all in the sitting room talking and making plans for the baby's arrival. Ji Shen had just picked up her teacup, only to double over, grabbing her stomach as if she'd been punched. She screamed aloud as warm water rushed from between her legs to the floor. It was followed by a series of prolonged contractions.

While Pei helped Ji Shen up the stairs to bed, Song Lee rushed to get the midwife. The wizened old lady finally sauntered in, saying, "Relax, relax, the first one never comes so quickly!"

Almost eleven hours later, the midwife cut an incision that lengthened all the way to Ji Shen's rectum. Only then did the baby finally arrive. Ji Shen tried to lift her head, smiling weakly when she saw her newborn son. "A boy," she whispered, her eyes looking up and finding Pei's.

"A boy," Pei echoed, placing the baby next to the exhausted young woman.

Pei couldn't help but remember her own mother, and the births Yu-sung had suffered through. All that pain, only to have five daughters and no sons to carry on her husband's name and help with the groves and ponds. In the end, she and Li had been the only two to survive. Pei's heart filled with yearning to know if her sister Li was still alive and well.

Ji Shen's moans brought her thoughts back to their cramped, warm room. Pei looked down to see the midwife frantically trying to stop the flow of blood from the incision. Song Lee had disappeared to fetch more clean towels. Pei's heart quickened to see how pale Ji Shen was and how her grip was weakening.

"What's wrong?" Pei screamed, wide-eyed with fear. "Do something! Do something!"

The midwife made a coughing sound as if something were stuck in her throat, but didn't answer. In the next moment it seemed as if she were trying to do a hundred things at once, mumbling to herself. Finally, she said the words aloud: "The bleeding won't stop." She removed a bloody towel from between Ji Shen's legs and replaced it with the last clean one.

Pei bent down to Ji Shen's ear. "You have to live through this," she pleaded. "There's still so much you have to do. You have to see your son grow into a man." The heat of the room was stifling with the sour smell of sweat and blood. "Ji Shen, can you hear me?"

The slightest whisper of a moan.

"Ji Shen! Ji Shen!" Pei's distraught cry filled the room.

Very slowly Ji Shen opened her eyes and smiled calmly at Pei, her head rising just a bit. "I'm sorry," she mouthed.

A last breath of words before her lids suddenly fluttered and her eyes rolled to the back of her head; the last of her spirit rose from her parted lips. Pei clutched Ji Shen tighter, refusing to let death take her. "Live! Live! Live!" The frantic chant, willing Ji Shen to return to life, as the baby squirmed beside her, making small gurgling sounds that sounded faintly like laughter.

The funeral was small and spare, the sky as clear as glass. Pei and the baby, Song Lee, Quan, and Ho Yung stood on the graveyard hill. Pei had borrowed money from Ho Yung to secure a plot and marble headstone for Ji Shen in a Chinese cemetery. It stood before them, soft gray swirls in hard white rock. A life—a loving mother who wasn't given the chance to love her son—reduced to an engraved name, the years of birth and death. Song Lee cried aloud as Ho Yung held gently onto her arm. Quan stood stone still, tears streaming down his face.

On this gloriously bright day, Pei held on tightly to baby Gong and said her final good-byes to Ji Shen, who for the last eight years had been the sole remaining member of her Yung Kee family. Pei kowtowed three times in front of the grave and felt the squirming bundle press against her. A hot sting of tears burned inside her but wouldn't emerge. Grief had numbed her. Nothing could have prepared her for Ji Shen's death. Now she felt the shadows of both Lin and Ji Shen hovering over her. Pei looked up quickly and thought she saw a thin woman in a red scarf watching from a distance, but when she looked again, the woman had disappeared into the bright sunlight.

The Language of Threads

During the nights that followed Ji Shen's death, Pei hardly slept. The heaviness of grief pressed against her and left her breathless every time she closed her eyes. Whenever she stepped out of the warmth of her bed to check on Gong, he, too, was awake in the dark silence, waiting. It was as if the memory of Ji Shen kept pulling them both awake. Pei understood her own deep longing, but how was it possible that a newborn child could already know that he had no mother to love him and no father to give him a name he'd be proud to carry on?

Pei watched the baby intently for any small resemblance to Ji Shen. The thick black down that covered his fragile skull. His pale, soft skin, and the tiny hands that reached out for Pei every time she came near. His small, dark eyes, which already seemed to know her from long ago. They were all a part of Ji Shen, and Pei felt a hot knot of tears pushing from behind her eyes every time she looked at him.

Every morning Pei wrapped the baby up in a blanket and took him with her to the Invisible Thread. Keeping busy was the only thing she could do. She sleepwalked through her days at the shop and occasionally even stuck herself with a needle in her daze. Ji Shen's death had been too unexpected, like a suddenly missed step. Hard and surprising. But every time Pei thought she couldn't pick herself up again, she watched Gong and saw how one life had unexpectedly taken the place of another.

Usually the baby stayed upstairs in his bassinet while Pei quietly mended beside him and Song Lee temporarily worked the counter. Pei was grateful for Song Lee's devotion, for all the sympathy she hadn't voiced, but simply showed by remaining with them. She felt Song Lee's sadness in the sighs that floated up from downstairs, as if each breath were too heavy. "Leave it, leave it," she heard Song Lee's indifference with a customer. The air no longer rang out with the music of Ji Shen's patient small talk. Pei swallowed and tried to fill the hollowness that threatened to over- take her. She peeked at the baby, watching for the slight rise and fall of his chest, always fearful that he, too, could be snatched away from her.

Each week Ho Yung and Quan came to the shop and visited the baby. As the days passed, Pei saw how each one brought a special gift of strength and character that would enrich Gong's life. He reached up to them, flailing his tiny arms, asking to be picked up; both men were careful and attentive to the delicate package they held.

One day, Pei left the baby in his bassinet behind the counter with Song Lee. "He has a high forehead," remarked the first cus- tomer to come in that afternoon. "A sign of great intelligence!"

"Don't let the gods hear you say such things," Song Lee snapped. "Anything can still happen with a child so young." Then she quickly added in a loud, clear voice so the gods would hear her, "This one's a scrawny little thing. Nothing much to look at!"

For the first time since Ji Shen's death, Pei wanted to laugh. She knew it was one thing to read a face and see its good fortune, another to say that fortune aloud and bring bad luck. It hadn't been five minutes since she'd brought Gong downstairs, and al- ready this new addition to their family had made his presence felt in the shop.

Sometimes Pei was surprised that the Invisible Thread kept flour- ishing, even when so much else around her seemed to have wilted. She reached into a pile of clothing that needed to be mended and pulled out a piece of bright blue silk, startled by its sudden rich color. It opened up to reveal a banner of embroidered flowers representing the four seasons. Pei fingered the worn threads of each flower.

> *A peony rising in spring.*
> *The lotus of summer.*
> *Autumn's chrysanthemum.*
> *The plum in winter.*

What once must have been a beautiful array of colors had faded and frayed over the years. Pei examined the pale bouquet against the bright blue sky. It would require a great deal of work to replace the intricate embroidery with new threads. Pei stood up and made her way downstairs.

"Who brought this in?" Pei asked, placing the blue silk banner on the counter.

"An older woman who was in a hurry," Song Lee remembered. "She wanted to know if you could replace each flower with new threads."

"I only mend clothing. This work would be too time-consuming, not to mention the cost."

Song Lee shrugged. "She said never mind the cost. She was willing to pay whatever you charged because she'd heard you did good work. She also said she wasn't in any hurry to get it back, so you could take your time." Song Lee glanced up at Pei. "Was I wrong to accept it?"

Pei fingered the faded threads and could already see the bright colors that would replace them. "No, you weren't," she smiled.

A month after Ji Shen's death, Pei still struggled with sleepless nights and a suffocating grief. During the day she threw herself into her work. At night, she sometimes fell asleep long enough to dream of Ji Shen alive again—sitting behind the counter at the Invisible Thread, talking and laughing with customers—only to be startled awake by the knowledge that Ji Shen was gone. "I won't let anything happen to either of you," she had promised;

the words turned over and over in her mind. The bed beside hers was empty, the dark house full of night cries.

Pei rose in the coolness to check on the baby, who had now fallen into regular sleeping habits. Pei's hands moved away from the soft baby skin to the smooth silk of the blue banner. She sat down beside the table lamp and quietly began to snip away the faded threads; they fell to her lap like blades of grass. Pei was determined to replace each flower, one thread at a time, as if she could control the flow of seasons. Gradually, all the colors lit up her dark nights—red, the summer of life; white the color of autumn; black of winter; blue of springtime; yellow that rose from the center of the earth.

Eventually, Ji Shen's death no longer kept Pei from sleeping, and even more slowly the language of threads spoke loud and clear against the bright blue sky.

Song Lee

Song Lee knocked lightly on Pei's door. Night after night she saw a slice of muted light coming from underneath that door. She knew Gong had been fast asleep for hours, knew Pei was trying to catch up with all the mending, which multiplied with each passing day. Song Lee held the cup of hot tea steady, and tapped again. When she heard Pei's voice whisper a response, she turned the doorknob and quietly entered.

"You're up late," Song Lee said. "Again." Even in a whisper, the last word echoed through the room.

"There's so much . . ." Pei answered, without glancing up, without finishing her sentence.

"I brought you a cup of tea."

Pei looked up and smiled. "Thank you."

In the flickering light Song Lee saw the fatigue that clouded her eyes, the grief still etched along the rims.

"You know . . ." Song Lee paused, then peeked at the sleeping Gong, who at two years old was a constant reminder of Ji Shen. He had the same full lips, and a slightly flat nose that Song Lee lovingly pinched together to give it height. She knew he was still young enough to change the fates. "It's time you found someone to help you with all the mending."

"Yes," Pei agreed.

Song Lee looked at her in surprise. They'd had the same conversation for almost two years now, with always a hesitant response emerging from Pei's lips. "Not just yet . . . Maybe later . . . I'll think about it." In the quiet room Song Lee heard Gong's even breathing. On the wall above his bed hung the blue silk banner with the flowers of the four seasons. The old woman had never returned to the Invisible Thread for it. Another abandoned child. Song Lee knew the hours Pei had worked on it, the colors carefully chosen to bring each flower back to life.

After a year's time, when Gong had begun to wobble and walk, Pei hung the banner on the wall of their room to keep him from grabbing at the bright material. It was a sign of renewal, a testament of their passage through a most difficult time.

"I'll begin looking for someone tomorrow," Song Lee quietly offered.

Pei nodded, then closed her eyes for a moment, her hand still pulling the thread through the silk jacket in her lap.

It didn't take long for Song Lee to get the word out that the Invisible Thread was looking for another seamstress: "Efficient, fast worker with a mild, easy personality. Bring a sample of your work." Song Lee interviewed each woman who stepped through the door to apply for the job. She had prided herself on finding the right domestic positions for her sisters; now she would do no less for Pei. Again she implemented her face-reading skills; she dismissed those with demanding, down-turned mouths, and the obviously devious ones who wouldn't look her directly in the eyes. Less than a week later, Song Lee had happily found the perfect seamstress to work alongside Pei.

Pei

"She'll be here any minute!" Song Lee's voice rang high in her excitement. She moved the clothes waiting on the counter into a tidy stack.

"Bring her upstairs when she arrives," Pei said. "I'd better start working." She was only too glad that Ho Yung had come to take Gong out for a walk.

Pei had just sat down when she heard the jingle of the bell on the front door. Song Lee and another voice filled the air with soft and polite words. Their hard, firm steps followed up the stairs. Song Lee and a thin woman in her late twenties emerged at the top of the stairs and paused.

"Come in," Pei said. She stood up, forgetting that her height immediately gave her a certain advantage.

Song Lee stepped aside. "This is Mai."

Mai bowed her head, nodded shyly.

"Please sit," Pei offered.

In one quick glance Pei saw a modest young woman with large deep-set eyes and a slightly protruding forehead, accentuated by hair tightly pulled back in a chignon. She clutched a sample of her work, which she offered to Pei—a pair of brown cotton trousers that, she explained, had been ripped at the knee. "The left knee," she quickly added.

While Song Lee excused herself to return downstairs, Pei and Mai made small talk, exchanging careful, courteous words they wouldn't remember in the years to come. While Pei spoke of the eight hours required, of the salary she could afford to pay, Mai listened quietly. Then, in a flood of soft words, she told her story. She'd been sewing and mending for her younger brothers and sisters ever since she was a little girl. Sewing was all she knew. It was what she loved. Now she had a husband who was ill, who could work only sporadically, when he was strong enough. She washed clothes, scrubbed floors, and emptied buckets of night soil. She didn't mind the work. It earned honest money to pay their debts. Her husband was a good man, but the fates had been unkind to them.

Pei listened and poured her a cup of tea. Mai's words were steady and matter-of-fact. She took small sips from the cup, then continued to speak. When her story ended, Pei watched the young woman's hands wrap around the half-empty teacup for warmth, for security. For the first time in her life, Pei realized she had the ability to change a life, change a fate.

As Mai paused to glance around the crowded room, Pei felt for the rip in the left knee of the brown trousers. They must belong to her sick husband. Pei's fingers could barely distinguish where the tear began from where it ended.

Mai was a true gift, a quick and efficient worker, who spoke little while she mended, and worked with such concentration that she might sit for hours without looking up. In the first few weeks, Pei taught her all the secrets of invisible mending. "Take the same thread from a seam or hem if you can; if not, make sure the material and thread match as closely as possible," she'd instructed. "The slightest difference in color can be as distinct as another language. Always study the pattern of the material and follow it as closely as possible." It wasn't long before Mai's work was almost as good as Pei's.

During her breaks, Mai relaxed, talked, and laughed, and lavished attention on little Gong. When they played, his squeals of laughter could be heard throughout the shop.

"I helped to raise my brothers and sisters," Mai said one afternoon, as if in apology. "I hadn't realized how much I miss having a child around."

"You would make a fine mother." Pei smiled. "There will be plenty of time for you to raise your own soon."

Mai shook her head. "I'm afraid that won't be possible."

Pei hesitated, then asked, "Your husband?"

"This time it's my fault," Mai answered, then picked up her mending and closed the subject.

The Invisible Thread continued to thrive—so much that Ho Yung began to talk about finding a bigger shop.

"This place is too small," he said. "There's no longer enough room for customers to even stand."

Pei looked up from her mending, acknowledging the clutter she'd grown used to. The racks of clothing; the papers piled up and weighed down by empty wooden boxes that once held spools of thread; Gong's makeshift bed, where he napped.

"It only takes a few minutes for customers to drop off or pick up their clothes," Pei said softly.

The door jingled open downstairs.

Ho Yung spread out his arms, as if he were about to embrace the small room. For the first time, Pei noticed how his body had begun to thicken and his hair showed a glimmer of gray. She thought of Lin, whose life was forever frozen in time. At thirty-eight, Pei was already five years older than Lin had been when she died.

"It's too small up here," he said. "You have another employee now."

Pei considered Ho Yung's point, the practical words that had cemented their business partnership and strengthened their friend-ship through difficult times. Sometimes Pei still caught a glimpse of Lin in him; sometimes she saw a kindness that was all his own.

"Isn't there some way we could stay here?" Pei asked. "There's only Mai and me." She couldn't explain to him what great comfort the fish store–turned–mending shop brought her.

Ho Yung paced. "We'll see what we can do," he said. Then, rather than hurrying off to deal with his family real estate business, he sat down in Mai's chair. "There's something else I'd like to talk to you about." His voice was even and serious.

Pei put down her mending. "Is anything wrong?"

Ho Yung cleared his throat. "You know my mother passed away last year?"

Pei nodded. Wong tai had been sick for a long time. Ho Yung had once told Pei that she was bedridden through most of the occupation. It was her choice, he'd said, as everything she did had always been, even when she slowly began to end her life, little by little. She refused to allow anyone into her room other than her sons. Then, gradually, she refused to speak, to listen, to eat, and, finally, to live.

"Did she ever forgive Lin for going through the hairdressing ceremony?" Pei blurted.

Ho Yung looked at her, surprised at first. "She was unable to," he said at last.

Pei's throat felt dry and scratchy. She still felt bad about not having attended Wong tai's funeral—for Ho Yung, if not for herself. But she simply couldn't pretend to honor a woman who had shown her only contempt. She wondered if the cold glare of hatred had clouded Wong tai's eyes one last time before she closed them for good. Everyone had saved face when Gong came down with a fever, enabling Pei to send her condolences without having to attend.

"Yes, well . . ." Ho Yung cleared his throat again. "My brother and his wife have their own apartment. I'm alone in a big house now, with much more room than one man needs, while you and Gong are cramped in one small room at the boardinghouse—"

"It's not so bad," Pei quickly interrupted. "Our lives are very simple. Song Lee helps out a great deal."

Laughter and voices floated up from downstairs. Mai had returned from her break.

"But is it enough for you? For Gong? He's growing up and needs more attention. A father's attention." Ho Yung swallowed. "What I'm trying to say is that I would be happy to have you as my wife and to raise Gong as my son."

Pei felt the blood pulsing through her body, the rush of warmth coloring her face. What was Ho Yung saying? She had gone through the hairdressing ceremony with Lin, given her life to the silk work. And though the sisterhood was only a vivid memory, Pei had never let go of her vows. She felt Ho Yung's eyes on her. Lin's eyes. There hadn't been a moment when she didn't trust him and care for him, but what she felt wasn't a wife's love for a husband.

"I . . ." she began.

Downstairs she heard Gong's chiming voice questioning. "Why? How?"

"I don't expect an answer right away," Ho Yung said. "It's something you might think about." He stood up quickly and tried to smile, though his eyes told her that he'd understood her thoughts. He leaned forward and touched her shoulder lightly. "I'll see you tomorrow."

Pei wanted to tell Ho Yung to stay, but the words caught in her throat. She watched as he crossed the room, disappearing step by step down the stairs.

The Letter

Ho Yung returned to the shop the next day, but stayed just long enough to deliver a letter for Pei that had arrived at his house. The warm September rains had begun the night before, drumming rhythmically against the roof, splattering against the windows.

"But who could it be from?" Pei asked, thankful that the surprise of the letter freed them from any discomfort they might have felt about his proposal.

Ho Yung looked down at the damp and dirty envelope with Pei's name quickly scrawled across the front, care of his address. "From someone who knew I would get it to you."

Pei balanced the envelope on her palm, her pulse racing. There was no telling how long the envelope had been in transit, but to judge by its soiled appearance, it was lucky to have reached her. Pei opened it carefully, pulling out two sheets of thin white paper covered with small, neatly written characters that she immediately recognized. All the years of silk factory ledgers and of notes scribbled in the margins of religious pamphlets that came to the sisters' house. And the carefully written address of Ma-ling's boarding-house.

"It's from Chen Ling," Pei said, her heart beating faster.

"From Yung Kee?" Ho Yung leaned closer, his damp raincoat falling against her arm, the warmth of his breath brushing against her neck.

"Yes," she answered, closing her eyes for a moment. The nearness of another body was something she hadn't felt in so long that its sudden comfort surprised her.

He stepped away, taking his warmth with him. "After so long?"

It had been almost eleven years since she and Ji Shen said good-bye to Chen Ling and Ming at the girls' house. Lin had just died, and the future in Hong Kong was no more than a dream.

"The letter was written three months ago," Pei said, her thoughts already drifting back.

Ho Yung cleared his throat. "I'll leave you to read it."

"Ho Yung—" Pei couldn't look into his eyes. "About yesterday . . . I can't."

"I know," he said quietly.

"Thank you." Pei looked up. "For everything."

Ho Yung smiled. He raised his hand in a slight wave and was quickly gone from the small, crowded room that she so loved. Pei heard the front door open, the rain splashing in the street; the smell of wet concrete rose up and entered.

Chen Ling, whose name rang like a bell. A voice returned from the past. The rank, damp dirt down by Baba's fish ponds, the hot, sweet steam of the cocoons boiling, the clinking of bowls at the sisters' house, sudden and distinct, settling inside her. Pei saw again the square-jaw and dark, piercing eyes of Auntie Yee's daughter, whose strength and passion had led them through a successful strike for better working hours and carried them through the dark days of the silk factory's demise.

Without a word read, so many questions were instantly answered. Chen Ling was alive. She *had* survived the war in that Buddhist vegetarian hall in the countryside. Pei could only hope Ming was with her, and that they had once again survived the Communist takeover. The thought filled Pei with joy. She paused to catch her breath, then sat down, unfolded the thin sheets, and began to read.

Dear Pei,

Where have the years gone? I hope you and Ji Shen are well and thriving in Hong Kong. I've sent this letter in care of Lin's brother. I found his card among old papers from the silk factory, and I pray to Kuan Yin that my letter will find its way to you. I still hold close the memory of you and Ji Shen leaving us so many years ago.

Ming and I continue to grow old in the countryside. It hasn't been a completely peaceful life. We haven't gone totally untouched by the madness of the world around us. Like all predators, the Japanese devils found their way to our hall, taking what they wished and destroying everything else. We hid in the cellar, warned just in time by a kind farmer whose wife often sold us their firewood. We emerged from hiding to find them hanging by their wrists from a mulberry tree, their throats slashed from ear to ear. Lives saved and lives taken within moments of each other.

And so we begin our lives all over again under Mao and the Communists. And you must be wondering why a letter now, after all these years. Words have never come easily to me. I've held in much more than I've ever let out. I've lost track of how many

*unfinished letters I've begun, telling you where we were and how
we were doing. And after the Japanese occupation, I no longer
knew how to reach you. Until Lin's brother's card came to me,
like the granting of a wish.*

*But to continue, Ming and I were in the village of Yung Kee
the other day to visit Moi. Yes, Moi still lives, as stubborn as she
ever was at the girls' house. Perhaps her stubbornness has kept
her alive. She went on and on about a woman who had come to
visit her a few days earlier. A woman she first thought had come
to steal from her. She stared too long at everything, Moi said.
"A sister?" I asked. Moi shook her head. "A sister, yes, but not
one of ours," she answered. "What are you talking about?" Ming
asked. Moi smiled at her secret, then said: "Pei's sister. Her real
sister, Li."*

Pei stopped reading to catch her breath. The blood rushed to
her head. Could it be possible that after so many years, Li was
alive and was searching for her?

"Where is she now?" Pei asked aloud, quickly scanning the rest
of the letter for the answer.

*She lives in the small village of Kum San about thirty miles
from Yung Kee. She is a widow. Her husband died four years
ago, right after the Japanese surrender. She walked all the way
to Yung Kee with hopes of finding you, of bringing you the
news of your father's death. I'm sorry that you must find out
like this.*

*Moi told her that you had gone to Hong Kong to begin a
new life. Li clung to the news with happiness. "Then the gods
have been kind to her after all," she said, with a wide smile.*

*Does it startle you that the past can be so close by? I still
feel Auntie Yee's presence at the oddest moments of the day. And
I often wonder if our paths will cross once more in this lifetime;
but then I realize that we will all meet again in a better place.*

Chen Ling

Pei let the letter fall to her lap and sat stunned. Chen Ling's words ran through her mind: Li was alive, and Baba had died. A life and a death on two thin sheets of paper. She hoped Baba hadn't suffered, hadn't died alone. With Ma Ma gone, she imagined, he must have spent all his time in the groves, only returning to the house to eat, to sleep, and finally to die. Pei closed her eyes at the thought.

And what of Li? Her sister was *alive* and looking for her. It had been thirty years since they'd seen each other. As a child, Li was the quiet, obedient elder sister Pei always tried to emulate, but never could. Pei was always the one in trouble, the one beaten for asking too many questions and not keeping her clothes clean, while Li silently stayed out of the way. Later, when they were put to bed, Li would roll over in the sticky darkness and stop Pei's tears by slipping a precious piece of sugar candy into her mouth.

This time, Pei cried tears of happiness.

Chapter Thirteen

1950

Li

The first letter had arrived like an unexpected gift. It was an early spring day and Li awoke with a strange sensation, a flutter of anxiety that came and went. Since the farmer had died four years ago, she moved about her daily routine, freed of the responsibilities that once kept her a virtual prisoner on the farm. Her sons were grown and gone, and the old farmer had died a slow and painful death. The house no longer felt like a jail. Its walls were simply a rough and faded shell, just as worn and old a relic as she'd become at the age of forty-one. Li's days passed quietly, the scars of her past life slowly healing. It had taken her a while to no longer feel afraid of the looming shadows that always came at twilight—the ghosts of the old farmer and his son, Hun, returning from the groves.

The knocking had startled her. It was solid and persistent. Li moved toward the battered door tentatively, thinking it might be Party members coming to have her relocated. The village letter writer, old man Sai, had warned of these visits. Li sighed and cracked open the door. But instead of the Party officials she'd expected to see standing there, she saw two peasant women, dressed in cotton tunics and straw hats.

The heavyset one spoke first. "We're looking for Mui Chung Li."

"She isn't here," Li answered cautiously.

"Do you know when she'll return?"

Li shook her head.

The woman smiled, not unkindly. "Will you give her this letter? It's from her sister, Pei."

She held out a blue envelope and Li's heart jumped at the sight of her own name, written in bold black characters.

"Pei?" Li had said, her voice rising at the sound of her sister's name. At first she hesitated to take the letter, thinking it might be some kind of trick. She thought about her sons, Kaige and Yuan, and wondered if the Party was somehow testing her loyalty.

"My name is Chen Ling, and this is Ming. We are Pei's silk sisters." The thin, quiet woman next to the heavyset one smiled shyly at the sound of her name. "Pei heard of her sister Li's visit to the girls' house and wants very much for her to have this letter. Please, we have come a long way to deliver it."

It had to be true, Li thought. It *was* a letter from Pei. Why else would these two women have traveled so far to bring it to her? Li swung open the door and sunlight flooded the dark room.

"I am Li," she confessed.

Chen Ling broke into a big smile. "I never doubted it for one moment."

"How could you know?" Li asked, her hand rising instantly to touch her dry cheek and the raised, puckered scar that ran down it to the corner of her mouth. More years had passed than she could remember since anyone had come to visit. She must look terrible in her coarse muslin tunic and trousers. Li took a step back into the house.

It was quiet Ming who then spoke up. "Because you and Pei have the same beautiful eyes."

                              *   *   *

Since Chen Ling and Ming's visit, Li had received two more
letters from Pei through old man Sai, who was also the uncle of
a high-ranking Party official. He had made it possible for Pei and
Li's letters to go back and forth unimpeded for the time being.
A red stamp of approval marked the front of each envelope. She
marveled at how her life could suddenly change after so many
years of stagnation.

Li set the three envelopes down on the scarred wooden table
and gazed at them in disbelief. Their lightness surprised her; how
could thirty years of questions and answers feel so weightless? Her
trembling fingers pulled out the sheets once again. Ma Ma had
taught her and Pei to read and write when they were young, but
she'd had little time to make use of her skills working on the
farm. Now, in the fading light of day, Li stared at the careful
lines and felt like a child again. It took the longest time before
some of the characters revealed a familiar shape and meaning.
What she couldn't read herself, Li had asked old man Sai to read
to her so many times, she had each sentence of Pei's letters
memorized.

"Tell me about your life. I've prayed for your happiness."

The old farmer she had married at the age of fifteen had stolen
her youth, then tried his best to squeeze the remaining life out
of her. Li's days consisted of cooking, cleaning, and working in
the groves; at night, she lay under him while he took his pleasure.
During the first year of her marriage, Li had thought daily about
ending her life. It would be as easy as throwing herself down the
well, or slicing her wrists with the kitchen knife.

Even now, with the old farmer dead and buried, Li still winced
at the thought of him and of their life together. There wasn't a
day that he'd been kind to her. When he didn't beat her or force
himself on her, he ignored her completely. His two children by
his first wife gave her little respect. How could they think of her

as their mother, when she was roughly the same age as they? At least the farmer's daughter had helped her with the household duties, until two years later, when the farmer gave her away in marriage. Li could still see the fear in the girl's eyes the day she rode off to join her new husband's family. Li wanted to say something to her, but knew she felt like an animal caught in a trap, wanting to gnaw off her own limb in order to get away.

But it was the old farmer's son Hun who became the real source of Li's misery. Even the worst beating the farmer could give her wouldn't have been as bad as the constant torment Hun inflicted on her mind and body. It began on the first day of her arrival, when the sixteen-year-old sneered at her and said, "You're nothing but a little whore. Don't think you'll ever replace my mother!" He hated her until he died, twenty years later, at the hands of a Japanese soldier. Li could never really call the Japanese "devils"; as she saw it, they had killed the real devil.

In the last days of his life, the old farmer lay screaming in pain and dribbling like a baby. Even then, he couldn't let go of his cruelty; it burned in his eyes as they followed her around the room. Li did what she could to make him comfortable, then watched as he clung to his pitiful life, afraid to let go.

"Do you have children? Am I an aunt?"

Li might have ended her life, if she hadn't soon become pregnant with her first son, Kaige. The idea that a new life could grow inside her, no matter how barren and desolate the life of the outside, renewed her spirit. Two years later, she gave birth to Yuan. The lives of her sons took precedence, while hers no longer mattered. Kaige and Yuan became the thin threads that kept Li alive.

Kaige was quiet and sensitive, though a hard worker and as good to her as he could be. As a boy, he could do little but hide when his father became enraged and beat Li. As a young man of eighteen, he worked quietly in the groves, but one night begged her and Yuan to go away with him, away from the beatings. Where? How? Li had asked. They had no money and nowhere to hide. The next morning, Kaige was gone. She saw his empty bed in the corner and heard a great howl surge through her body. After two months, though, she received word through a friend of Kaige's that he was fine. A year later, he'd joined the Communist Party, in which men and women were equal, and he'd found a new family of his own.

Her younger son, Yuan, was a happy, outgoing child. Li often thought it was her only compensation that a child conceived under such terrible circumstances could find such ease in life. She swallowed and remembered that terrible day as if it were just yesterday. She had come in from the fields to begin cooking their evening meal, dribbling cool water from the well down her neck; out of nowhere, Hun grabbed her from behind and dragged her into the barn. He'd still been angry with her from the night before. The old farmer had been berating him for not having fed the cow, and Li, who tried to calm little Kaige's squealing, began to sing softly to him. Hun had thought they were making fun of him and stormed out of the house.

"Now I'll teach you a lesson," he hissed.

Before Li had time to scream, he was on top of her, tearing at her cotton trousers and forcing her legs apart with one hand, while his other hand gripped her neck, choking the breath out of her. He rammed himself inside her with such force, Li wished his choking would kill her. She felt his grip tighten, her lungs losing their fight for air, but she scratched wildly at him when she thought of having to leave little Kaige. She choked red, then blue, giving up the struggle as her arms felt as heavy as lead. The world spun dark around her, and except for leaving Kaige, she couldn't imagine not being happier in the other world.

Then, suddenly, Hun let go. Li gulped air and began to revive. She coughed, alive again. Hun pulled away from her, then stood up and started laughing. "That'll teach you to laugh at me, you cow!" He yanked up his pants and glared down at her. The next time she opened her eyes he was gone from the barn.

Li lay gasping for air, unable to move; her desire to live slowly returned with each breath. When she heard the old farmer walking up from the mulberry groves, she forced her aching body up from the ground and into the house before he saw her. Another breath. Another beating. He never paid attention to the red prints around her neck, which days later turned to black and blue. Even to her, one bruise resembled any other.

Yuan was the child she gave birth to nine months later. During her pregnancy, Li thought she would hate the baby. How could she love the son of a devil? But his birth had been as easy as his temperament. As soon as Li saw his smiling eyes, she knew it was impossible for her not to love him. Yuan was the child that even the old farmer came to adore; Hun never realized the boy he hated so much was his own son.

"I can't imagine what you must look like. You were the one who had Ma Ma's beautiful hair."

Li touched her short gray hair. Ma Ma's beautiful hair was a distant memory. Li had worn hers short for more years than she could remember, since just after Yuan's birth. Her long hair felt heavy and hot during the hot summer when she carried the baby strapped to her back and worked in the mulberry groves. She went back inside the dark farmhouse and quickly cut her hair off with a kitchen knife. "What have you done to yourself?" the old farmer roared, and slapped her so hard she fell, cutting her cheek against the edge of the table. It bled for hours and she heard a ringing in her ear for days after. "If I wanted a boy, I would have married one!" Still, in Li's one open act of defiance, her hair remained short from that day on.

"I hope Baba died in peace. I was able to see Ma Ma one time before she died, when I was still doing the silk work."

Li never saw her parents again after her customary visit home after three days of marriage. Ma Ma knew the farmer had beaten her, and had quietly told her to stay home. "It's not too late," she said. "It will bring us no shame." Li had wanted to run and hold her mother, tell her how frightened she'd been and how the farmer had hurt her, but she couldn't move and the words froze on her tongue. It broke her heart to have to leave home again, but Li had refused to be a "return bride," to dishonor her family.

The news of her father's death came a lifetime later.

One morning after the farmer's death, Li had awakened to the realization that everyone in her life had died or drifted far away. Even Yuan had followed his brother and joined the Communist Party after the Japanese surrender; he now lived far away, near Chungking. She rarely saw him or Kaige anymore, though they sent her messages and small packages of food when they could.

At forty-one years old, Li was finally free to do as she pleased. As if some strange voice were calling to her, she was summoned to return to her childhood home. The next morning she borrowed an ox and cart to make the day's journey. As she approached her father's farm, a flood of memories returned. She saw again the two little girls running down to the fish ponds. Pei would lie in the red dirt, sucking on sugar candy and questioning Li as to what the fish were thinking about. Pei was always seeking answers to the unknown. Li had snapped back at her, but secretly wanted to see life just the way she did.

The morning young Li had awakened to find Baba and Pei gone, she knew her sister wouldn't be returning. She leaned over to find Pei's side of the bed already cold. Her mother sat by herself and could barely look at her when Li asked where Pei was. "She won't be back," her mother had said, her eyes red and filling with tears. "She has another life as a silk worker now." Li had been stunned. She hadn't even gotten to say good-bye, or to give her playful sister one last piece of sugar candy. Li distinctly remembered her silent mother putting a bowl of jook on the table for her, the soft crackling of the fire under the iron pot, and the hard realization of how quiet it would be with Pei gone.

Now, Li continued down the dirt road, and saw strangers moving about her father's land. They sadly told her of her father's lonely death six months earlier. But the good of it—they smiled up to her—was that her father's farm was now being used as a Communist collective. The following week Li went in search of Pei in the village of Yung Kee.

"I have a small sewing business here in Hong Kong, and a four-year-old adopted son named Gong."

Li smiled. She would never have expected Pei to have a business or a child. She saw once again the little girl with pigtails, who rolled in the dirt and moved quickly from one thing to the next, never settling down except to sleep. Li could never catch up, and simply took to scolding Pei instead: "You'll get in trouble if you dirty yourself! Ma Ma wants us back at the house for our lessons!" Pei listening and not listening.

For years Li had wondered why she wasn't the one given to the silk work. She was the elder daughter, the one who should have gone first, but was left behind. When she awoke alone in their bed that morning, she somehow knew that Pei had raced ahead of her again. Li was too slow, too cautious to ever catch up.

Li took a deep breath. She was happy that her younger sister had found such a good life in Hong Kong. Pei had her own business and a life Li could only dream about. And now, after so many years, Pei had stopped long enough to wait for her.

"Could life be so kind as to grant us another chance to see each other again? Now that you're alone, you could come to Hong Kong."

Li had grown so old and hard in the years since the sugar candy, fish ponds, and mulberry groves of their childhood. How would Pei recognize her? What would they have to say to each other after the novelty had worn off? She took a deep breath. Besides, the Communists had sealed all the borders since they'd come to power. She'd have to be smuggled by boat across the sea to Hong Kong.

In all her adult life Li had never been farther than the village of Kum San. At first, the idea of being smuggled on a boat and going to a large city with tall buildings and people from all over the world terrified her. Then she realized this might be the first time in her life she felt really alive. The numbness of the past years lessened with each letter. Li closed her eyes and could almost feel the warm blood rushing through her body. It was no longer an extravagant wish to think of seeing Pei again.

Li smiled to herself. She would not let the fates guide her through the rest of her life. Now there was Pei. She carefully put each letter back into its thin blue envelope, then stood up and lit an oil lamp. The dark room was suddenly awash in a flickering of light and shadows, though Li no longer felt afraid.

Ho Yung

Ho Yung watched Pei pace back and forth across the crowded room, moving in and out of the late-afternoon shadows. He knew she was more determined than ever to get her sister Li out of China and bring her to Hong Kong. She still held the pale pink blouse she had been mending when he bounded up the stairs to speak to her. He could see the tiredness around her eyes, the lines of her forehead wrinkling in thought.

Ho Yung sipped his tea and looked around the small upstairs room that still functioned as Pei's office and workroom. He had come to like the room as much as she did. Over the years, both business and personal discussions had taken place in the small, cramped room, surrounded by clothes, spools of thread, pins, needles, and jars filled with buttons, sequins, and beads. On another table was a piece of embroidery she'd begun and worked on religiously every time she had a spare moment.

By a stroke of luck and good timing, Ho Yung had been able to purchase the building next door. They'd simply torn down the common walls to expand the Invisible Thread, without ever having to displace Pei. In the new, larger building, Pei had living quarters upstairs as well as an expanded downstairs storefront. Pei had since hired two other seamstresses besides Mai and herself.

"I should go and get Li myself," Pei suddenly said.

Ho Yung looked up. "What good would it do if you both get caught by the Communists?" he demanded angrily. If anyone were to go, it would be he.

"She'll be too afraid to come out alone," Pei answered.

"It's too dangerous." His words were flat and final.

"Then what do you think we should do?" Pei asked.

Ho Yung took another sip of his tea. "We'll pay to have her smuggled out."

"Isn't that just as dangerous?" Pei asked.

Ho Yung had an answer ready. "But then we'd only have to worry about Li, not about both of you. The fewer people involved, the better."

Pei paced and stopped, then turned to him. "Just how dangerous would it be?"

Ho Yung pulled no punches, knowing that Pei needed all the details in order to make up her mind.

"People are being smuggled out of China every day. The lucky ones make it to Hong Kong and live in the streets or in squatters' camps. The unlucky ones are caught by the Communists, or drowned at sea. If Li were caught, she'd most likely be sent to a reform camp. Then we might not be able to find her again for years, if ever."

Pei sat down in the chair across from him. "I suppose we have no choice but to smuggle her here," she finally said, accepting the words as she said them.

"Let me see what I can do," Ho Yung said. He had already set up a meeting with Quan for the next morning. If anyone might know about hiring a smuggler with a fishing boat, Quan would.

Pei looked at him with gratitude. "Thank you, Ho Yung. For

all these years of taking care of the details." Her voice had a softness to it that took him by surprise.

"You don't have to thank me," he said, clumsily. He felt his face color, and looked away.

Ho Yung caught a taxi home. From Pei's office, they'd joined Song Lee and Gong for dinner. If he wasn't attending to other family business matters, he usually ate with them at least twice a week.

The warm September evening was still and calm, showing no signs of the typhoon season that was likely to begin any day now.

The heavy winds and rain would make it virtually impossible to walk down the street. Ho Yung rolled down the window and breathed in the tranquil night air as the taxi began its uphill climb toward Macdonnell Road.

As Ho Yung stepped through the iron gate of his old house, he made a mental note of all the repairs he needed to make after the rainy season—replacing the warped window frames, filling the cracks in the front steps, tending to the garden. He had to start paying more attention to his own life.

Once inside, Mui took his jacket, and Ho Yung went into the sitting room and poured himself a brandy. The pale brown liquid tingled, then burned his throat slightly as it went down. Two more sips and he could feel his entire body warming. Reinforced, he moved slowly toward the family photos neatly lined up on the mantel. He had only added a single photo in the past year, one of Pei, Gong, and himself, taken on Gong's fourth birthday. That same day, Pei had asked him to be the boy's godfather.

"I didn't know you believed in God," Ho Yung had teased.

"I believe that you would be a good father, God or no God attached," Pei answered.

He smiled at the thought. In the photo, Pei had only a slight, embarrassed smile on her lips, as if she'd been caught off guard.

He thought she was still very beautiful; her once-strong features had softened over the years, yet her inquisitive dark eyes had grown even more searching. He'd found Pei striking from the first moment he met her, back in Canton over twenty years ago. Tall and shy, she had accompanied Lin home for his brother Ho Chee's wedding.

Ho Yung turned to the photo of the young, smiling Lin. What had she felt upon returning to their opulent house in Canton? Lin had given herself to the silk work so that their family could survive. He remembered how excited she had been, moving through the house like a whirlwind, while Pei stood awkward among all the antiques and dark wood. Ho Yung had felt timid around Lin until she laughed at seeing how tall he'd grown, and said, "What happened to my little brother?" Then she took his hand and held it in hers, and in that instant, he knew how special his sister was.

And even then, Ho Yung could see that there was extraordinary happiness between Lin and Pei. It had taken him years to realize just how rare it was, this joy, like catching a shooting star or watching a flower just as it blooms. He took another swallow of brandy. Perhaps even from afar, he understood how Pei could cherish one person for a lifetime.

The next morning, Ho Yung walked quickly down to the harbor, already late to meet Quan. Quan made his living as a fisherman, and even after Ji Shen's death, he came to visit Pei and Gong whenever he was back in Hong Kong.

Life aboard the fishing boats began when most of Hong Kong was still asleep. Sometimes, when he'd had trouble sleeping, Ho Yung would get up and gaze from his bedroom window down to the harbor. He'd see the winking lights of the fishing boats going out to sea in hopes of a profitable catch. Usually Quan did most of his fishing out by the island of Lantau. It was Ho Yung's luck that he was back just now, visiting his family and staying on his uncle Wei's boat.

Ho Yung saw that harbor life was already in full swing. The smells and sounds of cooking and eating floated through the air. Men who had returned from fishing bathed from wooden buckets, while their wives scooped them bowls of thick white jook, flavored with dried fish and green onion. He passed children who had gathered their books together and were heading off to school, carrying tin buckets filled with rice and fish.

"Quan!" Ho Yung yelled, seeing the young man waiting down by the dock.

Quan turned around and waved for Ho Yung to join him. The past three years had been good to him as a fisherman. He'd made enough money to rent an apartment for his mother, brother, and sister in Causeway Bay, and even had some leftover money to put away. Now he wore a well-pressed white shirt and slacks.

"Well, look at you." Ho Yung shook Quan's hand and patted him on the back.

"You're looking rather prosperous yourself." Quan teasingly pointed at Ho Yung's stomach.

"Which reminds me—let me buy you some breakfast."

Quan nodded. "I want to show you something first." He walked a few feet down the dock, then stopped and pointed to a fishing boat. "How do you like her? She's all mine!"

Ho Yung inspected the good-sized boat. It was rusty in a few spots, but otherwise looked in good condition. "She's a beauty," he said, slapping Quan on the back. "Your family must be proud of you, I'm proud of you."

Quan smiled. "I can't wait to show Pei and Gong. The little guy will love it!"

Ho Yung knew how devastated Quan had been when Ji Shen died. The loss was so unexpected, like a light suddenly being turned out. It took time for each of them to find their way in the darkness. Quan had left for Lantau right after the funeral; he didn't come back to Hong Kong to see Pei and Gong until six months later. No one had worked harder than he had since then. Ho Yung watched the young man move from one end of the boat to the other.

"And look here." Quan pointed to the stern.

Ho Yung moved toward the back of the boat and saw the name "Ji Shen" painted in bright red letters.

"Do you think she would have liked it?" Quan asked, his voice slightly shaky.

Ho Yung breathed in the fishy air. "I think she would have loved it," he said.

They had breakfast in a small bird-walking teahouse not far from the harbor. Every morning men and women aired their birds by carrying them out in their cages and taking long walks. Then they gathered at one of the many bird-walking teahouses for their morning meal before returning home. By the time Ho Yung and Quan arrived, most of the early-morning bird-walkers had left, and only a few iron cages still hung from the hooks on the ceiling. Ho Yung ordered jook and long fried Chinese doughnuts, which they tore into pieces and ate with their jook.

"It would be easier if Pei's sister could get to Macau first," Quan said, as soon as Ho Yung explained the situation. "From there it would be simpler to arrange for a boat to bring her to Hong Kong." He swallowed a large spoonful of jook.

"How dangerous is it?" Ho Yung wanted to be able to answer this question the next time Pei asked.

Quan shrugged. "There's always danger involved, but many more people have made it out than have been caught."

"How soon could it be arranged?" Ho Yung fingered a water-mark on the table.

"For the right amount of money, it could happen within a few weeks." Quan scraped the last of his jook from his bowl.

"But it would be better if you waited until spring. It's already September, and the typhoon season is just around the corner. The winds will be high, and the rough waters are notorious. There'll be more chance of the boat capsizing than of the Communists ever catching them."

Ho Yung sipped his tea and watched Quan finish the rest of the food. He knew Pei would have to agree that there was no use in rushing to get Li to Hong Kong while the waters made the journey so treacherous. If they waited until early spring, they would have another six months to prepare. Ho Yung sat back and listened to the low murmuring of the voices around them, the clinking of bowls and dishes, the high-pitched whistle of a bird from the lone cage left hanging from the ceiling.

A Life History

Pei was having trouble sleeping again, the clearness of daylight giving way to the murky fears that always emerged at night. She wanted to sleep, deeply and tranquilly, conscious of nothing, but instead she lay on her back, listening to Gong's regular but almost labored breathing coming from the bed next to hers. Pei worried. The old herbalist said it was a chronic condition, which he'd most likely grow out of. "Keep the house clean, and have him drink this three times a week." He measured the dark leaves, dried flowers, twigs, and roots into separate packages. Song Lee kept their upstairs apartment spotless, boiled the tea, and prayed that the pungent odor wouldn't chase away any of their customers.

Pei turned on her side. Ever since Ho Yung had returned with the news that it would be another six months before they could bring Li to Hong Kong, she had been restless with fear and anticipation. Was it possible for her to come this close, only to never see Li again? Pei felt that old childhood urgency rising up in her, the conviction that if something wasn't done right away, it might never happen. She knew her thoughts were foolish but they possessed her nonetheless.

Something else had bothered Pei in Li's first letter, but she had dismissed it in all her happiness. The shaky, awkward handwriting obviously wasn't her sister's but had probably been dictated to a letter writer. Ma Ma had taught them to keep their characters neatly spaced and in straight lines. Li had always been the diligent one, who did what she was told. Even when she was a girl, her characters were uniform and exact.

Li's words turned over and over in her mind, always short and to the point. Pei was reminded of the quick, careful edge her father's words had had.

> *Yes, I'm fine. I have two sons, Kaige and Yuan. They are grown and have found lives of their own. I live a simple life, with few needs. I am happy that your life has turned out so well. Yes, I, too, hope that we will see each other again.*

Pei's worries multiplied. Li's letters never mentioned anything about coming to Hong Kong. Could the letter writer be trusted? How could Pei tell Li where to go and what to do, once all the plans were made to bring her to Hong Kong?

Pei pushed all the unanswered questions out of her mind. She had to trust that Li wanted to see her with the same urgency that she felt, the same strong pulse that wouldn't allow her to give up.

Rising into the cool night Pei checked on Gong, then realized what she needed to do. She crept down the stairs and back to her workroom. During the day, her life was abuzz with running the Invisible Thread and Gong's endless chatter. "What's that for?" or "Can we go out now?" He was already daring and inquisitive, and a constant reminder that Ji Shen was still close by.

Now with Gong and Song Lee asleep and the house quiet, Pei

unfolded a piece of red silk satin from her crowded worktable. It was three feet by five feet long, and divided into five panels. At first, months ago, she had planned on following a traditional embroidery pattern—evenly spaced lotus flowers or an iris-and-butterfly design like one she'd seen in the Chen household.

But something had happened when she sat down, facing the smooth red surface like an empty canvas, threading the needle and pushing it through the material. Pei had realized that a wall hanging of lotus flowers or butterflies would mean very little to her. It wouldn't tell a story or answer any questions. She suddenly thought of her mother's silk painting of five white birds, two of them in flight. As a child she'd stared at it for hours, never realizing that she and Li would be those two birds.

Pei had begun the first panel with two fishes, the symbol of abundance and harmony. Green and blue threads, with a touch of yellow and black. Night by night, the embroidery had evolved slowly, as if she were in a trance. The quiet embraced her. And even though it wasn't customary to embroider people and places, she wanted to leave Gong and his children something to remember her by. Before long, Pei had added the fish ponds, the mulberry trees, and the farmhouse, filling the first panel of the silk material.

Now, Pei flipped open the second panel, where she had pictured her life in Yung Kee. The girls' house, the silk factory, the sisters' house, and two girls watching it all, one taller than the other, with single black braids hanging down their backs. Each step had come to her like walking, a life history she saw slowly materialize with each careful stitch.

Pei fingered the two embroidered black braids, and smiled to think what Lin would have been like now, at forty-five. Pei imagined her thin and graceful, with a touch of gray coming in like Ho Yung's. She would still move softly and swiftly, so as not to disturb anyone. Her fair skin might have the wrinkles that came with time, but her eyes would remain the same—kind and full of spirit, as if to say, "Yes, tell me more."

Pei sighed, and touched her own graying hair. She'd lost weight and gotten old in the past year. It was Lin who wouldn't recognize her when the time came for them to meet again.

Pei looked down and smiled again. She had stopped working on the embroidery halfway through the third panel, just about the time Chen Ling's letter arrived and Li had suddenly returned to her life. Since then, there'd been so little time and energy to continue. Ma-ling's boardinghouse, Quan's rickshaw, the house on Conduit Road, and Mrs. Finch's Victrola awaited completion. Pei looked closely at what she'd already sewn, satisfied with her handiwork. Now it was as if she needed more than ever to tell the entire story.

She had six months to wait until she saw her sister Li again. That gave her the perfect opportunity to finish the panel. Pei sighed, unfolded the rest of the material, threaded a needle, and quietly began to sew.

Chapter   Fourteen

1951

Li

Li awoke before dawn and lay on the hard bed, staring into the darkness. Ever since she'd received the letter from Pei explaining how she would get to Hong Kong, Li hadn't been able to sleep well. Everything had been arranged by Pei; all Li had to do was make her way to Macau, where a boat would be waiting to take her across the sea to Hong Kong. She shivered at the thought of being surrounded by nothing but water, confined and unable to plant her feet on solid ground. Li couldn't think of a greater abandonment then being set adrift, rising and falling on the unpredictable waves.

When the letter first arrived, Li had tried in vain to make out the quick, neat rows of characters on her own. The short and long lines, dots and dashes, caught and held with familiarity, though there were too many characters she didn't quite grasp. She knew she was taking a chance bringing the letter to old man Sai, but his eyes told her that she could trust him. Finally, she had brought Pei's letter to him to read. He had laughed and said, "Another one? Your younger sister has more words than I have gray hair!"

But he stopped smiling once he began to read. His pipe bobbed up and down between his crooked teeth as he glanced up at her, and he lowered his voice for fear that someone in the village might hear. "Do you know what danger leaving involves?"

Li nodded. "Just read it once; I'll remember all the details," she whispered back. "I don't want to cause you any trouble."

Old man Sai shook his head and sucked on his pipe. "It's too late, you've already brought me into your schemes."

Li stood up and reached for the letter. "Then I'll find someone else—"

"Where do you think you'll find someone who'll read this letter to you and not turn you in to the authorities?" He waved his pipe and motioned for her to sit back down.

"You're the last one I would want to get into trouble," Li said softly. "You have helped me in more ways than you could know."

Old man Sai smiled sadly. "You deserve a better life than the one given you so far." He held the letter gently between his big knobby fingers. "Now, you must listen carefully to what I read to you, than return home and burn the letter. From that moment on, I will no longer be any part of this."

Li nodded. Because of Sai, she would have a chance for a new life in Hong Kong with Pei. He'd always been kind to her, even when she was married and only came into the village once or twice a month with her husband and sons to go to the market. Every time she hurried by his letter-writing stall, old man Sai smiled and told her, "Slow down, there's no one chasing you."

She used to smile shyly, but didn't dare say anything back to him, just pushed her two boys along. The farmer hated to be kept waiting. He gave her just enough money to buy the same supplies month after month—rice, salt, pickled turnips, and sometimes a bag of litchis if they were in season and he was in a good mood.

After a while, Li looked forward to the simple words that came from old man Sai; she made sure to pass his stall every time she was in the village. She longed for the sound of a calm, kind voice that she didn't fear.

Later, after the farmer had died, Li worked the farm and went into the village once a week on her own, taking her time—touching the smooth and bumpy skins of fruits and vegetables, seeing the small details she'd never before had the luxury to experience: the loud screeching voices buying and selling, the multicolored display of candy and paper kites, and the salty-sour scent of the bodies that pushed and pulled against her in the crowd.

The first time she'd dared to enter the ancestral hall at the end of the village, the cool darkness and the sweet smell of incense that curled into the air had filled her with joy. Li had stood in front of the burning incense and prayed for Kaige and Yuan. And just before she turned to leave, she prayed that some day she might be reunited with Pei.

Then, back outside in the bright sunlight, she walked directly to old man Sai's letter-writing stall and spoke to him for the first time. "How are you?" The words had sounded strange and foreign coming from her mouth.

Li watched as the dawn light slowly filtered into the spare room, staring hard to see everything in it for one last time. She had to remember, now, in order to forget—in order, finally, to let the cold harshness of her years here fade from her memory.

There was a dingy, tired look to everything, from the worn kitchen table to the threadbare blankets that covered Li's bed. It was as if the house itself had suffered some great illness, which lingered and festered in every piece of furniture, in the thin muslin curtains, in every crack between the boards. For twenty-seven years, Li had lived within it, willing herself not to die from it.

Li had come to the old farmer with virtually nothing, and she planned to leave that way, too. All she would take with her was what she could carry on her back. She felt a sudden sinking in her stomach. Again she heard old man Sai's voice reading

Pei's letter over and over, glancing up at her to make sure she remembered the date and time. Li could hear the seriousness of Pei's words, accentuated by old man Sai's own concern.

> *You will have to make your way across the Chinese border and into Macau. Follow the map enclosed to a small cove on the north side not far from the border; a fishing boat will be there at midnight. He'll wait for ten minutes past the hour, and if you're not there, he won't be able to wait. Please, Li, be there.*

When he was certain that she had the letter memorized, he wrote a quick response from Li to Pei. Then, old man Sai sat back and inhaled long and hard on his pipe.

"And once you have reached Hong Kong," he said in a low voice, "no one will ever chase you again."

Li leaned closer, smelled the sweet tobacco from his pipe. "Thank you for everything." She swallowed. "When you receive my letter, you'll know that I'm with my sister again."

"I look forward to that glorious day." He folded Pei's letter and map back into its envelope and handed it back to Li, his hand covering hers and squeezing it for a moment. "Don't forget to burn the letter."

When Li left the village that day, it was with a heavy heart. She was leaving the only friend she had, for a world she knew nothing about. She could already smell the letter as it burned, at first comforting and then frightening. The singed thin edges burning inward, the characters she had memorized disappearing and turning to ash.

Li started a fire under the iron pot for jook, just as she did every morning. When she'd eaten her fill and the fire burned hot and low, she unfolded and looked at Pei's letters one more time before placing them into the flames. Li walked away rather than watch, though she heard the crackle-pop as they flamed.

She looked at the map Pei had sent. According to Sai, it was a day and a half's journey by foot to the border. There'd been rumors, village gossip, about those who had tried to cross the border and failed. "They're interrogated for hours and hours, slapped and tortured by the Red Guards, until they confess to things they hadn't even done." Li folded the map and tucked it into her pocket. "Then they're paraded around the village with a sign hanging from their necks, telling of their shameless crime." As far as Li was concerned, worse things could happen.

On the kitchen table were her food and water. She hurried to pack them in a cloth bag. Enough for two days, and some to spare, just in case something went wrong. Li tried not to think of that. She grabbed Kaige and Yuan's letters, tied together in a small bundle. For a moment she stopped at the thought of leaving behind her sons, the two little boys she had always pushed ahead of herself. "Faster, faster," she whispered. "Baba gets so angry when we're late." She had kept them out of harm's way, so that the slaps and punches that came hard and frequent would fall on her body and not theirs.

Li smiled to herself. They were both grown men now and no longer needed her protection. She had prayed they would fly high and away from the pale, lifeless world she'd known all of her adult life. And they had, with wings she had managed to keep safe and strong. It was all the happiness she had thought she'd find in this lifetime.

Slowly and meticulously Li began to dress, one layer after another, three tunics in all, the entirety of her summer and winter wardrobe. She'd thought about buying something new to wear for when she finally saw Pei, somehow thinking that a new tunic might help to distract from the years and scars. But in the village that day, her reflection caught in a piece of glass told her another story. It would take more than a new tunic to cover the years of sorrow. Li stuffed her savings back into the pocket of her worn trousers.

Once she made it to the border, she'd have to wait until

nightfall before attempting to cross over into Macau. Li took a deep breath and trembled at the thought of what she was doing. For the first time in ages she felt the blood surging through her veins. Li slipped on her padded jacket atop her three layers of clothing, then made sure the fire had completely destroyed her letters from Pei. Only ashes were left. She opened the door and felt a cool February wind blowing, the sun struggling to break through the gauzy layers of cloud. Li swung the cloth bag over her shoulder, started down the dirt road, and never looked back.

The morning remained gray and heavy, threatening rain, the clouds so low Li felt a thick blanket just over her head. Each step brought a new discovery wherever she looked. The land she knew so well began to change its shapes and textures. At first hilly, with mulberry groves and fish ponds, then flat and wet, ripe for growing rice. She walked by a multitude of farmhouses just like the one she'd left behind, with generations of a family living in one open room. Voices stirred in the distance. She saw women and children out in the rice fields, stooped over in the meticulous planting, old before their time. Beyond them, a lone ox moved slowly across a field.

Farther along, Li found herself having to cross a stream. She paced along the edge to find the shallowest spot to cross and, when she finally gathered enough courage, held her cloth sack raised high over her head. At each cautious step, she was filled with fear that the water would rise up and swallow her. She thought back to how, in the prosperous years, her father would wade into his fish ponds, pushing the wire net heavy with fish to one side; Pei would jump in and imitate him when their parents weren't looking. Li had always watched from the edge, never daring to wade in.

She relaxed only when she'd made it to the other side, the water never reaching higher than her chest.

Li spent a damp and cold night among some trees along the road, afraid to sleep for fear that someone might find her and report her to authorities. She cushioned her body against the hard ground with grass and leaves, regretting that she hadn't thought to bring one of the threadbare blankets. Real and imagined sensations crept into the dark reverie of her half-sleep: the snapping of twigs, the scurrying of animals in the night, the deep, dank cold that chilled her to the bone, even before it began to rain.

By late afternoon the next day, Li was hot and exhausted. She carried in her cloth sack two sets of the clothing she had started out with, peeling off the damp layers as the day grew warmer. At the top of a steep, rocky slope she looked down and saw a lone guardhouse, with Red Guards patrolling along the barbed-wire fence that marked the border between China and Macau. It was difficult to see any difference from one side of the fence to the other. She stared beyond the barrier, at the swaying trees, the dry, rocky terrain, and the dirt road that was supposed to lead her to freedom.

Li would have to wait until dark before she attempted to cross the border. According to the map, she'd have more than enough time to make it to the cove, though it would be harder traveling in the pitch-black night, which hid even shadows. She'd be blind to the simplest dangers. With each step there was a chance that she might fall and twist an ankle, or hit her head and lie stunned or dead. Li told herself it wasn't any different from all the times she'd been sent out to dump night soil or fetch water in the dark of night.

She looked around her and spotted a shady area among some rocks. Li had never been so tired and hungry in her life. She hid herself among the rocks and pulled out the last of her rice and pickled turnips, washing them down with the tepid water she carried. Li felt time move in a strange way, as if one life had ended and another was about to begin, though she was still caught somewhere in between.

Li closed her eyes and waited for night to fall.

Pei

Pei hurried from one room to the next, making sure everything was just right for Li's arrival. She hadn't been herself for days, nervous and distracted, unable to sit long enough to get any mending done. Mai and the other girls smiled and accepted all the work Pei brought to them to finish. Even her own embroidering had been put aside, the fourth panel completed, the last an open space waiting to be filled. Song Lee clicked her tongue, shook her head, and took care of Gong. Pei realized the Invisible Thread would run just as smoothly without her.

Ho Yung had come to see her just that morning, carrying a small package. He and Quan had planned Li's escape meticulously. The fishing boat would drop Li off at the secluded beach of Shek O, on the tip of the island's western side, far away from inquiring authorities. All Quan and Ho Yung had to do was wait for Li to arrive and deliver the second half of the payment to the men on the fishing boat.

There had even been an answer from Li, putting to rest Pei's fears that her sister might be turned in to authorities if Pei's letter had fallen into the wrong hands. Li's words came back to her.

> *The letter writer has made sure I memorize all your instructions. There's nothing to worry about. Your words are safely locked in my heart. I never dared to believe that dreams could come true until now.*

"You see, everything will be fine," Ho Yung reassured her, after hearing Li's words. "How do you think Li has survived all these years without you?"

"What if something goes wrong? The boat—"

"Nothing will go wrong. You're just making yourself crazy, not to mention all of us!"

"I suppose you're right."

"Quan and I will pick you up first thing tomorrow morning. It should take a little over an hour to drive to Shek O. And now that it's settled, I wanted to give you something." He handed Pei the package he was holding, flat and square and quite heavy in her hands.

Pei felt her blood rise to color her face. She had received so few gifts in her life that the gesture still embarrassed her. "What could it be?"

"Open it and see," Ho Yung answered.

Pei hesitated, then carefully unwrapped the package to find the silver-framed photograph of Lin as a child. She stared at it for a moment, then looked up at Ho Yung.

"I thought you might like to have it." He ran his fingers through his graying hair.

Pei was at a loss for words. She stared into Lin's eyes; they had been gentle even in childhood. "You can't imagine how much," she finally said. She leaned over and kissed Ho Yung on the cheek.

Pei had been in and out of Li's room, just across the hall from the bedroom she shared with Gong, at least twenty times. She couldn't stop worrying about where Li was at that very moment. Was she cold and frightened as she waited to get on a boat that would take her across the sea to a sister she barely knew?

Sometimes, Pei found herself just standing there, wondering if she'd forgotten anything. In truth, she had forgotten everything, and all their childhood secrets now came tumbling back in bits and pieces.

For years, Pei hadn't thought about the ghostly fortune-teller who had determined their fates just by the touch of his fingers upon their faces. She could still feel the tingling sensation, but struggled to recall his exact words about Li: "Two sons. Illness, but she will survive." She was eight and Li was ten then. The fortune-teller's words were as foreign as another language. How could Pei know that they would come true, with two sons named Kaige and Yuan, and a marriage that became a long illness worse than any death.

Pei ran downstairs and brought up a vase of fresh flowers to put in Li's room. Five minutes later, she hurried back in to open the window in case it was too hot. Pei stepped back and hoped Li would like the pale purple gladiolas. She couldn't remember ever having flowers in the house when they were growing up. It seemed as if everything that was alive in their childhood had dried up, died, or been given away. She and Li were no exceptions.

Stolen Crossing

Li heard voices in the shadowy night. Guided by a sliver of moon and a huge round light beside the guardhouse that swept the barbed-wire fence and beyond in every direction, like a big white eye that could see everything, she made her way carefully down the rocky path. Then she moved away from the voices; dirt and rocks slid beneath her weight. She hoped to cross over to the Macau side farther down the path and away from the guards. According to the map, a jagged line of guardhouses and barbed-wire fence ran all along the border, as far as the eye could see. It stopped only when the land touched water on one side and mountains on the other.

Li had studied the movements of the guards and the light. It took the men one hundred and sixty-eight paces to walk from end to end of the area they patrolled. She had to take advantage of the monotony of their job, find the crack to crawl through when their backs were turned. She could easily count to one hundred before the guard returned her way again.

One, two, three, four, five . . . Li moved as quietly as possible, waiting until the guard walked away from her and back toward the guardhouse before she descended the final few feet to the fence. *Eight, nine, ten, eleven* . . . She made it to the barbed-wire fence, where her hands reached out and touched the savage wire thorns. *Fifteen, sixteen, seventeen* . . . She slid her cloth sack between the fence to the other side, then felt the barbs sink into her palms as she spread the wire strands wide enough apart to squeeze through. *Twenty, twenty-one, twenty-two* . . . She crouched to avoid the eye of light that raced her way. *Thirty-three, thirty-four, thirty-five* . . . Her trouser leg caught on a wire thorn and tore as she pulled her left leg through; The barb ripped into her calf. She bit down on her lip rather than scream. *Forty-one, forty-two, forty-three* . . . The light fell on her just as she rolled out of its touch, chasing her like a rabbit running for its life. *Forty-nine, fifty, fifty-one* . . . Her heart pounded so loudly, she was sure someone would hear her. *Sixty-three, sixty-four, sixty-five* . . . She lay perfectly still until she was sure no one had seen her. *Seventy-six, seventy-seven, seventy-eight* . . . Her leg throbbed. She heard faint voices in the distance. The light raced back in her direction. *Eighty-four, eighty-five, eighty-six* . . . Cloth bag in hand, she ran as fast as she could, putting distance between her and the border before the guards found the material from her trousers pinned to the barbed wire, before they knew that she had inched through a crack right before their eyes. *Ninety-eight, ninety-nine, one hundred* . . .

Li kept running until she could no longer run and the eye-light blinked and disappeared behind the dark trees. She fell to the ground where she stopped. Her palms stung as if she held a bee in them. She was glad it was too dark to see the gash that ran down her calf. Anyway, there was no time to stop and tend to her wounds. Somehow she'd have to find her way to the cove. Li took out Pei's map, held it up to the thin moonlight, uncertain now of where she was and which direction she was supposed to go. She stumbled around in the dark, then just stopped and closed her eyes. Real darkness. When she opened her eyes again, she could make out the shadows of trees, the edges of rocks. Seeing at night was a different way of seeing. Finally, she found her way back to the dirt road. According to the map it headed directly to the cove; and if not, she was certain at least, that it headed somewhere.

The darkness offered a particular comfort, shielding her from all terrors rather than revealing them. Li didn't dare stop to rest though she was exhausted, her legs and back aching. She'd lost track of time. Then, as if she'd been strangely guided there, Li reached a clearing on the left side of the road. She paused when she heard the surge of water below, a spray of salty sea air blowing in her direction. Li held the map up: She'd found the spot. A narrow, steep path led down to the cove. She looked for any sign of a boat down below. All she saw were the dark shadows of rocks and the thin whitecaps.

When Li reached the bottom of the path, the sea breeze felt cool and clean against her stickiness. It was the first time she'd ever been so close to the sea. She had stepped down onto the sand, sinking into its softness, when someone grabbed her from behind. A fishy-smelling hand covered her mouth. Li tried to scream, then kicked and shoved her elbow into the body restraining her.

"I'm here to take you to Hong Kong," the man whispered roughly.

Li stopped struggling, and he released her. She turned around to see a coarse-looking man with a scraggly beard. His small narrow eyes watched her closely.

"Hurry," he commanded, marching down the sand toward

the water. Every once in a while, he turned his head to spit into the sand.

Li followed after him, wondering if it was wise to put her life in the hands of such a terrible man. But she had little choice. Behind a large rock, Li finally saw the fishing boat that was to bring her to Hong Kong. It was no more than a large sampan, bobbing in the rough seas like a child's toy. The man didn't stop to wait for her, but kept walking into the sea, swimming the last few strokes to reach the boat, and was helped up by another man waiting on board.

Li hesitated. She had never learned how to swim and this wasn't a shallow stream, but the ocean. She would surely drown before she got to the boat. For a split second, Li thought about turning back. She could always tell the Red Guards it was all a mistake and pray that they'd let her go home.

The man yelled something to her. Li looked up and saw him waving his arms for her to come. She took a few steps forward, the cold water washing over her shoes. She kept going as the salt water rushed up to her knees, sharply stinging the cut on her leg. Li clutched her cloth sack tightly as the waves slipped in and out, rising with each step she took. When the water had risen to her neck, a big wave washed away her sack, splashing into her eyes and mouth. Li froze and couldn't move any farther.

"Come, hurry!" the man yelled, the words carried to her on the ocean spray. Li's feet had turned to stone, sinking into the depths. The next thing she knew, the man was beside her, his arm wrapped tightly around her waist as he swam her limp body to the boat. She swallowed salt water, coughing it back up as the younger man on the boat reached over and pulled her aboard. Li stood on deck, weaving from side to side with the constant rocking motion.

"You'll stay down here," the younger man directed. He removed the heavy wooden cover to the fish hole and directed Li to hurry and climb down. She was shivering, standing on the windy deck, the two men obviously annoyed at her slowness.

"Now!" the older man yelled.

He held a lantern over the hole so she could see the wooden ladder and find her footing. Only when Li descended the slippery ladder into the dark, stinking hole did she realize there were other people waiting down there, the flicker of light illuminating their ghostly faces as they blinked. Before they were returned to darkness, the wooden cover closing with a final thud over their heads, she saw a handful of adults and a child. Her foot left the last rung and touched water, knee-deep by the time her two feet were planted firmly on the bottom of the boat. She couldn't stand up straight, and stooped low against the ceiling. Though she had seen at least five other people crammed into the small hole, no one said a word. It was darker than any night, and when she tried to take a step in any direction, she ran into an arm or a leg.

"I'm sorry," she whispered.

A child whimpered.

"Over here." A woman's voice. "To your left."

Li inched left and felt a body move over with a soft sweep of water, so that there was enough room for her to squat and then sit. The burst of fresh air that had come in when the wooden lid was lifted was now gone. The hot, humid air stank of fish and sweat and she didn't dare imagine what else. The gash on her leg burned as she sat in the tepid water up to her waist. She was so thirsty that her throat felt like sand.

"How long have you been waiting here?" Li asked, the words coming out slowly.

"Hours," the woman's voice said.

"Are there any more coming?"

A man laughed sarcastically. "Where would they put them? Six adults and a child stuffed into a box. As it is, we're one step away from suffocating!"

"Then save what little breath you have left!" the woman next to her snapped.

"They take our good money and crowd us in a hole for dead fish," the man persisted.

"Ssh!" Another voice.

The child moaned, "I don't feel good."

"Soon, soon," her mother's voice said soothingly.

The boat creaked and suddenly groaned to life. It jerked once or twice, then began to move slowly.

"We go, we go," the mother repeated.

Li could barely see the outline of the mother's pale hand rise up and down again as if she were about to sing a song. But the dark hole was silent, the bobbing of the boat growing as they sailed out to sea, rolling and rising with each wave. Li felt her stomach rise and fall along with the boat, and braced herself to keep from toppling onto the woman next to her. She leaned back against the damp, slimy wall. Her clothes were soaked and every muscle in her body ached. The air was so thick, she felt as if they were all sharing the same breath. She sucked in her share, trying hard to stay conscious.

"I feel sick," the child whispered, breaking the dark silence.

"No, you're fine," the mother whispered back. "Think of happy times," she said encouragingly.

Li closed her eyes and tried to think of happier times. Her leg burned and felt numb. Happiness was always a word just beyond her reach. She thought of scant moments with Kaige and Yuan when they were small, then had to travel all the way back to her childhood, to afternoons when she and Pei were finished with their chores and could run outside to play.

"This way, this way!" Pei would call. "Come see the babies."

Li followed without question. They wandered way down into the mulberry groves, farther than their parents had ever allowed them to go.

"It's too far," she said.

Pei didn't pay any attention. "When you see the birds, you'll know it was worth it."

Li wasn't sure it would be worth Baba's strap, but she kept walking. At the very edge of the grove, Pei cleared away some tall brush to expose a nest of twigs and grass, two chirping baby birds peeking out.

Li fell to her knees. "How did you know they were here?"

"I heard them calling for their mother. She always goes away at this time of the day to find them food."

She wanted to touch them, but Pei stopped her. "The mother will know we were here and she might not love them anymore."

Li's hand stopped in midair. She couldn't imagine a mother not loving such tiny, helpless creatures. They watched the little birds reach out toward them, their beaks opening and closing, opening and closing.

The sound of the child throwing up woke Li. A sour smell filled the thick air. Li felt something in her own stomach turn again, a bitterness rising up to her mouth even as she tried in vain to swallow it back down again.

Six or seven hours later, when the blessed stupor of half-sleep finally came to Li, she was abruptly awakened. The wooden cover scraped open and a sudden flow of fresh air and daylight entered the hole. It took a few minutes for the fresh air to revive the passengers. Their slow, lethargic movements made Li realize how close to being dead they really were.

"Everyone out!" the man yelled down to them.

Li blinked against the light. For the first time, she was able to see the people with whom she'd made the journey. There were two men, an older woman, two younger women, and the little girl, who appeared only semiconscious. Her mother was patting her cheeks. "Up, up, we're here, we're here," she repeated. One by one they climbed up the ladder into the daylight.

Once on deck, Li saw that they weren't *there*: no tall buildings, no Pei waiting for her. The boat had pulled close to shore, where another boat waited. Li looked just bewildered enough for the bearded man who had saved her life last night to point to it and explain: "That boat will take you on to Hong Kong. Still a good two hours away." He poured a mouthful of water into a tin cup and let her drink from it.

Li looked up and tried to smile, to give him some small sign of gratitude, but he had already turned away.

The last leg of the voyage was luxurious compared to what they had endured earlier. They gulped down mouthfuls of fresh air as if to store it for later, before descending into another small, dark hole. But this one was dry, and they were given a lantern to see the extent of their exhaustion as they sat squeezed side by side. The child had fallen asleep again on her mother's lap. The old woman pointed to Li's leg and said, "You'd better have that taken care of."

Li smiled at her concern, then finally dared to look down in the flickering light to see the swollen wound. A jagged line, not like the puckered curve that ran across her cheek. There was only a slight throbbing now to remind her of it. Li was too tired to think about anything but sleep.

The dull thuds of footsteps on deck and muffled voices yelling from above let them know that Hong Kong was in sight. They were told they would be released near the beach village of Shek O, on the other side of the island. Li's heart raced. She wished she still had her cloth sack with some clean clothes to change into. Her white tunic was soiled and her trousers torn. Pei wouldn't recognize her—or worse, wouldn't want to.

Again, they were hurried up on deck. The mountains of Hong Kong rose before them, greener than Li had expected. In the distance she saw a group of people gathered together at the edge of the rocks, waiting. She paused for just a moment, balancing herself against the side of the boat, wondering if Pei was among them, and how would Pei recognize her after so many years? The unkindness of life was etched so deeply into her face.

The fishing boat anchored offshore, only this time Li didn't hesitate to enter the cold water. She leaped in and thrust herself through the water, arms and legs working with all the strength she had left. The waves pushed her back then forward, until her feet touched the rock and sand bottom. She wiped the water from her eyes, the glare of the sun burning. Li heard the splashing of the others behind her and in front of her as she struggled to walk the last heavy steps onto the beach. Every muscle in her body hurt as she stumbled and fell to her knees. From the corner of her eye, Li saw a woman running into the water toward her, a tall shadow lifting her by the arms and holding her against the warmth of her own body. Li looked up into the woman's eyes and knew instantly it was Pei.

"You're here," Pei whispered just once, her fingers touching the scar on Li's cheek so gently it felt like a flutter of small kisses.

Chapter Fifteen

1951–52

Pei

"There will be illness, but she will survive": The fortune-teller's prediction for Li didn't come true until she arrived in Hong Kong. The years of being battered and bruised had toughened her body and spirit to fight for each day of survival. The moment she relaxed into the warmth and comfort of family, she fell ill. And after so many hours aboard the cramped fishing boat, wet and exhausted, a terrible infection developed from the cut on her leg.

It took Li three months to recover fully, with Pei at her side day and night. Song Lee watched her like a hawk and rushed down to the old herbalist every week for blood-strengthening teas. Each day, she made sure Li drank down the dark, muddy-looking liquid. When she saw the color begin to return to her cheeks, Song Lee clapped her hands in triumph and said, "You can see her energy returning gradually, a good sign that it will stay with her. If it comes too fast, it can be deceiving."

And slowly Pei and Li began to know each other again, catching each sigh and gesture, trying to remember what they were like as girls and learn who they'd become as women. The words came haltingly at first, and then they wouldn't stop. Like water, they filled two thirsty throats. In between the discoveries were pockets of stillness, memories that stayed silent and secret, along with the curiosities and wonder that didn't.

Li smiled and sat up in bed a month after she'd arrived. "You were always tall."

"And you still have Ma Ma's fine hair."

Li shyly touched her short gray hair and shook her head. "I feel too old. Like something broken."

Pei sat down on the side of her bed. "Then it's time for you to mend," she said, placing her hand on top of Li's.

Li leaned back against the wall, her scar almost translucent in the white sunlight. "When I awoke that morning and you had already gone with Baba to the silk village, it was as if I'd lost a part of myself."

"I thought you would be happy to have me out of your hair!" Pei teased.

"Yes"—Li smiled—"you were a handful. But you were the one who helped me to judge my own worth. If you were naughty, I was obedient, if you ran too fast, I slowed down. With you gone, I was alone. Ma Ma was burdened with everyday life, Baba had his pond and groves. The quiet in our house was deafening."

Pei swallowed. She hadn't known. She'd always thought their lives would be easier without her. "I didn't know," she whispered. "At first I thought I was being punished. Given away because I never listened."

"And I believed I was being left behind," Li said sadly.

"Is that why you married the farmer?" Pei asked. She unconsciously moved to touch the back of her chignon.

Li paused for a moment and closed her eyes. "There weren't many choices left for me." She opened her eyes and turned her head so that the smooth edge of her scar showed.

Pei stood up and opened a window. She didn't want Li to see the tears brimming in her eyes. "It's milder today." She cleared her throat.

"I've always wondered, Pei . . ." Li began; then she leaned

forward and waited for her sister to come close again. "What was your life like, doing the silk work?"

Pei answered thoughtfully, "It was lonely at first and very hard." She walked back to the bed. "Then the girls' house and the sisterhood became the home I no longer had, and the family in which I learned about life's injustices and love's kindness."

Pei reached for Li's hand and looked into her sister's familiar eyes, dark brown and knowing that a life was filled with many stories—myriad of parts that made up the whole. She would tell Li all of her stories one at a time, and each day from that moment on, they would create new ones together.

Li

It was as if she'd awakened from a long, endless nightmare to finally be in Hong Kong with Pei. After she'd recovered from her illness, Li walked slowly forward into her new life, taking tentative, careful steps. It took a good week for Pei to persuade her to go downstairs and venture into the Invisible Thread. She sat quietly behind the counter with Song Lee, seeing more people in one day than she'd seen in months back on the farm. Li was amazed at how efficiently her sister ran the business. Including Song Lee, she had four women working for her. The seamstresses worked upstairs and laughed and talked as they mended. Whenever Li offered to help, Pei insisted she take it easy for a little while longer.

Each day was a new adventure, and Li was like a child again, learning the simplest tasks with all the modern conveniences that only served to confuse her. Water flowed right into the house, then could be boiled without starting a fire. Light filled a room from a small bulb in the middle of the ceiling. And the first time she went to the market with Pei and Song Lee, the automobiles and crowds terrified her. Unlike her small village market, where a few stallholders sold chickens and vegetables, this market was as large as the entire village. It sold everything Li could imagine, from fresh beef and pork to vegetables and fruits, and even a slithery snakelike fish called an eel.

But nothing puzzled and intrigued Li as much as the *din wa,* the telephone. The voice that floated out without a body made her think a spirit was trapped inside. The first time Pei talked to Li on the telephone, Song Lee had to promise her Pei was all right and just calling from Central to see if she needed anything. "Talk to her, talk to her!" Song Lee pushed the black receiver into Li's hand, and showed her which end to press against her ear and which to speak into.

Although Li gradually began to understand the fast-paced Hong Kong way of life, she was like a spooked horse that could never stand still—always nervous and cautious. She didn't go far from the Invisible Thread, except to walk the three blocks to pick up seven-year-old Gong from school. She had eagerly volunteered one afternoon, when Song Lee was too busy at the shop. Fetching Gong gave Li a chance to make herself useful, as well as to get to know the boy. From then on, it became her afternoon task.

She would stand several feet away from the front entrance where a crowd of amahs and well-dressed Hong Kong mothers waited to pick up their children. Li felt awkward and embarrassed among them, with her scarred face and plain clothes. She didn't quite fit in either category.

"Auntie Li, why do you always wait out here?" Gong asked, wide-eyed and serious, one day.

"I was afraid you might not see me in the crowd," Li answered.

Gong looked up at her. She knew he hadn't been able to take his eyes off the puckered scar since the day they'd met.

"Does it hurt?" he asked.

Li smiled. "Not anymore. Do you want to touch it?" She leaned down to him.

Gong raised his index finger and followed the curved road along her cheek. "Is that why you stand so far away?"

Li hesitated, thinking it was because of so many things, including the scar. She wasn't sure how to explain such complicated feelings to a little boy, who was not unlike her Yuan. Then, before Li said anything, Gong had his own answer.

"Because it's how I could always tell it was you in a crowd," he said, taking her hand and pulling her down the busy street.

The Letter Writer

That night, after Gong was put to bed, Pei was quietly working on the last panel of her embroidery, the panel detailing their reunion. Li sat down at the table across from her with some paper. Pei looked up to see her sister troubled about something.

"Is anything wrong?" she asked.

Li cleared her throat. "I need to ask you a favor."

"Of course, anything." Pei stopped embroidering.

"Will you teach me to write, the way you told me Lin and Mrs. Finch once taught you? Like Ma Ma once taught us? There was never any time on the farm. . . ."

Pei smiled. "Yes, I'd be happy to teach you," she said, thinking how Ma Ma would have been surprised to see her teaching Li. Pei reached for the paper.

"Thank you," Li said softly.

"Let's begin with your name." Pei wrote the quick lines and dashes, like a dance on the white paper, and then she numbered each stroke so Li could follow in the right sequence. "Now you try," she said, and pushed the sheet back to Li.

She watched Li press attentively down on the page, her face set hard in concentration. In neat, careful rows her name filled page after page, late into the night.

* * *

Pei taught Li five to ten characters at the beginning of each week. Every day she sat down with Gong and they both practiced, an old student and a young one side by side. By the end of each week, Li had written each character hundreds of times, committing it to heart and memory. Pei had never seen anyone work so hard.

After three months, Li began to recognize some simple characters on street and shop signs—"Stop," "Go," "Enter," "Gold Mountain," "Silver Palace." Sometimes Pei would turn around to find Li had stopped in the middle of the block, trying to read a menu or sign on a door. Pei knew that each time Li recognized a word, she was seeing the world in a new way.

After six months, Li could compose very simple lines. One morning she came to Pei with a neatly folded piece of paper in her hand.

"Will you look at this?" Li asked. "Just to see if it makes any sense."

Pei was on her way down to the Invisible Thread, after dropping Gong off at school. She was already late, though she knew Mai and Song Lee would have everything under control.

"What is it?" she asked.

"A letter long overdue," Li answered.

When Pei read the spare lines her sister had meticulously written, her eyes clouded with tears.

Dear Old Man Sai,
I have found my way home safely.
Thank you,
Li

Chapter Sixteen

1973

Pei

Pei stared out the train window and watched as a scattering of last-minute passengers rushed to find their cars. Moments later, the train jerked to a start, then maintained the same rhythmic rocking and rattling for the almost three hours to Sumzhun, where she would walk across a short bridge separating the Hong Kong and Chinese borders. Then Pei would take another train to Canton. After an overnight stay, she would catch a bus that would take her the rest of the way to Yung Kee.

Since the American president Nixon had visited China a year ago and met Mao Tse-tung, China had opened her doors a crack, just enough for Pei to return to Yung Kee one last time. Pei couldn't imagine what the village must be like after thirty-five years, or what remnants of her past she hoped to find, but the desire to return had begun to bloom inside her like a flower that had long been dormant. As far back as Pei could remember, her past had always been inextricably tied to her present, and the future was what followed. There were so many threads that she could never really sever, even with Lin long dead and Li in Hong Kong helping her run the Invisible Thread.

She had hoped to see Chen Ling, and had written to her several times, but hadn't heard from her since Ming's death. Li had also planned to go, wanting desperately to see her sons and grandchildren, but Kaige and Yuan couldn't make the journey from Chungking because of their work, and then Li's rheumatism flared up, making it difficult for her to walk. Song Lee had then volunteered to accompany Pei—but, already in her mid-seventies, soon realized that she was too old to make the long trip. She mumbled to Pei over and over again, as if angry with herself, "The mind's willing, but the body isn't."

That left Pei to make the journey alone.

A few days before she'd left, Ho Yung had come by to see her. She could tell by the heavy step on the stairs that he was coming. He had never married and was a priceless friend. When she counted her good fortunes, Ho Yung stood out. He had walked with her through life, never pulling ahead or falling behind, but keeping in perfect pace.

"Are you sure you want to make the trip alone?" Ho Yung asked, always her protector.

"I'll be fine," she reassured him.

"If you wait until next month, I'll rearrange my schedule and go with you."

Pei put her hand on top of his, gave a warm squeeze. "I need to do this now, and alone."

Ho Yung nodded. "Just like always." He smiled.

Out the train window, the outskirts of Kowloon sped by. When they entered the flat open space of the New Territories, Pei leaned back and closed her eyes, shifting uncomfortably in the new suit she'd bought for the trip. At sixty-two, she was still a handsome woman, standing tall and straight, trying to grow old as gracefully as Mrs. Finch. Pei was entering the last years of her life in relative contentment. All life's benevolence balanced against the blows it had struck. Gong had grown up to be a decent young man, who had studied architecture and was about to be married. Yet she still felt a small stab in her heart every time she thought of how proud Ji Shen would have been of him.

Pei opened her eyes with a start when a staticky voice announced that they'd arrived in Sumzhun. She carried only a small canvas bag. It was a short walk across the concrete bridge over the dry ravine separating one guardhouse from the other, the past from the present. Groups of people trudged across carrying gifts and packages, voices lowered, hoping not to be detained with something deemed suspicious—a clock-radio, a camera, razor blades. Pei walked briskly ahead of the crowds, stood in line, stared the guard hard in the eyes as if to say, "I'm not hiding anything," and heard the dull thud of the stamp passing her through.

The train to Canton was yet another step back in time. Pei saw for herself how China had stood still while others rushed right past. Even the train moved at a snail's pace, and Pei imagined she might get out and run faster. She stared at the white doilies that covered the back of the seats. The pale green walls and lace curtains made her feel as if she were in someone's sitting room. The faint smell of mothballs emanated from the seats. A woman dressed completely in white pushed a rattling cart down the aisle, serving hot tea from silver thermoses.

As the train slowly inched its way through the countryside, Pei saw the mahogany-colored earth of her childhood. It was just as she'd remembered it. She saw again her mother and father, and the land they had tended and worked so hard just to scrape by. As a child, she'd known nothing of what a drought or flood meant to their existence. All she knew was that every crack in the dry dirt meant less food and more worries, while at the same time the jagged lines made for her a new puzzle in the ground, and the rain-soaked earth provided new ponds for them to play in. Could she have once been so young and naïve?

*   *   *

By the time the train pulled in to Canton, it was late afternoon. Ho Yung had arranged for her to stay at a good, comfortable hotel, and though she was uneasy spending so much money for just a bed to sleep in, he assured her that she could well afford to stay three days. Pei smiled at the thought.

The station was crowded and noisy. People pushed and shoved from all directions to get where they wanted to go. Voices shouted over the loudspeaker, announcing arrivals and departures. Vendors sold steamed buns, paper toys, and candy all along the walkway. Pei couldn't move two feet in any direction without being solicited to buy something. She picked up her step and headed for the line of mismatched bicycle-rickshaws waiting along the curb.

The next morning she caught an early bus and was on her way to Yung Kee before the sun had fully risen. Sitting on the hard wooden seat, she watched the morning light slowly bring into focus a world that had never been far from her heart and mind. In the bright light, the fish ponds gleamed mirrorlike, surrounded by mulberry groves.

Pei sat across the aisle from a woman who smiled at her every time she glanced her way. She was obviously ready for some early-morning conversation, while Pei struggled to keep the silence of her own thoughts. Except for the two of them and another man sleeping up front, the old bus was empty.

"Tso sun." The woman leaned toward her.

Pei had to respond to the good-morning greeting. "Tso sun."

"You're going to Yung Kee?"

Pei nodded.

"More people returning now," the woman added, loud enough to wake the sleeping man.

"Do you live there?" Pei asked.

The woman spoke with her hands, making small circles in the air. "During the week I take care of my grandson. My daughter works in a silk factory there."

"Silk factory?" Pei repeated, surprised.

"It used to be work for only the unmarried girls," she confided. "Reeling the silk was wet work, and people thought it might interfere with having babies. But now any woman can do it. It's hard to pay attention to the old superstitions when production for the masses is what counts."

Pei tried to appear interested as the woman rattled on, her hands dancing in front of her. How times had changed from the days of the old superstitions that had forged a sisterhood of silk workers, who lived, worked, and even died together. Pei swallowed, glanced past the woman out the window.

The last time Pei had been in Yung Kee was 1938, and her sadness then was so thick she couldn't see beyond it. Lin had died, and she and Ji Shen were running one step ahead of the Japanese. By then, Yung Kee had become a big, rambling town, far removed from the small dusty village where she'd grown up. The silkwork had kept it flourishing and Pei remembered being amazed at its immensity.

Now, from the window of the bus, she saw its dusty edges and faded colors. Clearly, Yung Kee was in the midst of transformation, with new buildings tucked here and there among the old ones. It was just another Chinese town that had somehow managed to survive a lifetime of changes, buoyed by a silk industry that stubbornly continued. Pei swallowed, her mouth dry and bitter. It had taken her thirty-five years to return and say good-bye.

She leaned forward in the bus and tried to figure out where they were. New shops and open stalls selling fruits and vegetables lined the streets where once there had been nothing. She would have to rely on her memory to get her through the maze of streets and bicycles to the girls' house. Stepping down from the bus, Pei nearly missed being hit by a young man on a bicycle. He turned around long enough to shake his fist at her and then continued on his way.

She stood at the side of the dirt road, cleared her mind, and found the direction by recognizing the straight line of tall trees that still shaded one of the roads leading away from the market. In the past, all the times she'd walked down this same street, she'd never paid the least attention to it. Now she saw how many of the big houses that still stood were in need of repair. Jasmine and litchi still grew wild and abundant. Pei walked faster, the fine dust resting on the tops of her shoes. Rounding the corner, she still expected to see Auntie Yee, Chen Ling, and Ming, young, eager Ji Shen, her calm, knowing Lin. Instead, she saw only the two-story red-brick building that was the girls' house.

The Girls' House

The wooden fence that had once surrounded the girls' house was gone. Pei imagined it must have been priceless firewood during the occupation. Weeds and foliage littered the front courtyard where she'd once sat with her father and Auntie Yee. The house itself was a shambles; the front steps had disappeared. Instead, several tree stumps of different heights led up to the front porch. Auntie Yee had kept the house spotless during Pei's childhood; the scent of ammonia had never been far from her dreams, and the wood floors gleamed even in the rainy season. Seeing it in such ruins made her heart ache. Pei closed her eyes and wished that Lin were there with her.

Sudden loud voices came from inside the house. She started for the front door, only to be startled by someone speaking from behind her.

"What are you doing here?" The voice was sharp and familiar.

Pei turned around quickly. It took her only a moment to realize that the wizened old woman standing in front of her was Moi. And once again Pei felt like the little girl who stood to one side as Moi dragged her bad leg through the kitchen of the girls' house, never allowing any of them to enter. Year after year she had cooked wonderful meals for all the girls lucky enough to stay with Auntie Yee.

Pei stood for a moment in disbelief. Moi must be in her nineties. Pei had never expected she would still be alive. Her heart skipped a beat to think Moi had survived through such difficult years.

"Moi." The name rolled softly off her tongue.

"Who wants to know?" Moi snapped, stepping closer to get a better look.

"I'm Pei," she said, hoping her name might conjure up some small memory in Moi's mind, though the girl she'd been had long since turned into a tall, gray-haired woman. "I stayed here at the girls' house with Chen Ling and Lin."

Moi stared at her with suspicion, then turned away as if she were having a conversation with the air around her. "Yee tells me you are one of our girls. The tall one."

Pei looked around. "Auntie Yee?"

"She comes to me often," Moi said, and gestured for Pei to follow. She turned, dragging her bad foot, down the path that led to the back of the house.

Pei quickly followed. What had once been a flourishing garden was now a jungle of weeds and shrubbery. Hidden in it stood, a small shack constructed, with the resourcefulness Moi had been born to, of flattened tin cans, cardboard boxes, and wood scraps. Characters in red and black hinted as to what the packages once held: oranges, bananas, a thermos. Outside the door were two wooden crates.

"Sit, sit," Moi mumbled, pointing to the crates.

Pei did as she was told. Moi stepped into her small house and ladled water from a metal drum into a pot, clanking it down on a small camp stove.

"Who's living in the big house?" Pei dared to ask.

Moi clicked her tongue. "Families assigned by the village work force," she answered, clear and precise.

Pei looked into Moi's alert eyes and saw that she wasn't the confused old woman she pretended to be. She understood everything that was going on around her. Whether she wanted to listen was another matter.

"Have you seen Chen Ling?"

"Out in the countryside. Sometimes she comes to visit. It's not so easy anymore. We've all gotten old." Moi sprinkled tea leaves into two cups, then poured hot water into them. From an old footlocker, she pulled out a bag of peanuts and filled a chipped rice bowl.

"Are you all right here?" Pei grieved to see Moi living in such squalid conditions. If she had known, Pei would have brought gifts from Hong Kong to make Moi's life easier.

Moi pulled out another crate from her shack and sat across from Pei. She had shriveled to the size of a child. "Yee and I have survived it all," she finally said. "No one can take me away from here. They let me be. Just waiting for me to die so they can take what little I have."

Pei smiled. "You were always stubborn."

"It was always Yee who was the stubborn one, not me," Moi said, with renewed energy.

Pei sipped the tasteless tea.

"Why have you come back?" Moi suddenly asked.

"To see the girls' house," Pei answered. "To see what was left of Yung Kee and the sisterhood."

"Everybody's gone," Moi said quietly. "The silk work is something else now."

Pei looked at Moi through the cloudy sheen of tears that suddenly covered her eyes. "You're still here."

Moi laughed. "There's not much left of me, either. Not that it matters." She offered Pei a peanut, then picked one up and freed it from its shell. "I'm not long for this life; Yee has as much as told me so. It's just a short time before I join her and all the others."

"Don't say that." Pei leaned closer to Moi, remembering the jars of dry food Moi had given her to carry all the way to Hong Kong.

"Nothing to be afraid of. It's okay to leave one world for another." Moi smiled. "Even when the Japanese devils descended upon the house like locusts, I wasn't afraid. They thought they could take everything away from me, but they couldn't. They laughed at me, and they took or destroyed all the food I'd gathered, but it meant nothing. Because everyone and everything that has always been important was right inside here!" Moi put her hand over her heart. "And they could never take that away from me."

Pei swallowed, tears pushing against her eyes. "You don't have to stay here anymore, you could return to Hong Kong with me. I could file the paperwork over there. . . ."

Moi laughed. "Aiya, what would I do there? My home is here. It always has been." She chewed thoughtfully on a peanut. "I don't need much."

"No, you don't." Pei smiled.

They sat in silence, simply taking comfort in each other's company.

Pei stayed with Moi until late afternoon, when she had to catch the last bus back to Canton. She could hardly bear to leave Moi behind. The old woman was Pei's last link to the girls' house. Moi walked her out to the street, wearing a threadbare padded jacket. Pei made a mental note to replace it as soon as she returned home, and to send along a new teakettle, teacups, and bowls.

"You must promise to take good care of yourself," she said, and grasped Moi's hand in hers.

Moi nodded. "You and Lin will always be here," she said. She lifted her hand over her heart.

It was the first time Moi had mentioned Lin. Pei glanced down at Moi's serious, thoughtful face. She had seen so much and said so little throughout the years.

"Go, before it gets dark," Moi said, with a quick wave of concern.

She watched Moi slowly limp back toward the house, still in charge after all these years. "I'll come and visit again," Pei called after her.

Moi turned back once and smiled, just before she disappeared behind the girls' house.

Pei paused a moment in uncertainty—the past quietly tucked away, the late-afternoon sun warm against her back. She twisted Mrs. Finch's emerald ring on her finger. She wasn't scheduled to return to Hong Kong for another two days, but there was nothing left in Yung Kee she needed to see. She could visit Lin's grave tomorrow morning if it was possible to get through the gates of their old house; then she'd catch a train home. Everyone she loved was in Hong Kong, waiting for her.

As Pei walked down the street, the smell of wild jasmine grew stronger, wrapping itself around her. She stopped and drew in the fragrant memory of the sisterhood and Lin, stirring and settling somewhere deep down inside of her.